INVASIVE SPECIES

INVASIVE SPECIES
BOOK 1

JOHN WILKER

Rogue Publishing

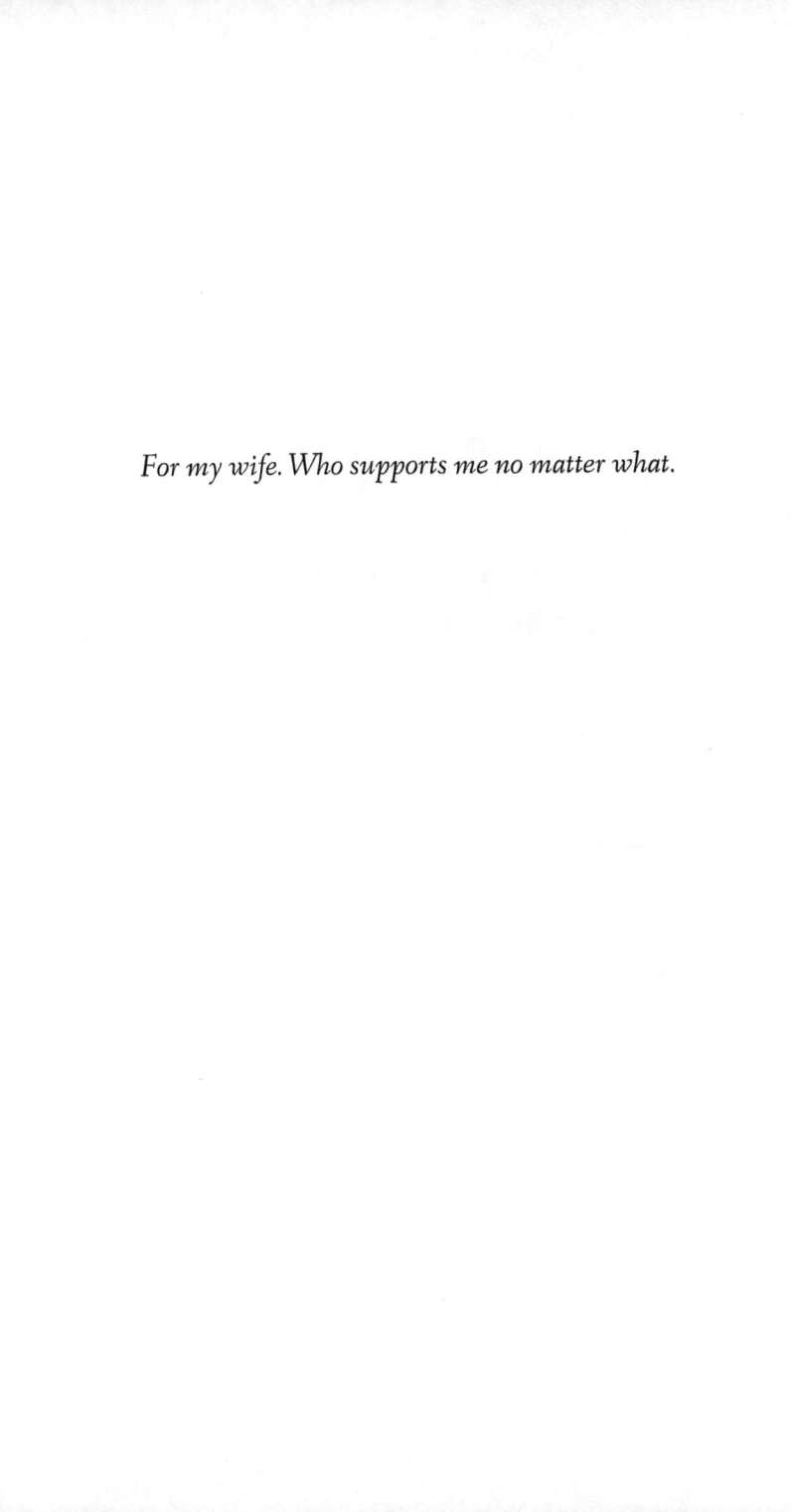

For my wife. Who supports me no matter what.

CONTENTS

You're about to embark on a fun adventure!

When you're done reading, I hope you'll take a minute to leave a review!

If you liked the story and want more, joining my newsletter is a great way to get free samples, and exclusive short stories, and other goodies.

PROLOGUE

"GOOD EVENING, ladies and gentlemen. From Studio Sixty, I'm Laura Bertram." The anchorwoman reached up to adjust her bobbed hair. The studio was awash in neon, the screen behind the anchor desk showing an animated world, slowly spinning amid a sea of twinkling stars.

Her co-anchor ran a hand through his salt and pepper hair before smoothing his mustache. "And I'm Mike Spencer." He turned to another camera. "The United Nations has released its plan to deal with asteroid LV-426." His relief was plain on his face.

Laura nodded as the camera switched back to her. "It's a desperate plan, but with only fourteen days left before the 'planet killer,'" she made air quotes as she said that last part, "impacts the Earth, and all other attempts having failed...Well..."

She turned to another camera, knowing an info-graphic was being added to the feed. "Several UN nations, under the coordination of U.S. Space Command, will be launching the world's remaining nuclear missiles toward the asteroid."

Mike picked up the story. "The missiles are scheduled to launch at midnight Eastern Standard Time. It will take nearly ten days for the weapons to reach LV-426, which is just barely enough time to destroy or divert the asteroid."

"If all goes well," Laura added, "The missiles will shatter the asteroid far enough out so that any remaining large pieces will be spread apart and pass Earth with room to spare."

She smiled. "That's the hope."

The camera turned to Mike. "In other news, the Global Climate Panel has finished its meeting and will announce what, if any, accords they came to in order to address the planet's worsening environment."

"GOOD EVENING. I'M LAURA BERTRAM." She cleared her throat. "Flying solo tonight as my," a cough this time, "colleague, Mike, is out sick today."

After taking a deep breath, the newswoman said, "It's been eleven days since the missiles were launched at asteroid LV-426. I'm sure that for you, as for me, the wait has been..." She composed herself. "A struggle. Well, the wait is over and the news isn't good. We've learned from sources inside U.S. Space Command that the missile attack against the asteroid was..." Her eyes fell to the desk. "Unsuccessful." She paused again, taking a deep breath. "This explains why U.S. Space Command and all other authorities have been silent."

Finally, she looked back to the camera. "Our anonymous source tells us that more than half of the missiles missed the asteroid completely due to some type of miscalculation in the targeting. Apparently, all of the missiles were needed in order to shatter the planet killer. There are, it seems, no missiles left on Earth that can do the job."

She opened her mouth to continue but stopped, a shudder interrupting. After taking a deep breath and tilting her head back to look at the ceiling, she continued, "The asteroid is shattered, but not enough. We're told that instead of the expected hundreds of smaller pieces, most of which would pass harmlessly by us or burn up in the atmosphere, LV-426 has broken into closer to a dozen or so larger pieces. Most are expected to hit Earth's atmosphere." She gave in, letting a low sob escape. "And few will burn up."

"HELLO. I'M..." The man paused. His shirt was rumpled and sweat stained. "It doesn't matter. This may very well be our last broadcast." He busied himself moving out of the way a coffee cup that looked like it was from the previous night. "The station received an updated its list of potential Impact Zones." He squinted past the camera. "Marcus? Put up the graphic."

On the screen behind him, a slowly spinning globe appeared. One at a time, red icons appeared, first in

China, then progressing across the globe in a nearly straight line. The last icon appeared a few hundred miles from Mexico City, near the southern tip of the country and the Gulf of Mexico.

"Rioting is being reported in cities around the globe centered around the projected Impact Zones." He shuffled the papers before him absently. "We'll stay on the air and update these projects as long as we can. The first impact is estimated to be in fifteen hours. Civilian authorities are doing their best to evacuate, but I'm hearing that Aswan and surrounding cities have completely fallen to chaos." He looked right at the camera. "God save us all."

PART 1

CHAPTER ONE

"STOP PUSHING, *amigo*. They won't run out of beer."
Paco Rosales looked over his shoulder at his friend and
teammate, Brandon Sinclair. The streets of Denver were
crowded and noisy this time of day.

Brandon ran both hands through his light brown hair.
"Yeah, but we're not drinking it right now." He looked to
his right, to the small blonde woman with a lopsided pixie
cut. "Right, Luce?"

Lucy scowled at her much larger associate. "Friend"
was still too strong a term as far as she was concerned.
The three of them were a fire team, had been since they
started their third year at the academy, two years ago. She
still wasn't sure Brandon was worth her time.

Cadets at the North American Coalition Armed
Forces Academy were put into groups of three on the first
day of their third year. Once their core education was
complete, cadets hoping to be suit pilots were grouped
into fire teams. Fire teams stayed together until they

retired or enough of them died that any survivors had to be reassigned.

The North American Coalition Armed Forces Academy, NACAF, learned that teams of three worked best and that forcing them to bond in their final two years at the academy strengthened those bonds.

The three of them were surrounded by nearly a hundred other cadets all making their way out of the downtown Denver Academy complex main gates into the neighborhood surrounding the academy. Finals were over, and it was time to drink and celebrate.

"If everyone beats us, we'll be standing all night," Brandon said. He gave Paco another shove and urged Lucy on with him. She rolled her eyes but picked up her pace. Brandon wasn't wrong about having to stand, and she wasn't interested in that. There were hundreds of bars in downtown Denver, but everyone at the academy preferred one specific bar.

The trio elbowed its way through the crowd, making its way to the street. They were in the middle of the pack. Their last lecture was in one of the furthest buildings from the main gate.

"Come on!" Paco motioned to an alleyway. "We can cut down here. Get to the Kaiju first."

Lucy eyed the alley. "I'm sure there'll be tables left if we just go the regular way." She could smell the alley from where they were.

Brandon grinned. "Come on, Luce. Just step lightly and breathe through your mouth." He headed down the alley, banging his fist on a dumpster as he passed.

"I don't want to taste it!" she protested, following the

two men. It hadn't rained recently, so the Denver alleys were especially ripe.

"Where you three going?" Chad Lundgren shouted. He and his teammates were passing the alley, moving toward the next corner. As one of the tallest cadets in their class, barely making it into the suit pilot course, Chad assumed the role of class leader—and bully. In any gathering of cadets, Lundgren stood almost three inches above the rest. How he fit in a pilot's crèche was beyond Brandon. He ignored the other man, urging his friends on.

Paco waved to Chad. "See you at the Kaiju! Last one there buys the first round!" He sprinted down the alley. Paco was the shortest of the three friends, at a relatively diminutive five foot four. Despite his small stature, he was fast and had mastered using his low center of gravity in hand-to-hand combat.

The Drunken Kaiju—named after a popular Japanese term for massive monsters—

among a few other bars, was a popular haunt for academy cadets. When the Kaiju filled up, cadets spilled out to the others. Brandon favored the Kaiju and convinced his team in their first year together that the Kaiju was their favorite as well. It had been their go-to watering hole ever since.

The Kaiju was a two-story building in the middle of the block. Most of the block had been renovated over the years, but not the Kaiju. Its old red brick facade was smeared with decades' worth of graffiti and probably worse. Rumor had it the building had been a brothel back in the day.

By the time Brandon the others stepped inside, several groups of cadets were already seated or standing at the bar on the first floor. Paco led the team upstairs, not even trying to find a spot on the first floor. The second floor didn't have a bar but had far more comfortable booths. Exiting the stairwell, he pointed a corner booth. "See, told you."

The trio sat down as Chad and his team came in, several other cadets on their heels. Paco waved. They scowled, taking seats at a table in the middle of the room. There were way fewer comfortable chairs at the center tables. The room was quickly reaching its maximum legal capacity.

A shadow passed over the building, causing the room to fall silent. Brandon glanced out the window and whistled. "Soon enough, we'll be up there." He inclined his head.

A massive NACAF air carrier was passing overhead, its powerful gravity lift engines thrumming. The vessel looked like a skyscraper lying on its side, nearly a kilometer long, bristling with weapons and antennas.

Paco leaned over him. "The *Roosevelt*. Nice."

The NACAF *Roosevelt* drifted out of view behind several nearby office buildings. The sound of her passing faded as she slid out of view. Over the years, downtown Denver had grown up and out. Most buildings in the lower downtown core, as well as in surrounding districts, were between seventy and one hundred stories tall.

At a kilometer in length, the second-generation air carrier was a masterpiece of engineering, a collaborative effort between VarTech and the surviving nations and alliances of the world. Massive thrusters at the vessel's rear provided propulsion while grav-lift engines, a proprietary and top-secret technology of VarTech, kept the huge vessels aloft.

Most of the technology used in the fight against megafauna was VarTech's, and they aggressively kept it need-to-know.

THE WAITRESS, a new girl Brandon hadn't seen before, dropped off the next round of drinks. She looked around the room. "You three ready to get out there and bring the pain to some monsters?" Everyone in town could spot a suit pilot—cadet or otherwise. Given the space constraints, pilots trended on the shorter side and their height capped out at five-ten. Any three people of shorter stature together were almost certainly a suit fire team.

Brandon flashed a grin, slightly messier after three rounds. "Oh, yeah. We're gonna kick some megafauna ass!" He turned to Paco, hand in the air. His friend slapped his hand against Brandon's. They both let fly with an improvised war cry.

Lucy rolled her eyes, turning to the woman. "Postings are tomorrow." She took a sip of her water.

The other woman inclined her head. "Well, good luck tomorrow." She turned and headed for the stairs to pick up her next tray of drinks.

Lucy looked at her teammates. "Think we'll get the *Roosevelt*?"

From the middle of the room, Terrence Danville, one of Chad's teammates, scoffed. "You three? The *Roosevelt*? You'll be lucky to get a groundside posting in Minnesota." He raised his glass in mock salute.

While there was an NACAF base in Minnesota, it was the farthest base from an Impact Zone. To the best of Brandon's knowledge, no suits were assigned to it. North America had lucked out, as far as such things went, with regards to the asteroid impacts. The nearest Impact Zone was the southern tip of Mexico. It was also the last Impact Zone in the chain that devastated Earth's atmosphere and surface conditions.

Brandon raised his own hand in salute. The single finger variety. "Suck it, Terry."

While most of the cadets ignored Chad's antics, Brandon let the other man get under his skin—and Chad, and his team, knew it.

Chad came from Wyoming, which, other than dealing with massive immigration over the years, had suffered few, if any, ill effects of the impacts. Life in Wyoming was no different now than it had been before anyone had heard of LV-426.

The *Roosevelt* was the flagship of the NACAF and the most desired posting there was, regardless of role. As such, the competition was fierce. Each air carrier had room for only four fire teams, twelve mechs in all.

Chad was about to say something when a hush fell over the room. The displays mounted in each corner of the room were showing the logo for Global News One.

Paco checked his watch, then looked at Brandon and Lucy. "Not a normal broadcast." To reinforce what he said, BREAKING NEWS streamed across the bottom of all the screens.

In the early days post impact, many nations not directly struck by an asteroid fragment fell into chaos; the asteroids kicked up massive dust clouds. The dust clouds ravaged global infrastructure and the environment. It was even worse for nations that suffered an impact directly. It didn't take long for the UN to splinter. In its wake, alliances formed. Rumors and misinformation spread through unofficial news sources because many of the national news outlets were offline. Slowly, as things came together, many national and international news outlets came together to form Global News One.

When the earliest signs of megaflora showed up, it became clear that having a well-connected worldwide news network was beneficial to everyone. Now, outside of regional outlets, GNO was the single source of most people's news and current events.

The screen switched from the logo to a dark-skinned man in a well-tailored salmon suit. "Good afternoon. We're interrupting local programming with a special update."

Brandon looked at his friends. "What the hell?" The entire second floor had fallen quiet. Lucy waved a hand at him, making a buzzing noise. He frowned at her but said nothing more.

The newscaster continued, "A strike force from China's *Yangtze Kiang* is missing and presumed lost. Three fire teams went into the alien jungle after receiving distress calls from several nearby villages." He turned to another camera as a stock image of a VarTech

AC-01 air carrier, the precursor to newer ships like the *Roosevelt*, appeared over his shoulder. The first generation of air carrier used four massive turbo fans to provide lift. There was no scenario where one of those snuck up on anything. "People's Navy Carrier *Yangtze Kiang* lost contact with the group of suits three hours into their recon mission. They were en route to a pair of villages just inside the Chinese's impact plus fifteen Exclusion Zone, near the remains of Nanjing."

The newscaster again turned to a different camera, the images over his shoulder switching to an aerial view of what had to be China but wasn't identified. "The ship dispatched its remaining fire team to investigate, but so far they've not found any sign of the first group." The image changed to a still of a burned-out group of huts. "Both villages appear to have been wiped out."

The newsman was replaced with what Brandon assumed was camera footage from the carrier. A massive multistory jungle of alien plants filled the screen with slashes of bright oranges, purples, and greens. Occasionally, the massive shape of a Category 3 megafauna would rise out of the foliage to munch on a bright orange leaf or snag an elephant that had wandered too far into the alien flora.

"The Chinese assure us that nothing unusual has been reported in the area and that this is likely a technical issue." His look made it clear what he thought of that explanation, but he said nothing. He nodded to the camera. "Back to your regular local programming."

"Fucking Chinese," Chad scoffed. "Second rate suit drivers from shit villages."

Brandon turned in his seat. "Shut the fuck up, Chad." He added a sneer to the other man's name. "Your racism is showing."

Lucy turned to Terrence. "Terry, your friend is making you all look bad." She smiled her most innocent smile. "Maybe do something about that."

Chad stood and leveled a finger at Brandon. "Don't worry, enclave baby. The Chinese can't hear us." The moment Chad found out that Brandon hailed from the walled enclave of Vail, he never missed an opportunity to use whatever derogatory nickname he could think up on the fly. Unlike Wyoming, Vail had refused any and all immigration and even gone the extra step to build a wall around most of the town. The wealthy wanted little to do with the world's woes.

Before Brandon could shove Paco out of the booth to meet Chad's unspoken challenge, Paco put a hand on his arm, shaking his head. He looked at Chad and smiled. "Chad, *amigo*. Those pilots went through the same training as us and deserve at least that much respect. No?"

Chad made a face, running a hand through his thick black mane. "Whatever." He turned to his team. "We'll never see these losers again after tomorrow. Probably end up in secondhand suits guarding Vail or some other nothing job."

"*Pendejo*," Paco muttered under his breath.

Brandon's cheeks were blazing. "I hate that fucking guy." Chad's team had spent the last two years tormenting Brandon and his team every opportunity they got. To be fair, they tormented almost every other fire team at the academy, feeling themselves the pinnacle of academy achievement. They focused on Brandon and the others more because they knew it bothered him.

From another booth, Becca Dunbar, an engineering cadet, asked loud enough to be heard, "Wonder what really happened? Three fire teams...That's a lot of suits to lose in one go."

"And a lot of firepower. What can take out nine mechs?" someone asked from one of the tables in the center of the room.

"Without being seen?" someone else added.

Lucy turned her glare from Chad and his team to Becca. "Looked like they were well into the Exclusion Zone. Maybe just got overwhelmed?"

"Wonder why they went into the Exclusion?" Paco said.

"Guessing we'll never know," Brandon replied.

The world had rallied to fight the slow invasion of the megaflora and fauna, but many countries and alliances still kept each other at arm's length.

"NOW ENTERING DENVER AIRSPACE, CAPTAIN," the helmsman announced from one of the forward stations of the NACS *Saratoga*'s bridge.

Captain Thomas Bartell turned from the station he was leaning over, watching a junior officer show him the latest border data they'd recently received from Command. "Thank you, ensign." Looking to his executive officer, he said, "Link, has Denver Base sent over the resupply schedule?"

Commander Lincoln—Link—Willis smiled. He held up a tablet. "Your ears burning, sir? Just came in a few minutes ago. Almost done reviewing." He held up a tablet. "Looks pretty good. We should be in port for only two weeks."

Bartell nodded. "Excellent. We're due down south on the fifteenth. Might be cutting it close, but that's fine, the *Detroit* can linger a day or two if needed."

The ship's XO nodded his agreement. "We have the send off party for Bravo night after next." He knew the captain hadn't forgotten, but it never hurt to be sure.

NACAF was the unified military force born from America and Canada's disparate services. Every time one of its fire teams rotated off an air carrier, there was a party. Surviving a tour was not that rare, but rare enough.

Suits were the front-line force against the ever-encroaching megaflora and the much worse megafauna. Giant alien plants and animals the likes of which humanity had never seen, they were born of the fragments of the asteroid LV-426 and spread around the globe.

Bartell grinned, thinking about the last rotation party. "Haven't forgotten. Be nice to not have the party in the hangar. I reserved the rooftop of the officer's club."

Willis' eyes went wide. "You go, sir."

Denver was home to not just the academy but a regional military base just to the west of the city in what used to be an air force base.

The captain accepted the tablet from his XO.

Looking it over, he said, "Good timing. Denver's graduating class gets their assignments tomorrow. We'll have a new Bravo Team when we head out."

"We're gonna need suits for them," Link said.

The captain nodded, rubbing his chin. "Yeah..." He tapped his chin a few times before looking at the tablet in his other hand. He swiped on the screen a few times, tapping here and there. "Looks like we can pick up three new," he looked at his XO, "to us, suits." He shrugged. "Better than nothing."

"Don't forget Charlie Team. Doc says they'll be down two for a while; Peterson and Mduba are going to have to be transferred off-ship if they have any hope of making a full recovery."

Bartell grunted. "Let's keep Charlie Two aboard. She can work with the newbies as a training officer."

Willis nodded. "Sounds good. I mean, she'll hate that, but you know..." He grinned. His captain nodded. Fire teams lived and died together. Charlie One and Three had been heavily damaged just outside Mazatlán. A trio of Category 3 monsters ambushed Charlie Team. Bravo had deployed to back them up.

The *Saratoga* had been on her way back from what remained of Northern Mexico and the now abandoned city of La Paz on the Baja peninsula. The cities and towns of the peninsula had been thought safe; most megafauna didn't seem to like water, so the narrow Gulf of California been a natural border. That was until a Category 2 waded out of the water and laid waste to most of La Paz and several surrounding towns before the *Saratoga* arrived to kill the creature.

Everything about the operation was going by the numbers until four Category 3 megafauna followed their friend out of the Gulf, catching Charlie Team and the *Saratoga* by surprise.

The Category 3s rushed Charlie Team, damaging Charlie One immediately and putting the mech out of the fight, her pilot's crèche ripped open. Bravo, the standby team, dropped.

Before Bravo hit the ground, two of the new monsters leaped onto Bravo Three, pulling the suit off its deployment line and driving her to the ground. The suit never even fired a shot; the two creatures ripped it to pieces.

The remaining four suits fought like hell to buy the people of La Paz time to escape, but in the end, the two remaining Bravo suits were destroyed, their pilots dead. Charlie Three's pilot, Carol Mduba, was barely conscious, her suit half submerged in the ocean.

By the time the *Saratoga* was crossing into Arizona, word was already spreading through the NACAF that the entire peninsula would have to be evacuated. Hundreds of thousands of people were about to be in need of a new place to live. It wasn't until after the battle that clean up teams realized the entire gulf was choked with a mutation of the all too familiar vines that always signaled the coming of the monsters. The vines seemed to be impervious to saltwater now, and one of the dead kaiju had what looked like rudimentary gills. If the oceans didn't stop them, the spread of the alien life could go in any direction.

It was always the same. The vines crept forward, choking off plant life and providing the environment needed for the megafauna to look for new territory. Slow terraforming, the science types called it. Creatures ranging from ten feet in height to nearly sixty came out of the jungles and established nests, burrows, and whatever else alien monsters slept in. They devoured every native plant and animal in their path, then repeated the process, creeping ever outward from the five Impact Zones around the world.

From the front of the bridge, the operations watch stander said, "Sir, we're passing over Denver now."

Off to the right and ahead of the ship, NACAF Base Denver was visible. A two-kilometer-tall mushroom-shaped structure that served as the command center, cargo area, and docking facility for the air carriers can came through. Four evenly spaced indentations served as docking ports, allowing four of the massive ships to visit at one time.

"Looks like *Roosevelt* is in town," Willis said, nodding to the tower and the air carrier snugged into one of the docking ports.

Bartell smiled. "Denver's gonna be busy the next few days."

"And nights," Willis agreed.

THE KAIJU WAS the first stop of the night, but once the cadets realized two air carriers were in town, they quickly migrated to spots the crews of those ships were known to frequent.

For Brandon and the team, that meant a booth with a

few engineering cadets at a nightclub a few blocks away. The Dusty Rose wasn't exactly top shelf as clubs went, but the owner was a former suit pilot, so NACAF officers drank for half off any time they were in town. Pilot hopefuls paid full price.

"Look! I think those're *Roosevelt* pilots!" Paco shouted, nudging Brandon repeatedly.

"Dude, you're gonna give me a bruise," he said, then added, "Yeah, you're right, though." Once pilots were assigned a carrier, they were issued a leather bomber jacket like pilots in the wet navies wore. Patches for each posting were added to the right arm. The two women and one man all had four patches, the most recent being the *Roosevelt*.

Paco pushed Brandon until he got out of the booth. "I'm going to go say hi."

"Fanboy," Lucy said before raising her glass to take a sip of something bright blue. She turned to the two other cadets that joined them when they left the Kaiju. "So, you two excited about tomorrow? Any thoughts on where you'll end up?"

The tall brunette smiled. "Hoping for the *Saratoga*." She nodded to her friend. "Bernadette's angling for a spot at the R&D shop in San Diego."

Bernadette nodded, both hands on her pint glass. "They're doing some really cool stuff with suit-to-pilot interfaces."

Brandon turned. "What's to improve? With the suit and the brain cap, they move like we do."

Bernadette nodded her agreement. The pilot's suit and helmet, called a brain cap because of the thousands of tiny electrodes that read the pilot's brain waves, allowed a suit to operate like an extension of the pilot's body. While the pilot was securely ensconced in the crèche, the multiton mech around them responded to their every thought and muscle twitch. "Sure, but there's a 0.0021 second delay. What if that was gone?" She cocked her head as she took a sip of her beer.

Brandon scrunched his brow. "Uh, I guess that'd be good?"

Lucy rolled her eyes. "How're they going to do that?"

The other woman set her beer down. "Apparently VarTech is working on some next gen superconductive filament. Supposed to be as close to instantaneous data transfer as we're likely to get."

Paco interrupted them, pushing Brandon up against the first engineering cadet. "Scoot. *Vamos.*"

Brandon smiled at the woman. "Sorry. I don't think we got your name." He blushed.

She grinned. "Rashida." The song playing loudly over the dance floor changed. "Come on, pilot." She leaned forward to look at Paco. "Back out you go."

"*Ay, caramba,*" Paco groaned, making way so the pair could slide out. Sitting back down, he eyed Lucy, then Bernadette. "So, wanna know what they're like?"

"Who?" the two women said as one.

Paco frowned. "*Roosevelt*'s Alpha Team!" he said.

The two women rolled their eyes. Bernadette nudged Lucy, nodding to the dance floor. Lucy nodded vigorously.

Paco watched the two of them go. He reached for his glass when a meaty paw landed on his shoulder.

"Hey, *amigo*. Mind clearing this booth?"

Paco turned, looking up, and up, and up some more into pale blue eyes set against dark skin. A man in a sport coat and jeans looked down on him. Not NACAF. "Sorry... *amigo*. My friends are coming back, just on the dance floor." He nodded toward the gyrating bodies on the floor.

The big guy nodded. "But my friends and I are here now." He had two other men and three women with him. He grinned and made a shooing motion at Paco.

CHAPTER TWO

THE BIG LOCAL cocked his head, waiting for Paco to move. "Come on, little fella. Move along."

"*Perdóname*," Paco said.

"You heard me, little guy. Do you not speak English?"

Paco smiled and reached up, placing his hand on the other man's. He reached the man's wrist and gave a twist, forcing the much larger man to his knees.

The three women took a step back as the big man's two friends took steps forward, both their faces showing a mix of shock and rage.

Paco eased out of the booth, hand still locked on the other man's wrist. "Sir, I tried being—" he released the man's wrist, ducking as the man's other hand came out of nowhere for a right hook. Paco took a step back.

On the dance floor, Brandon looked up at Rashida's smiling face, then glanced past her to spot what Paco was up to. His face fell. "Excuse me." He rushed off the dance floor. He saw Paco barely dodge a right hook, only to take a jab from one of his opponent's friends. Swearing under his breath, Brandon broke into a run.

Paco grunted but turned with the blow, coming around to drive an elbow into the man who'd sucker punched his side. All three men had at least a foot on him. He continued his spin, coming around again to sweep the man's legs out from under him. Before he could turn to the man who'd started it all, Brandon flew through the air to tackle the instigator.

Paco grinned as Brandon rode the much bigger man to the ground, raining blows on his face and neck as he did so. By the time the pair hit the ground, the instigator was unconscious.

Paco turned to the two friends. The women that had been with them were nowhere in sight. "Surely you don't need your asses kicked to learn the lesson, right? *Amigos*?" He smiled the smile he often gave his *abuelita* when she caught him stealing cookies.

The two men looked at Paco, then their friend at Brandon's feet. They moved off, scooping their friend under his arms to drag him away.

Paco turned to Brandon. "I had that."

"Sure, you did, pal." He turned, looking for Rashida on the dance floor. She spied him and waved him back onto the floor. He waved to Paco as he headed back into the dancing crowd.

Paco shook his head and slid back into the booth.

IN THE DAYS POST IMPACT, it became clear to most of the nations of the world that another system was needed—of government, of military, of everything. The UN was in disarray; member nations far from Impact Zones felt that those directly impacted should take care of themselves. Those directly affected were in desperate need or had collapsed into anarchy completely.

The first few years were mostly recovery. The shock waves from the impacts wiped out everything in a hundred-kilometer radius. After that, ash clouds from each impact clogged the skies for years. Several countries ceased to exist, with little to no fanfare.

Once things settled enough for the world to catch its breath, fences went up around the Impact Zones and rebuilding started.

Then the megaflora appeared. At first, it was nothing more than an odd colored plant here and there. Many assumed they were terrestrial plants, mutated by the various exotic energies the asteroid fragments brought with them. They were wrong.

Then those same odd colored plants grew to one hundred feet in height, sporting palmlike fronds with razor-sharp edges. Some had vines, thicker than a man's thigh, that crept in all directions, choking off the native plants.

The megafauna appeared shortly after that. At first it was just the occasional odd looking creature wandering out of the new alien jungles that were spreading from the Impact Zones. Then it was violent and hyperaggressive monsters that stood two, three, four stories tall and devoured any terrestrial creature they encountered. The hyperaggressive monsters threw the entire food chain into chaos, turning apex predators into prey for the first time.

By then, it was too late. The local governments nearest the Impact Zones were already stressed to breaking. The UN was a ghost of its former self. Without the UN, many nations decided that smaller, local alliances made more sense. Some formed out of necessity, others out of fear their members would be weak on their own.

With those alliances came new militaries and even new commercial ventures: the North American Coalition, South American Alliance, African Union, and so on.

VarTech rose quickly as the preeminent technology firm of the post-LV-426 world. They weren't the first company to capitalize on discoveries from the alien plants and animals. They were the most aggressive at mergers and acquisitions. It was VarTech's weapons division that helped humanity finally push back the aggressively invasive alien plant life.

Suits. The forty-foot-tall mechanized warriors were inventions of VarTech. Air carriers...VarTech. VarTech helped humanity turn the tide against the slow but unstoppable creep of megaflora across the globe. In some instances, humanity was even pushing the invasive alien plant and animal life back.

How exactly some of their technology worked was a closely held secret. The military flew the carriers and piloted the suits, but VarTech and VarTech only kept them operational.

"WAKE UP."

Brandon rolled over, mumbling things about Paco's family and upbringing. Sunlight was streaming through the narrow window near the ceiling, the shaft of light striking his face, eliciting more grumbling.

The other man shook him again. "Get up, *cabrón*. It's assignment day." More mumbling from Brandon. Paco rolled his eyes. The two had been roommates since entering the NACAF academy. Brandon was a lot of things; morning person wasn't one of them. Especially after a night of drinking.

Paco could only imagine what life was like in Vail, but it obviously didn't involve getting up early, unlike the farm communities south of the border where Paco grew up. The wealthy enclaves were a mystery to most; those in rarely left, and they rarely let outsiders in.

Paco jumped up onto Brandon's bed, straddling his friend. Then he started jumping up and down.

Brandon sat bolt upright, shoving at his friend. "I'm gonna puke!" he groaned through clenched teeth. Paco jumped off the bed as Brandon scrambled from the bed, barely making it to the small restroom in time.

"Postings go up in thirty!" Paco shouted over the sound of retching. Something unintelligible was shouted back. "I'm not waiting for you. Lucy is meeting us in twenty at the quad."

Brandon leaned out of the small head. "I hate you."

"Love you, too, *amigo*. I'll be downstairs."

The academy dorm building was split down the

middle at the elevator lobby. Men on one side, women the other. Since the NACAF was quasi-military, funded and partially run by VarTech, the rules weren't quite as strict as in the older militaries, but comingling was still not encouraged.

Brandon took a quick, cold shower, popped a few generic headache pills and headed out after Paco. Most of the building was empty, the cadets all in the quad waiting for assignments.

Lucy's floor was three below Brandon and Paco's. The door slid open, letting her in. Brandon smiled. "Hey, Luce. Paco said you were meeting us in the lobby."

She looked him up and down. "You look like shit." Before he could answer, she continued. "Pilar was having a...a moment. She needed a little pep talk."

He shrugged. "At least I match how I feel. She okay?"

She shook her head. "Well enough. She thinks she's gonna get assigned to one of the bases in Oregon."

"At least it's pretty there."

She turned to look at him, shaking her head.

The lift doors slid apart. Paco was waiting for them in the lobby. He waved to them, holding the exterior door open. "Come on!"

When the old militaries found themselves unequal to the task of fighting what amounted to alien plants and animals, the various coalitions in partnership with VarTech formed new military organizations. With VarTech as a guiding force, each coalition and alliance's military looked and operated in a similar fashion. Each was separate but interchangeable.

The NACAF Denver Academy rotunda had a view

to the west of the Rocky Mountains and the high rises of Denver to the east. The academy occupied what was once an amusement park and sporting arena complex. The arena was still there, serving as a training complex for suit pilots. Further south and west, the spire of NACAF Base Denver resembled a termite colony surrounded by fliers of all shapes and sizes. The two massive air carriers, *Roosevelt* and *Saratoga*, occupied the two topmost docking ports.

Massive screens mounted to the sides of the various academy buildings were showing a rotating NACAF logo and countdown timer; five minutes and thirty-four seconds until assignments were displayed.

The NACAF had a fleet of eight air carriers, which each carried four three-unit fire teams. The competition for those spots was fierce. Cadets that weren't selected as suit pilots served aboard the carriers in other capacities or at the ground bases that bordered the Exclusion Zone.

Lucy pointed at the towering screen nearest them. The NACAF logo was gone.

Speakers mounted above each screen played the tone that every cadet knew all too well, the happy little ditty that signified the beginning of class.

"Here we go," Brandon said.

Lucy shushed him.

The screen went black.

"NACAF Academy Denver cadets. Please stand by for postings," a voice boomed over the rotunda from hidden speakers.

Paco looked up and toward the nearby air carriers, their powerful grav-motors thrumming away. "I hope we get the *Roosevelt*." Their team, nicknamed the Vultures, was neck and neck with Chad's Tigers for the top ranking of their class. It was anyone's guess where the two teams would end up.

Chad, Terrence, and Marcus sidled up to them. Nodding, Chad said, "Losers."

Brandon returned the nod. "Shit heads."

The screens around the common area came to life. Each graduating team was listed on the left by their team nickname.

The Tigers were listed first.

Chad turned to Brandon and winked as the assignments began to appear on the right side of the screen.

"THE *SARATOGA* ISN'T SO BAD," Lucy offered.

The three of them were standing at the base of the NACAF Denver tower. Directly overhead, the two mighty air carriers hovered, and smaller ships were coming and going, bringing supplies and personnel to and from the massive warships.

Brandon scoffed. "Sure, but it's not the *Roosevelt*, which is what I...we deserve." How was he supposed to be noticed and promoted, if not on the fleet's flagship? He had to make his parents proud. A loud sigh escaped his lips. He'd just have to show the *Saratoga*'s field ops commander how good he was.

Other than his team's not getting the top billing, the rest of the assignments went as expected. Chad and his team got the *Roosevelt*; another team two rungs below them got a slot on the *Armstrong*. Two other teams were assigned the forward base in Chihuahua, Mexico. Everyone else went to bases around the southern NAC border as support teams. A few lower ranked cadets ended up at bases to the north.

"You ever wonder how they work?" Paco asked, interrupting Brandon's pouting over their assignment. "The air carriers, I mean." He pointed up at the two ships. The low thrum of their grav-lift motors had become nothing more than background noise.

Lucy led the trio into the reception hall at the base of the tower. "Sure. Who hasn't? I hear even most of the engineers on the ships don't know exactly how the grav-motors work." She squinted up at the two ships. "Still incredible."

Brandon made a low noise. "VarTech and their secrets."

"How does that even work? I mean, the NACAF run the ships, right?" Paco asked. "What happens if something goes wrong?"

People could feel the thrum of the two ships' grav-motors on the ground, nearly three-quarters of a kilometer away.

Lucy shrugged. "Guess we'll find out."

A NACAF trooper standing near an electronic signboard with *NACS-03 SARATOGA* emblazoned across the screen greeted the trio as they approached. "Orders?"

Lucy stepped forward before Brandon could fish his NACAF-issued tablet out of his thigh pocket. "Pilot, first class, Lucy Jones, reporting in."

Paco and Brandon offered their devices as well. The

trooper took each device, scanning it with the terminal built into the lectern he was standing next to. After a series of beeps, he handed each unit back to its owner. "Welcome to the *Saratoga*." He stepped aside. "Lift is through there. The quartermaster is set up and will give you your uniform and gear before you go up."

Paco was beaming. "*Maravilloso.*"

Brandon gave him a gentle shove. Lucy was already halfway to the thick hatch that led to the smaller secured waiting and reception space and the lift that ran directly to the docking level the *Saratoga* was moored to.

Each docking arm had its own dedicated lobby and lift, allowing crew to bypass the office and administrative levels, getting quickly to and from street level.

The quartermaster was set up with a table and shelves lined with shipboard uniforms, boots, hats, and more. He handed each of them three sets of basic duty uniforms, a pair of boots, a hat, and a ruggedized wrist computer called a comm. It worked like their tablets but was much more powerful and was directly connected to the NACAF secure data network.

They'd receive their skintight one-piece jumpsuit affectionately referred to as "second skin" from the field ops commander aboard the ship. Someone at the academy would have already uploaded their measurements and brain scans.

After getting their gear, the trio filed into the waiting lift, a pair of crewmen joining them. One of the crewers turned to the group. "New pilots, huh? Excited?"

Brandon grinned. "Yes, and yes. Ready to show the coalition what we've got." The two crewmen exchanged a knowing look. Brandon's cheeks burned, realizing they'd heard it all before from every new group of suit pilots that had come aboard in the past.

The silence was getting awkward. Paco broke it with, "What do you two do?"

The one who spoke earlier said, "Weapons department. Gunnery mates."

The lift slowed, nearing the docking level.

The other added, "We keep the lower guns in order."

The doors slid open, revealing a small vestibule with a single desk. Beyond it was a long, enclosed gangway with the hull of the *Saratoga* visible at the end.

The two crewmen exited first, offering their comms to the man at the desk for scanning. The guard smiled, waving them through. He turned to the three new pilots standing awkwardly just outside the lift doors. He motioned them forward. "Come on, newbies. She don't bite."

Lucy drew herself up and pushed past the two men. "Pilot, first class, Lucy Jones, reporting." She held out her tablet. Their comms wouldn't work until activated aboard ship.

The officer scanned each of their tablets, then said, "Welcome aboard the NACS *Saratoga*. Make sure you high five the hull when you pass through."

Paco had started forward, then stopped. "I'm sorry. What?"

Brandon looked the man over. "What're you talking about?"

The guard shrugged. "Tradition. Every new crewmember does it. It's what keeps us in the air."

"Wouldn't that be advanced technology that very few people understand?" Lucy quipped.

The man shrugged. "That and the love of every person who serves aboard her." He gave a mock high five to himself, both hands clapping over his head. "Go on."

The three new crew members walked across the gangway to the waiting air carrier. Reaching the thick exterior hatch, Brandon paused and looked back at the guard, who nodded, making a *go on* motion. Extending one arm, he leaped up to slap his palm on the hatch's top.

Back in the vestibule, the lift doors parted and Commander Willis stepped off, seeing the three young people straining to jump and smack their hands on the top of the hatch. He watched one man make two attempts before successfully slapping reaching the top. The woman did not even try jumping, making the men boost her up.

Willis turned to the man at the desk. "Lieutenant Xi, did you—?"

"Yes, sir," the guard answered, a grin splitting his face from ear to ear.

Willis sighed. "Just high fives?"

The other man clucked. "The last group, bunch of wrench turners. Got them to kiss the forward side of the hatch."

Willis groaned, holding out his comm for scanning.

CHAPTER THREE

THE BOARDING HATCH the team entered through was in the forward quarter of the air carrier on the ship's main deck. The forward section was primarily mechanical bays and storage, with the rear two-thirds taken up by the hangar where the ship's twelve suits and their repair bays were.

After walking through a handful of hatches, winding their way through storage areas and mechanical bays, the team stepped out into the main hangar bay.

"Damn," Brandon said.

The center of the ship was a hollowed-out metal cavern three decks tall, lined with repair bays and gantries. A crane rumbled along an overhead track, moving several fully loaded pallets from the bed of a cargo lifter.

Crewmembers in powered load lifters were clanking this way and that, moving equipment around ahead of the ship's departure. The hangar was a hive of mechanized activity.

Standing silent sentinel, twelve massive suits lined the port and starboard bulkheads— the *Saratoga*'s four fire teams: Alpha, Bravo, Charlie, and Delta.

"Wow," Lucy whispered. Her two teammates nodded.

"Wonder which ones are ours?" Paco said.

"Watch out, newbies!" someone shouted from behind them. The trio jumped to the side just before a cart loaded with boxes zipped past.

Brandon pointed to a threesome of war machines standing closest to the massive aft hangar bay doors at the ship's rear. "Those look the newest."

They looked at the trio of suits. Each gleamed in the overhead lighting and stood silent, menacing vigil. The nearest was a pale blue beast of a machine with matching missile racks on its back and a forearm-mounted Gatling gun on its right arm.

Lucy turned to him. "You think we'll get new ones?" She shook her head. "No way."

"Hey, you three!" someone shouted. A broad-shouldered man, skin like midnight, approached them. He looked each one of them over, then said, "Pilots?"

They nodded, eyes wide.

"Deck Chief Diallo." He turned and motioned for them to follow. "Come on," he barked.

The three new pilots rushed after the brusque deck chief. He didn't look back to confirm he was being followed. Instead, he pointed to a trio of suits closer to the forward end of the hangar; they looked like they'd seen better days. "These're you." He spied their crestfallen expressions and chuckled.

"They look like hell," Brandon said in a low voice.

"Because they've been through hell," Diallo scolded.

He pointed to a matte black suit with an armored sail behind its head, left arm lined with armor plate, and a deployable blade. The right arm was obviously from a completely different suit. "Midnight Tango," he said. Three large holes ran diagonally from right shoulder to left hip. Diallo didn't explain them. The three new pilots recognized the wounds that likely killed the suit's pilot.

An orange and blue suit with massive three-fingered hands stood next to Midnight Tango. Large fins stood behind its shoulders, linked to thick pistons connected to its arms. Brandon nodded at it. The thing could punch. Its shorter than normal legs made it look like a massive metal gorilla.

Diallo nodded. "Crusher Maverick."

"Dibs," Paco whispered.

Lucy elbowed him.

The deck chief pointed to the last suit in the trio. It was dark blue with a stylized falcon in white across its chest plate. A pair of particle cannons were mounted on each shoulder. "Valiant Azure."

He turned to Brandon and the others. "You'll get briefed on them soon. Feel free to linger here, but," he squinted at each of them in turn, "no touching!" He didn't even wait for them to nod, turning and stomping off toward the newer suits they'd been ogling earlier. He was barking at some technicians before he was ten feet away.

Brandon looked up at the dented and aging war

machines. He should have known better. New pilots fresh from the academy—new suits don't go to newbies.

He took in each machine. "They could have at least cleaned them."

Lucy was staring up at Valiant Azure. "I think it's beautiful."

Brandon turned toward Midnight Tango, the remaining unclaimed suit. It needed a good cleaning, and its right arm looked like it might fall off, but...He cocked his head to one side.

"YOU THE NEW PILOTS?" a woman in a red technician's jumpsuit asked as she approached the trio, still gawking at their new-to-them suits.

Lucy stepped forward, offering her hand. "We are. Lucy Jones."

The woman nodded. "Jennifer Morris. VarTech." She pointed at the logo on her breast. "I'll be your tech aboard the *Saratoga*." She gave a half-hearted salute, then pointed to the gantry behind the suits. "Your official briefing isn't until tomorrow, but I can give you the high-level tour if you like." She nodded to the three machines. "I need to get them cleaned up still—"

"Oh, thank God," Brandon said. He glanced at Midnight Tango's dented and grimy armored chest.

Morris shook her head. She pointed at Midnight Tango. "Mainly short- to mid-range capabilities. It's got two six-round BFG-9000s with penetrator rounds, one in each leg." She pointed at the panels on the upper thighs of the mech. Squinting, Brandon could make out the seams through the grime.

Morris pointed at the arms. "Its armor is Mark Three. Not the newest or the toughest, but it's been around the block and is still standing."

The pride in the technician's voice was obvious to all three pilots. This woman lived and breathed keeping these suits in the fight.

"So, Jenny—" Brandon wanted to ask about the suit's mismatched arm.

"Jennifer." Her expression flat, she added, "Not Jenny, Jen, J-Dog, Jenny from the Block, or anything else."

Paco leaned in. "Did someone really try to call you J-Dog?"

Ignoring him, the technician turned to Valiant Azure. "Long range. It's meant to hit from a distance." She pointed to the shoulder-mounted particle cannons currently aimed up: their standby position. The powerful arms that moved them tucked into the suit's body. "Those particle cannons are new. Well, new to us. Mark Fours."

Lucy whistled. "Mark Fours?"

Jennifer smiled. "Yup. Salvaged from a gunboat we came across in the Exclusion Zone. The original Mark Ones it had were glitchy and under-powered. These," she grinned, "you'll like 'em."

Lucy nodded her agreement.

Morris continued. "Forearm-mounted beam cannons for close-in fun. They won't penetrate a Category 3's hide, at least at first, but they'll sting." She gestured to the suit's arms. "And," she smiled again, pointing to the mech's thighs, "cluster munitions." Each thigh had a flat rectangular launcher mechanism mounted on it.

Paco nudged Lucy. "Damn, *chica*!" She turned, a smile on her face. He looked at the technician. "Me next."

Jennifer rolled her eyes. "Crusher Maverick." She pointed to the machine Paco had claimed. "Close-in fighter. Built to grapple with the big ones. Category 3s." She pointed to the thick arms and hands of the machine. "More power in those arms than in the other two combined. Twice the number of artificial muscle strands in each arm. Plus beefed-up hyper torque drivers in the shoulders." She looked at Paco. "Only light energy weapons in the pauldrons. Hope you like boxing."

Paco grinned. He was the academy champion.

The trio spent an hour going over the nonclassified ins and outs of their new-to-them suits with Technician Morris until she finally said, "Okay. I've got to get these cleaned up. I'll see you three once we're underway."

Brandon smiled. "See you in a bit, J-Dog." He winked.

She frowned. "No."

He waved.

In the hours they'd spent in the hangar, the ship had come more alive. Crews, both new and returning, packed the corridors, heading for their bunks and duty stations.

Lucy dodged a harried looking crewmember who didn't even slow down as they rushed past them up the corridor heading toward the forward section. She looked at the wayfinding markers on a nearby bulkhead. "I think we need to go three decks up."

"You think?" Brandon teased.

She gave him a look. "I'm not the team map reader. You're welcome to take over."

Brandon held both hands up, palms out. "Lead the way."

Eventually, they found themselves on deck 4 forward, in what was clearly the low-ranking officers' country. Lucy pointed to a door. "This is us."

While academy dorms were not coed, quarters aboard NACAF ships were, especially among suit fire teams. A single suite-like space was assigned to each three-person element, the idea being to facilitate even closer bonding between the pilots.

Paco pushed open the door to their new home. He whistled. "I like."

Lucy looked over his shoulder. "Not bad, all things considered."

IN THE DAYS of ocean-going navies, fighter pilots were the superstars of the boat, the small group of specially trained warriors with the skill to pilot the expensive war machines of their time.

Post impact, that celebrity status shifted to suit pilots, those with the ability, and the physical size, to let their mind transfer into a forty-foot-tall metallic monster. No longer towers of physical power—suit pilots couldn't be taller than five foot ten.

The quarters assigned to fire teams were maybe not

luxurious but better than your average air navy sailor could expect aboard the tight quarters of an air carrier.

Paco rushed past Brandon, shouting, "Dibs!" as he pushed open a door to one of the bedrooms.

"They're all the same, man," Brandon shouted after his friend.

He and Lucy followed their friend into the room. Each fire team berth was three small bedrooms lined up along one wall of a sparse central lounge space, just big enough for a small sofa and desk. Brandon looked at the two remaining doors. "I don't care," he told Lucy.

She headed for one of the two unclaimed doors, opened it, tossed her duffel in, and said, "Done."

Paco emerged from his room. "These are pretty nice."

Brandon eyed his friend as he dropped onto the couch. Not the most comfortable thing he'd ever sat on.

Someone knocked on the door. "Anyone home?" a voice called.

"Come on in!" Brandon shouted from the couch built into the bulkhead.

Lucy and Paco leaned out of their respective doorways.

"Hi," a woman that looked like she was pushing the height limit for pilots, said as she led two other people into the small room. Six people made the room feel crowded. She smiled. "I'm Grace. Grace Abumwe." She offered her hand.

Lucy got to her first, her pale hand contrasting with Grace's much darker one. "Lucy Jones." She nodded toward her friends. "Brandon Sinclair and Paco Molina."

Grace introduced the rest of her team, Alec Lefebvre and Jacob Parsell. "Delta Team. We're across the hall."

Brandon grinned. "We're the new Bravo Team."

Grace nodded. "Big shoes. Bravo were good folks."

"You knew them," Lucy said.

Jacob nodded. "Yeah, served with them the last two years. Great pilots."

Grace pursed her lips then finally said, "We were supposed to be the ready team that day. I had some kind of stomach bug."

"Bad kimchi," Alec offered.

Grace made a pained face.

Alec shook his head, and sandy blonde hair, longer than regulation, fell to his shoulders. "*Très tragique.*"

Brandon shrugged. "Guess that explains our suits."

"Spare parts, *mon ami*," Alec said. "All three Bravo suits were," he searched for the right words, "a total loss."

Grace shook her head. "Anyway. Welcome to the *Saratoga*. Want a tour of the ship?"

Lucy nodded. "That would be great!"

Alec grinned. "We know where all the best hidey-holes are." He winked, causing Lucy to find the deck very interesting as a blush crept up her cheeks.

Brandon resisted the urge to give his friend a hard time, instead nodding to the door. "Lead the way."

VIRIDIAN SLAMMER DUCKED under the long-armed swipe of Crusher Maverick. "So close," her pilot chided. The lithe green suit pivoted out of Maverick's reach, jabbing the larger shell once in the chest. The sound of metal on metal rang.

"You're quick!" Paco said as he stumbled backward. The millions of sensors in his second skin and thinking cap translated to a pressure in his chest.

Valiant Azure appeared from behind the bulkier Maverick. The blue and white suit spun, her right leg coming up into a kick that almost connected with Slammer's torso, had the other mech not deflected the blow with her arms, sending Azure stumbling.

"Nice move," Stacy Decker, pilot of Viridian Slammer, said over the squad channel.

Bravo Team and Stacy—Charlie Two—were in complex rigs that deck hands had wheeled into the center of the *Saratoga*'s mech hangar. Each simulator unit resembled the secure pilot's crèche in a suit. Thick data cables connected each unit to a central control interface.

The other pilots and many hangar crew members gathered around large displays showing the simulation in progress.

When Midnight Tango got a lucky shot in—a punch that sent Viridian Slammer stumbling backwards—everyone in the hangar let out a whoop.

In the simulation, Azure was keeping Slammer busy. Brandon guided Midnight Tango around the training area's edge. The green armored mech tilted as Azure moved in to grapple, reaching an arm under Lucy's suit, toppling the enormous machine.

Before Azure hit the deck, Brandon charged again.

Viridian Slammer turned in time to see the oncoming matte black shell.

"Oh, crap," Stacy said as the two mechs collided with an ear shattering gong. The two machines went down in a tangle of limbs. Slammer reached up, trying to get a grip on the large sail behind Tango's head.

"Oh, no you don't!" Lucy shouted. Metal hands, painted blue with white accents, grabbed Slammer's arm, pulling it away from Tango's head.

Over the squad channel, the field ops commander said, "Stand down. Well done, Bravo Team."

Everyone's helmet visor went dark, then turned transparent.

As the simulation pods opened, Stacy said, "Echo that. You three did pretty good. Not perfect, but better than other greenies I've met."

"Thanks," Lucy said as she slipped her thinking cap off and eased herself out of the rig and onto the deck.

"I'm sure we'd have done even better if we'd had weapons," Brandon groused. This exercise focused on their hand-to-hand skills. Each simulated suit had its weapons locked down.

"Anyone can point and shoot," Charlie Two replied. As she jumped down to the deck from the simulator rig, she added, "Pilot's lounge in twenty. Debrief and beers." She didn't wait for an acknowledgement, heading for one of the forward hatches.

"Copy that!" Brandon said. He was furious and embarrassed but knew no one could see his face, so he didn't bother schooling his expression. After taking a calming breath, he hopped out of his rig and pulled his helmet off. "That was fun."

"I think we did pretty good," Paco said, joining Brandon and Lucy near the control terminal for the simulators. He looked around at the monitors and the crowd of *Saratoga* crewmembers slowly returning to their duties. "Guess we put on a good show."

"Hope they enjoyed," Brandon said. He looked up at the twelve massive mechs looming over them all. Their three were a bit cleaner than they had been when they'd boarded the ship, but not much.

Spying Technician Morris near Midnight Tango's foot, Paco called out, "Jay Jay. I think the left hip joint might be sticking. Is that a known thing?" They built the simulations on live performance data from the suits. It made for a great way to test suits without powering them up and stomping around the hangar.

She looked up from her tablet and nodded. "Yeah. I'll take a look. It does that sometimes."

"*Gracias*," he shouted.

Fifteen minutes later, Bravo Team and Charlie Two were sitting in the corner of the pilot's lounge that had a pair of large chairs and a sofa around a wall-mounted vid screen. Stacy pulled up a recording, selecting from one of the hundreds of virtual cameras' angles available.

Lucy leaned forward. "Wow. The fidelity is incredible. I mean, I expected the sensory feeds to be hi-fi, but even the recordings? Cool."

Stacy nodded. "They make the virtual trainings invaluable. We can examine every move from hundreds of angles." She picked up a tablet from the coffee table and said, "Okay. Let's dive in."

"Be gentle," Brandon said with a smile.

"No chance," Charlie Two replied with a smirk, a slight twinkle in her eye. He blushed.

CHAPTER FOUR

"ATTENTION. Attention. All hands prepare for departure," the 1MC blared.

Commander Willis turned to his captain. "All sections report ready for departure, sir."

Captain Thomas Bartell nodded, then turned to the conn team. "Conn, release moorings."

The ensign at the ship's conn nodded. "Moorings released. Course?"

"San Antonio," the captain answered. He turned to his XO. "You read the report?"

Willis nodded. "No contact in a week. That's not good. Think it's like those teams that vanished in China?"

The *Saratoga* rumbled as her antigravity drive powered up. Through the bridge's forward window, he could see the ship's forward cannons near the massive ship's bow. Most of the air carrier's weapons were mounted on her underside, where they could be brought to bear on megafauna on the ground.

From the bridge, the massive air carrier's forward

section was a metallic gray expanse. Sensors and access panels dotted the artificial landscape. The NACAF Denver tower docking arm receded as the mighty ship slowly turned its bow south, the deck tilting slightly as the ship spun in the air.

Bartell shook his head. "I hope not. But who the hell knows with this alien mess? The megafauna are as hard to understand now as when they arrived. And seem to be getting smarter faster than we are."

"If it was an attack, it's been a while since we've seen one of this scale," Commander Willis said. He tapped his chin. "Reminds me of La Paz."

The captain nodded his agreement. "Or Puerto Vallarta." Out the window, the *Roosevelt,* still docked to the tower, her forward guns in their locked position, looked magnificent. He smiled.

Willis grimaced. "Okay, maybe it's not as rare. That's kind of terrifying."

His commanding officer grunted.

Taking what militaries around the world knew about aircraft carriers and mixing with VarTech's highly classified technology had resulted in hovering rectangles that bristled with guns, missile launchers, antennas, and more.

"They should have just abandoned Texas. We coulda used tactical weapons to keep the area a no-man's—no-monster's—land," Willis said.

In the fifteen years since impact, the slow but as yet unstoppable spread of megaflora had taken more and more territory. Year after year, cities and towns north and south of the impact crater were abandoned when the fight against the alien plants and animals was lost.

"You've met Texans," the captain answered.

The world tried nukes and weapons—conventional, chemical, and biological. Most had little to no impact or caused too much collateral damage. The alien plants always, slowly, returned, taking more and more ground, out-competing native plant and animal species until they were killed or driven off. Once the megaflora were established, it was impossible to reclaim that territory.

The world post impact was becoming more and more resource constrained. Much of China and a large portion of Africa and the Middle East had fallen. As megaflora spread and consumed more land, refugees flooded the less-affected countries. Between focusing on keeping megaflora at bay and dealing with millions of refugees, building out high tech industry often took a backseat. Any and everything else was even less of a priority.

"We're on course, sir," the helmsman announced.

"Half thrust until we're clear of Denver's airspace. Then full speed ahead," Captain Bartell said. He turned to the communications station. "Let Command know we're en route to investigate Forward Operating Base San Antonio's silence."

"Yes, sir," the ensign at the station replied.

The pair of powerful jet turbine thrusters at the rear of the ship roared as they cycled up.

Willis handed him a tablet. "Latest reports." Every country and coalition shared data freely to ensure no one was caught by surprise. Data was collated weekly and disseminated to bases and ships.

"Damn." The captain looked up from the device.

Commander Willis nodded. "I heard a rumor that the

VarTech nerds think another evolutionary surge is coming. Bangkok and Beijing are reporting mutations."

Bartell shook his head. "We can barely keep up with these things as they are. If they keep evolving every couple of years..." He sighed. "Shit."

His executive officer nodded.

"ETA?" the captain asked, offering the tablet back.

Willis consulted the device. "Four hours."

Under their feet, the rumble of the *Saratoga*'s thrusters ramping up to full power could be felt. Combined with the antigravity motors that few understood, the massive engines could get an air carrier up to just above 0.5 Mach. Not as fast as commercial aircraft, but no slouch for something their size, lacking an ounce of aerodynamics.

DOWN IN THE ship's hangar, the four fire teams were gathered in a loose circle of folding chairs in the center of the massive metal cavern. Alpha One, Molly Chen, said, "I hear San Antonio Base is gone."

"No way," Grace said. She leaned back in her chair, tilting it rearward on its back legs. "San Antonio means Houston means Austin." She looked around at her fellow pilots. "Plus, we'd have heard."

Molly shrugged. Brandon watched the more experienced pilots' banter. Alpha and Delta Teams had been aboard the *Saratoga* for two years each. Charlie Team had almost as long a tenure but currently was down to one suit, Charlie Two. Stacy Decker. The other two pilots had been injured in the same attack that led to the three Bravo Team pilots being killed and were convalescing back in Denver.

It was clear to him that these men and women were close, which only made him feel more like an outsider. He glanced over to Lucy who was chuckling at something Alec Lefebvre had whispered. She'd bonded with the Delta Team pilot when they discovered their shared history growing up outside Winnipeg. No one else was from Vail.

Shipwide scuttlebutt had it that Commander Tanner, head of field ops, had put in for replacement pilots for Charlie Team, but all the graduating class cadets had already been assigned. Until two pilots were found, Charlie Team was on ice and Stacy was acting as training officer.

"Think it's infested?" Paco asked, adding, "Monsters, I mean."

One of the pilots from Alpha—Brandon thought his name was Rick or Vick or something—said, "Yeah, probably. That is, if it fell." He looked to his team leader. "I'm not sure I buy it. I mean, San Antonio? Come on."

Everyone fell silent.

"What was the force strength at the FOB?" Lucy asked.

"Just one fire team," Grace answered. She shook her head. "They should've had more than that." Everyone nodded. "Especially after the city fell. Keeping that area clear is—was—more than a three-suit job."

THE RUINS of Joint Base San Antonio lay spread out below the *Saratoga*. Purple and orange vines as thick as a man's torso snaked across the facility. Reinforced concrete was no match for the alien plant life; entire buildings had already been toppled. The vines came first, then the tree analogs sprouted, shooting hundreds of feet into the air. Then came the monsters.

The base fell a few years ago, but the NACAF had been doing its level best to keep the city safe. That all ended a month ago.

"Still can't believe it," one crewmember said. She was staring at one of the monitors showing a view from one of the underside cameras. She turned to the crewman next to her. "I was born here."

In the distance, the downtown core of San Antonio was crumbling, a mass of glass, steel, and odd-colored vines and trees. Occasionally, a creature not from Earth would lope, slither, or crawl from one building to another.

In the days post impact, a surge of refugees from Mexico swamped the United States' southern border. The North American Coalition was still forming and there was little either Mexico or the U.S. could do to slow the flow of people seeking safety to the north.

The southern reaches of Mexico, Belize, and Guatemala were nearly wiped out by the asteroid strike, and those few that survived that devastation fell to the airborne dust and alien particles that rained down for months.

A widening gap of alien life isolated North and South America from each other every year.

When it was clear that San Antonio was going to fall,

the NACAF set up a small forward operating base to monitor the northward creep of megaflora.

The senior communications officer looked up. "I'm not getting an answer from the base."

Commander Willis frowned, checking his tablet. "Supposed to be a fire team and a couple dozen NACAF support folks and some VarTech folks. Hundred souls, give or take."

"I've got eyes on the base," another bridge officer called out.

Captain Bartell nodded to the display nearest him. "Put it up here."

The screen came to life, showing the ruins of the operating base. The buildings and suit hangar were in shambles—vines clinging to the sides, pulling the buildings apart. Smoke was still drifting from some of the debris. Of the three-suit fire team, there was no sign. The suit hangar had a massive hole in its side.

"What on earth happened here?" Bartell wondered. "The monsters have never strategically attacked a base before."

Lincoln nodded, running a hand through his light brown hair. "We should investigate."

The captain took a long, slow breath. "Yeah." He strode toward the forward stations. "Helm, bring us over Forward Base." Turning back to Commander Willis, he said, "Prep a team."

Willis nodded. "Yes, sir."

THE PILOTS HAD MOVED their vid-feed watching to the pilot's lounge off the main hangar deck. Brandon and the team were with the other three fire teams, watching San Antonio and the remains of the NACAF Base on the camera feeds.

Someone whistled and said, "Damn."

One of the Alpha Team pilots said, "I remember when San Antonio had a population in the millions."

Brandon looked over at the man. He did look old enough to have seen San Antonio pre impact. It was the only time the city boasted a population that high. After the asteroids, those who could, moved north as refugees from Mexico flooded the city on their own way north. *How long had Alpha Team been on the job?*

"Look!" another pilot shouted. Delta Team. Brandon couldn't remember his name. So many new names.

One of the large monitors was showing the ruins of a suburban neighborhood. Homes and buildings were smashed to pieces. Bodies were scattered everywhere. A haze of smoke lingered everywhere, blanketing the entire town.

"They didn't even have time to flee," Grace Abumwe said in a low voice, as if the dead would hear.

Further along, the remains of a megafauna lay sprawled across what had once been a park. The thing's bright orange blood was a bubbling pool. Next to it was the lower half of a suit: gray with bright red accents.

"Crackers, that's one ugly monster," someone said.

Another said, "Category 3, at least."

"Can you tell which suit that is?" Sophie Belanger from Alpha Team asked.

One of the Deltas, Alec Lefebvre, asked, "Do we know which team was stationed here?"

Several voices commented that they couldn't identify the suit, nor did they know which team was supposed to be guarding the base. Everyone fell silent as the mangled remains of the top of the suit came into view, still unidentifiable, draped across the roof of a warehouse.

Someone groaned.

The room's loudspeaker crackled, breaking everyone out of their dark thoughts. "All pilots to your shells. All pilots to your shells. Alpha Team, you drop in five. Delta Team, you're on standby."

The six pilots of Alpha and Delta stood and bolted out of the lounge.

Brandon looked at Paco and Lucy. "What crap." He leaned back in his chair to gaze at the ceiling.

Lucy reached over and gave Brandon's chair a shove, causing him to jerk before falling over, his chair slamming to the deck.

Paco reached over and put a hand on his friend's shoulder. "We're all suiting up, *amigo*." He glanced over at Stacy. "Sorry, *amiga*."

She gave him a half-hearted smile and shrug. "I'll be there if needed." She turned and led them out into the hangar.

The hum of micro fusion reactors was already echoing around the massive space. Alpha and Delta suits were powered up, flexing arms, shifting from foot to foot as their pilots integrated with the massive machines.

Brandon stopped short as one of Alpha's suits stepped from its rack into the middle of the hangar.

"Fire team Alpha, prepare for drop!" the speakers in the ceiling blared. Brandon turned to look up at the large windows that let the field ops center look out over the hangar.

Two more suits stomped into the center of the hangar.

Along the bottom of the *Saratoga,* three of six armored hatches slid open revealing chutes.

Each Alpha Team suit stepped up to a circular hatch outlined in yellow and black. From the ceiling, a trio of tethers made of high tensile steel lowered to the deck, a thick magnetic latch at the end. Each Alpha Team suit grabbed a tether and attached it to the back of a teammate. All three suits took up position next to one of the circular hatches.

Each hatch slid open, revealing a tube lit by four light strips that ran straight down, ending at the open sky and ground, at the end.

Bravo Team powered up their suits but remained in their docking cradles, watching as Alpha Team, as one, stepped into the open portals in the floor, dropping out of sight.

"Have fun," Brandon said.

THE LANDING FIELD of Forward Operating Base San Antonio was cracked and devastated, the tarmac torn up by vines and enormous claws.

The shuttle touched down with a crunch. Before the engines even started to spin down, the rear hatch dropped, allowing twenty well-armed marines to disembark and spread out around the craft.

Commander Lincoln Willis stepped off the ramp as the senior marine approached. "All clear, sir." A trio of VarTech scientists cautiously stepped out of the shuttle, following the commander.

Half a kilometer away, three forty-foot-tall metal warriors landed with ear-splitting thuds on the cracked tarmac. Straightening, the three suits brought their powerful searchlights online. Tacit Ronin, Alpha One, turned to look at the shuttle, nodding her massive head. Alpha Team moved to take up position around the base, their footfalls loud in the eerie silence of the deserted base.

Willis watched the three war machines move off in different directions, then turned and nodded to the marines and VarTech scientists. "Okay, let's go."

The base command center was a two-story concrete structure, created with fast setting materials with an eye toward function over everything else. It looked as much like a bunker as anything else. Of the few buildings that made up the FOB, it was the only one that was still standing. The marines entered first, securing the heavily damaged lobby.

Willis and the VarTech team followed. The former whistled. "Damn." The building's exterior sported several gouges, likely made by enormous claws. By all rights, the interior should have been mostly untouched, but it was anything but. The lobby resembled the set of a postapocalyptic horror movie. Several bodies and parts of bodies were strewn about, marines and science types alike.

The commander turned to the lead marine. "Spread out. Divvy up your team. No squint goes unescorted."

The three VarTech employees rolled their eyes but nodded to the marines and split up. Willis fell in with the senior-most researcher, Becca Otinabe. "You know of anything in particular VarTech was up to here?"

She shook her head. "Even if I did, I'm sure it's classified."

Willis rolled his eyes. VarTech was joined at the hip with most of the world's militaries but did what, when, and how it wanted. "We are on the same team," he said under his breath. He saw her roll her eyes.

The command building was divided into several sections between the two floors and the partially excavated basement level. Willis, Otinabe, and seven marines emerged from the stairs into the lower level. The emergency lighting cast everything in a sickly red light.

The petite scientist panned her flashlight around. "Not spooky." From up ahead, something metal fell to the ground with a thud. "Spoke too soon." The marines snapped into action, moving ahead of the scientist and commander. Two marines stayed back, while the other five moved to secure the basement level.

"Found the backup battery. Should have minimal power in thirty seconds," one of the marines shouted.

Moments later, the flickering red emergency lighting was replaced with slightly less-flickering standard lighting. The brighter lighting revealed the blood smears that covered the floor and walls.

Willis turned to his companion. "Not sure this is better."

Before she could answer, a helmeted head leaned out of one of the doorways. "All clear, Commander. No sign of monsters, big or little."

From another doorway someone added, "You mean besides this?"

Willis and Otinabe rushed to the door and looked in. The marine in the room was pointing his rifle at a table with a dissected creature sprawled out across the top. Long limbs dangled over the sides. A Category 1 creature by the size of it.

Willis turned to Otinabe, who shrugged. "Never seen one like that." She moved next to the table, her eyes never leaving the creature. The marine took a step back, making room for her, his rifle never wavering. Otinabe smiled. "Half of its guts are in buckets over there." She pointed. "I think you can lower your rifle."

The marine cocked his head then looked at Willis, who nodded.

Willis looked around the room. "What was VarTech up to down here?"

Otinabe looked up from the dead creature. "You know everything down here is classified." She coughed, glancing at the marine. "Sir."

Willis looked at the ceiling, multiple expletives on the tip of his tongue. VarTech wouldn't let anyone that wasn't VarTech get anywhere near anything they did. Whatever they were up to down here, if Otinabe figured it out, she wouldn't share.

"Uh, got something back here, too," one of the marines called out.

Willis pointed to a terminal in the corner. "Okay, get what you can. We're not gonna be here long." The scientists nodded.

The marine who'd called out was standing outside the last door in the hallway—the farthest corner of the underground section. As Willis reached her, she tilted her head toward the open door.

Willis looked inside and swore. Whatever the room's purpose, it was lost into the massive sinkhole that filled most of the room, and some of the room next to it, the wall between them sagging toward the dark void.

"Uh, Doc. Otinabe? Come take a look at this, please."

The VarTech researcher leaned around Willis to look in the room and gasped. "Well, damn."

CHAPTER FIVE

CLAW MARKS WERE CLEARLY visible along the perimeter of the hole. Otinabe leaned down to shine a flashlight on a set of marks where she was standing. "These look like they match our little friend in the other room."

Willis shook his head. "These things tunnel now? In large numbers?"

The small scientist stood and looked up at the commander. "I need to get back to the ship."

Willis smiled. "Finish getting everything you can out of that terminal in there. I'm going to check the base commander's office." He didn't wait for a reply, leaving the scientist and her marine escort. Snapping his fingers at the two marines in the hallway, he said, "You two. With me."

Otinabe turned to her marine. "Let's go."

Commander Willis stepped into the base commander's office and found it in better shape than he expected, based on the hallway outside. A dozen marines gave their lives keeping this room from danger. No sign of the base's commander, though.

There was a layer of dust over everything, but that was the state of the entire facility. Multiton monsters fighting multiton robots tends to dislodge dust at an incredible pace.

The computer was online, but it looked like the commander executed a purge before the base fell. Why? The monsters couldn't operate computers. Could they? He shuddered.

"So, they found the first one, then what? The rest tunneled in and wiped everyone out?"

"Sorry, sir?" one of the marines asked from out in the hallway.

"Just thinking out loud," he replied. Tapping the screen a few times, he smiled. Sure enough, the security recordings weren't part of the normal purge routine. He pulled up the day that recordings stopped.

On the screen, he watched as ugly little monsters like the one dissected in the basement poured out into the building. Marines and VarTech scientists fell at the tidal wave of vicious creatures.

Then, one of the outer cameras spotted it: the first megafauna. A Category 3 charged out of the alien jungle. In another window, a similar beast emerged from behind one of the buildings of San Antonio. How it got so close, Willis couldn't be sure.

"Christ," he whispered. He watched as the fire team assigned to FOB San Antonio scrambled to action. Two suits were powering up when the nearest megafauna crashed through the hangar's side. It tackled one of the suits. The impact threw its pilot clear of the craft before she could reach her pilot's crèche.

"My God." He watched as the creature stood atop the downed suit, beating it with both fists. It turned to the still powered down suit, the pilot visibly trying to climb the damaged gantry, backhanding the machine. The suit came free of the gantry, toppling.

The third suit unleashed a salvo of weapons fire, driving the beast back out of the hangar the way it came in. The gray suit with red accents followed, its weapons blazing.

THE REMAINING fire teams were in the pilot's lounge watching Alpha Team patrol the remains of Forward Base San Antonio.

"Damn, that place took a beating," Jacob Parsell, Delta Two, said.

The screens showed a split view from each of the three suit's external cameras as well as overhead views from *Saratoga*'s myriad cameras. Several shuttles and various ground vehicles lay scattered across the damaged tarmac.

"Think we'll see the other two suits somewhere?" Brandon asked out loud, to no one in particular.

On the screen, Void Romeo—Alpha Three—stepped into what remained of the suit hangar. "Found the other two suits," Victor Isaacson announced. The feed panned around the massive space, settling first on one suit, then the other.

"They didn't even have a chance," Brandon said. He pointed to the body of one of the pilots, mangled near the foot of her suit.

Grace shook her head. "Megafauna don't sneak attack."

"That we know of," Paco said. Everyone turned to look at him. "What?"

"He's right," Brandon insisted. "This is different. How do monsters get the drop on us? Those pilots weren't even in their suits."

The speakers in the ceiling crackled. "All decks, all decks. Prepare for departure."

When that announcement ended, Commander Tanner came on the speakers only in the pilot's lounge and the cavernous hangar beyond. "Prepare for suit retrieval operations. Repeat, prepare for suit retrieval."

While most of the pilots remained seated, watching the video feeds, Brandon got up to go watch Alpha Team return to base.

Orange warning lights were spinning in the corners of the hangar floor as well as several key areas where the crew moved around the hangar.

Three thick cables lowered from the hangar ceiling. A moment before the thick magnetic tethers hit the hangar deck, three massive circular hatches slid open. The cables continued to unspool, lowering the cables down to the ground seventy meters below.

Jennifer Morris walked up to stand next to Brandon. "Amazing we can just reel them in, right?"

Brandon didn't turn his head. "Yeah. Like fish. Those tethers ever fail?"

The VarTech technician shook her head. "Not that I can recall." She nodded toward the trio of thick braided cables as they twitched and went taut. "Same stuff makes up the muscle strands in most current suits."

This made Brandon turn. "Really?"

Jennifer nodded. "Yup. Lotta the same tech is used between platforms." She smiled. "I can't say much more than that, sorry."

Brandon shook his head. "How do they get away with that?"

"What?"

"The secrets. I mean the NAC, the South Americans, Pacific Alliance, African Union, all of them. They all work with VarTech and VarTech keeps all of them in the dark about how the tech works."

The technician shrugged. "What's the alternative? Work with MechDyne? They're generations behind us. Their load lifters and smaller stuff is great but they're nowhere near VarTech in terms of suits."

Brandon ran a hand through his hair. "Wonder why?"

The three cables sang as they reeled in suits that weighed tons. Without warning, three metal warriors popped up from the hatches in the floor. As soon as they cleared the deck, they spread their feet just enough to straddle the openings as the powerful winches released the magnetic tethers and the hatch in the deck slammed closed.

The sound of three suits dropping to the metal deck rang throughout the hangar. Brandon winced.

Jennifer grinned, then headed off to see if the Alpha Team technicians needed any help.

Brandon watched her go, his last question still on his mind. Why did VarTech have such a lead on suits, and other specific tech, but wasn't that far ahead in other areas? He shook his head.

Alpha Team made their way to their docking cradles.

ONCE THE SUITS and ground team were back aboard the *Saratoga*, Captain Bartell made contact with NACAF Command in Calgary.

Admiral Lancaster nodded. "We assumed as much, but it's good, as such, to confirm." She sighed and shook her head. Her mid-length curly hair bobbed as her head moved. She looked at Bartell. "Were you able to account for all the base personnel?"

"No, ma'am," Bartell replied. "There was too much carnage and damage to the facility. But we scanned with everything we have. We used all of our high-gain microphones to listen for anyone trapped in the rubble. Nothing."

The older woman nodded. "Very well. I've got new orders for *Saratoga*."

Bartell leaned forward. "Yes, ma'am?"

"There's a town. West of your position. Piedras Negras," the admiral said.

The captain reached for his tablet. The admiral continued, "Right at the old border. Technically behind it now. NAC helped reinforce it three years ago. Quiet since. No sign of megaflora."

Bartell wasn't sure where this was going. "And?"

The woman on the screen pressed her lips into a thin line. "We've lost contact."

Bartell sighed. "Think it's related to San Antonio?"

She gave him a noncommittal shrug. "Maybe? I feel like something is going on, but fuck if I know what it is, and VarTech isn't being super helpful at the moment."

"Are they ever?"

"No. But this feels like more than normal VarTech fuckery." Bartell had forgotten how salty the old admiral was. He liked it and her. She always did her best to give it straight to those under her command. This felt like one of those times. She continued, "If it is, we need to figure out what's going on, and fast. When word gets out that FOB SA fell with very literally no warning, the news is gonna have a field day. The new round of idiot wall builders will go nuts."

Bartell shook his head. Wall builders. How they thought walls were the answer when all the very clear and very deadly evidence pointed to the opposite, was beyond him, but it seemed like every other election, someone was certain they had the plan—the thing no one else thought of, that would make their wall different from every other wall every other nation and alliance had tried at one time or another in the last fifteen years. Anything so long as it wasn't spending money on the thing everyone knew worked: flying aircraft carriers and giant robots.

"A fast cargo hauler is on the way with some of the

parts you requested. Might as well hang tight where you are until it arrives, then get moving for Piedras Negras," the admiral said. When he nodded, she closed the channel.

Thomas Bartell leaned back in his chair for a few moments, thinking over what had just been discussed. With a sigh, he heaved himself out of his chair and made for the exit of his ready room.

The bridge was the usual hive of activity. Officers occupied every station, and most stations also had a second officer nearby conversing with the watch stander. He spied Commander Willis near the map table in the center of the aft section of the bridge conversing with someone. Bartell was blanking on her name, from the tactical division.

"Sir?" Willis said, seeing his commanding officer approach. The tactical officer moved off to join her colleagues.

Bartell looked at the map table. "There's a courier en route. Priority one to get it offloaded fast when it arrives." His XO nodded, so he continued, "New orders. Some town on the other side of the old border. NAC helped them fortify a few years ago, been relatively quiet since." He locked eyes with his XO. "They went quiet a week ago."

"That timing seems...suspicious."

Bartell nodded. "Yeah."

Willis gave him a look, then shook his head. "Let's not jump to conclusions, sir. Could be nothing."

"You think we're that lucky?"

The commander nodded, conceding the point. He

looked down at the map table and tapped a few commands into the control panel. A green icon appeared with a range indicator next to it. "Looks like we'll be here for another two hours."

The captain nodded. He turned toward the forward stations, raising his voice. "Helm, distance to...what was the town called?" He glanced down at the map table, spotting it. "Piedras Negras."

The young ensign at the helm tapped commands into her station, then looked over her shoulder. "Fifty minutes. At standard cruise. Thirty at full speed."

Bartell smiled. "Hold that plot. We'll leave as soon as the supply ship departs."

"Yes, sir."

CHAPTER SIX

THE AFT HATCH of the main hangar was wide open. The dusky southern Texas sky filled the opening like an oil painting.

Despite pilots enjoying extra special status aboard ship, even they were banned from the hangar when cargo operations were underway. The same orange strobes that announced impending suit drops were spinning away, now announcing the imminent arrival of a cargo shuttle.

Air carriers were expensive even when measured against the old wet navy aircraft carriers. Keeping them moving at the edges of the NAC where monsters were was paramount, which meant a network of craft that could carry cargo quickly from bases in the interior of the territory to the border regions was a must.

NACAF cargo couriers were huge semi-aerodynamic rectangles with immensely powerful engines. They could cover a lot of ground quickly. Couriers were the lifeblood of the NACAF, moving personnel and equipment around so that carriers could remain near the borders and the threats beyond.

Courier NC-12 lined up directly aft of the *Saratoga* on a slow and easy approach. Deck hands in the hangar watched as the big craft slowly closed the gap.

Four powerful lift engines, similar to, but smaller than *Saratoga*'s, pivoted on articulated gimbles at each corner of the craft, allowing it to hover as it crept closer to the bigger craft.

"All hands. All hands. Prepare for courier docking," the overhead speakers announced. The NC-12 was barely fifty feet from the short flight apron at the carrier's rear. Everyone in the hangar jumped to action, preparing to secure the courier to the deck the moment it touched down.

The big courier ship slid inside the hangar, barely clearing the massive hatch's top. The craft was nearly as long as the hangar itself. As it progressed deeper into the hangar, a series of warning blasts from external horns sounded. Moments later, the lift engines wound down and the cargo vessel settled on thick struts that let the ship rest barely a meter above the deck.

Deck hands swarmed the craft the moment its engines went quiet.

Up in the Field Ops Command Center, Commander Tanner watched the activity below. From the forward end of the cargo vessel, several power loaders were removing a matte gray suit arm. He turned to one of his subordinates. "Who's that for?" He spied two men, each carrying a fleet issue duffel bag over a shoulder heading for the hatch that led to the lift connecting the Field Ops Command Center to the hangar.

The young officer frowned, brushing a stray lock of hair from her forehead before checking the tablet in her other hand. "Morris, sir. For Midnight Tango."

Tanner glanced to the Bravo Team section of the hangar and the glossy black suit with the damaged arm. He nodded. "Let her know she can get to work in an hour."

"Yes, sir."

The hatch to the command center slid open to allow the two men from below to enter. The taller of the two stepped forward. "Malcolm Taggart reporting for duty." The other snapped to attention next to him. "Brady Davidson reporting for duty."

Tanner nodded to both. "Welcome aboard the *Saratoga*." He turned to the man next to him. "I'll be back in a bit." He didn't wait for the young officer to respond, turning back to the two new arrivals. "Come on, I'll show you to your teammate."

"Thank you, sir. What can you tell us about her?" the dark-skinned pilot, Davidson, asked.

Tanner grinned. "She's tough as nails and won't hesitate to have your back in the field. Just don't fuck with her."

"But she's not team lead?" the other pilot said.

Tanner looked over his shoulder. "Not for lack of training on my part. Just so we're clear. You both come highly recommended and your experience aboard the *Detroit* speaks highly of you, but Stacy Decker has earned team lead. Command hasn't seen fit to act on my recommendations yet."

"Good to know," Davidson said.

UP ON THE BRIDGE, Captain Bartell watched as the cargo courier slid out of the hangar deck an hour after it had set down. "Chief never disappoints." The nimble craft pivoted in the air just off the massive carrier's bow then accelerated away on to its next assignment.

Commander Willis nodded. "Pretty sure he would have pushed it off the deck himself if his people didn't get it done on time."

The courier cleared the carrier's aft, turning slowly to point north.

"Captain, the chief of the boat signals that we're ready to get underway," one of the junior officers at the comm section announced.

"Acknowledged," Bartell said, then turned to the forward stations closest to the massive transparent front section. "Helm, set course for..." He turned to Willis. "What's it called again?"

"Piedras Negras."

Bartell nodded. "Piedras Negras."

"Course set, sir."

"Let's get moving," Bartell said.

The powerful thrusters at the *Saratoga*'s rear below and on either side of the rear hangar entry throttled up with a rumble.

The camera view of the hangar showed the massive rear door sliding closed. Bartell could almost hear the loud thud of the door closing several decks up on the bridge.

LUCY SMILED at the team's technician. "Jennifer, these look amazing!"

All three Bravo suits looked brand new. Well, five years old but cleaner than before.

"Hey, wait a minute." Brandon had his head cocked as he looked Midnight Tango up and down. "That's not the arm it had when we came aboard." He pointed to the mech's right arm. When he and his team came aboard and first saw their suits, the matte black mech's arm was mangled, barely connected at the shoulder. The forearm armor was stripped away, revealing the thick artificial muscle strands, oozing some sort of orange lubricant.

The new arm, flat gray, not black, looked brand new. Actually brand new, like from a factory. The pauldron was emblazoned with the NACAF logo.

Paco walked up to Midnight Tango, standing under the new arm, looking up at it. He could see something near the back of the gray armored hand at the wrist. "What's it do?" he asked.

Jennifer smiled. "Deployable triple-bonded metal blade with braided steel high tension cable. Fifty feet. Can retract from fully deployed in twenty seconds." She was obviously proud. "Was able to call in a favor before we left Denver. Took a while to get here, but the cargo shuttle caught up to us after we left San Antonio."

"Sweet," Brandon said.

The hangar loudspeaker crackled again. "Bravo and Delta Teams, prepare for drop. You're backing up Alpha."

Jennifer turned to look at the three pilots standing around the matte black leg of Midnight Tango. She looked at them. "Well? That's you!" She pointed at Tango. "Suit up!"

Brandon turned to his two friends and teammates. "Let's go!"

They ran to the ladders mounted on the bulkhead behind their suits as orange lights around the hangar strobed and Alpha's pilots ran to their suits. Next to each ladder was a small changing room where their bespoke pilot's suits, or second skins, were stored. They each ducked in, getting out of their shipboard coveralls and into the skintight garments as quickly as possible. One of the things drilled into cadets at the academy was how to get suited up as quickly as possible.

Almost at the same time, the three pilots stepped out of the changing rooms and headed up their respective ladders.

While all suits were more or less the same height, about forty feet, not all of them had the same dimensions. Paco stopped climbing his ladder, stepping onto a platform lined up with an open hatch in his suit's back, the secure pilot's crèche. Several hinged armored panels exposed a human-sized indentation, with matching arm shafts extending deeper into the machine. Crusher Maverick's shorter legs and longer arms meant the crèche was several feet lower than those of his friends. He looked up, spotting both of them still climbing their respective ladders and chuckled. "That's why I picked the stubby one."

He eyed the crèche. Sensor contacts were arrayed in a grid along every centimeter of the memory foam lining. The first time he stepped in, the onboard computer mapped every inch of him. Every time he got in, the crèche would hold him firmly and safely in place. No one wanted to scoop a pilot out of the crèche. He walked far enough to look around Maverick's wide frame. "Hey J-Mo! This padding looks good! *Muy lindo!*"

The VarTech technician scowled up at him.

He looked up at the platform a few yards above and forward of his, where Lucy was standing. "Ready, Luce?"

She looked down at Paco, a lopsided grin on her face. She nodded and gave him a wave, then stepped from the platform to the opening in her suit's back. Her arms slid into the waiting receptacles like she was giving Valiant Azure's power core a hug. As the memory gel pressed in around her, the sensor contacts in her suit clicked into place with their match in the in the crèche. Behind and above her, an umbilical deployed connecting to the top of her helmet. The crèche was airtight when sealed, but ports all along the suit's torso provided filtered air to the pilot.

Brandon watched Lucy and Paco step into their suits. Turning to his own shell, he took a deep breath and stepped into the pilot's crèche.

As his suit locked into the crèche, the multiple armor panels in Midnight Tango's back folded into place, securing the crèche.

The suit's power core moved from standby to full power, bringing systems online and flooding Brandon's sensorium with input. His skin tingled as current ran through the suit's systems. He flexed his right hand, or rather his suit did, but the sensors in the massive metal hand fed data to his nervous system as if it were his own hand. His helmet's visor flickered and came to life showing not just the view from the massive machine's head, but a full heads-up display with weapons status, suit integrity, power core operation, and more.

He was really glad the suits didn't have faces that could mimic their pilots because he knew his would have an incredibly goofy grin on it. "Here we go!" Brandon shouted, stepping out of his docking cradle.

ONLY VARTECH KNEW how the suit-to-pilot interface worked. The theory shared among pilots and everyone else who wasn't VarTech was that the connections on the pilot suit transmitted nerve impulses between the pilot and the machine. The helmet they wore fed them a view directly from the machine's optics.

The part no one outside of VarTech understood was how the pilot's second skin immobilized the pilot while still allowing nerve impulses to move the suit itself. Pilots felt like they were running, even though their bodies were motionless. Their head never moved, even when the suit turned its head.

Midnight Tango took a step forward. Over the team

channel, Brandon said, "Bravo Team. Sound off. Bravo One."

"Wait, why are you Bravo One?" Lucy asked, stepping out of her crèche, Valiant Azure putting her hands on her hips.

"I'm a natural leader," Brandon replied. Midnight Tango turned its head, cocking it.

"I have far higher scores in leadership," Lucy quipped, stepping past him toward their assigned drop chutes.

"What about me?" Paco demanded. Crusher Maverick joined Valiant Azure, grabbing ahold of the tether and attaching it to Azure's back. Lucy returned the favor, attaching Maverick's tether.

Brandon guided his suit to the third drop chute. He turned so that Lucy could attach his tether. He was about to announce their readiness when Lucy said, "Bravo Team. Ready to drop."

Midnight Tango's head turned, its pilot scowling as first Valiant Azure then Crusher Maverick stepped into their drop chutes, the super strong cable singing as it unspooled. Scowling, Brandon stepped into his chute, seeing Delta Team drop as one down their chutes.

Barely three seconds after stepping into the chute, Midnight Tango was in free fall, popping out of an opening in the bottom of the *Saratoga*. Brandon saw Maverick and Azure below, their tethers rippling as the heavy suits plummeted to the ground.

"Alpha Team reports several contacts due east of our position," Commander Tanner, the head of field operations, announced on the channel.

The *Saratoga* had slowed down to investigate signs of megafauna movement southwest of San Antonio. It was difficult to tell but looked like the creatures that attacked the forward base had come that direction, and the dry riverbed the ship was hovering over was littered with tracks, supporting the idea. A small town, Piedras Negras, was a few miles distant.

The two cables next to Brandon snapped taut. He looked down and saw his two friends kick up dust clouds as they landed with a fraction of the force they would have, had the tether not slowed them to almost a stop five meters above the ground.

A second later, his own tether went taut, yanking backward as his fall slowed to a survivable speed. With a click that reverberated through his suit, the tether came free and he dropped the last five meters.

Midnight Tango hit the ground, dropping into a three-point crouch.

"Fancy," Paco drawled.

"You'll have to teach me that one," Jacob Parsell, in Coyote Zulu, said.

Brandon beamed. "Sure! It's really—"

"I wasn't serious."

"Oh..." Tango rose to his feet.

The hulking suit stomped off, the feed belts for his forearm-mounted chain guns swaying.

Valiant Azure dropped a metal hand onto Tango's shoulder, sounding like two train cars colliding at full speed.

"Bravo, head west and secure sector three," field ops ordered.

Before releasing an explosive sigh, Brandon silenced his comm system. Toggling the comm system open again, he said, "Copy that, Command."

Midnight Tango turned to Valiant Azure and Crusher Maverick and made a *let's go* motion, hitching his thumb over a shoulder. The three suits stomped off in the direction of Alpha and Delta Teams.

The team's technician came on the channel. "If it helps, while you're down there, you can practice with your new arm."

Brandon grinned. "Oh, yeah."

CHAPTER SEVEN

WHEN THEY REACHED their assigned sector, Lucy turned, her suit's enhanced optics zooming in on the action across town. Inside Valiant Azure's head, behind her light blue optic mesh, heavy duty lenses shifted and whirred. They looked like eyes but were so much more.

Delta Team's Sierra Slammer was grappling with what looked like a Category 2 megafauna that resembled a cross between a polar bear and an orca—that was thirty feet tall. The creature had risen out of the sandy riverbed to charge Delta Team minutes after they reached their assigned position.

Sierra Slammer ducked under a savage swipe from a clawed flipper like appendage, one of five. The creature released a horrific sounding wail a moment before Slammer rose faster than something that big should have been able to, driving a pair of blades that extended out of his forearms up and through the creature's skull.

Alpha Team's Stalwart Rook stormed out of the neon-colored jungle, half covered in pale blue bodily fluids and alien organs, function unknown. Her right hand was in its war hammer configuration. The mighty suit's left arm looked worse for the wear.

"So cool," Lucy whispered.

"What?" Brandon asked.

She snapped her optics back to normal, turning to Midnight Tango. "Nothing." The other suit's head cocked to the side. Better to not let Brandon know how much they were missing out on. Alpha and Delta seemed like they had things under control over there.

Bravo Team found themselves standing in the remains of a small park. Brandon walked a couple dozen yards from his team to stand next to a ruined building. Across the street were the remains of the town's movie theater.

"Okay, here we go," he said as much to himself as to his friends.

Midnight Tango raised his right arm. In Brandon's field of vision, a blinking red targeting reticle appeared. He'd experienced it hundreds of times in the simulators at the academy, but it wasn't the same. He could feel the reticle blinking, a slight pulse in his eye, but not. As he moved his arm, he felt the pulsing change as the reticle blinked from red to green.

With a thought, he released the metal blade housed in his forearm. There was an audible click as the blade left its housing, then fell to the hard packed dirt below with a thud.

Over the team channel, Jennifer Morris laughed. "It's not spring loaded." He could hear Lucy and Paco chuckling. Jennifer added, "You deploy it as you're moving. Inertia takes care of the rest."

"How do I target, then?"

"You can see the targeting reticle. You probably felt it as you moved your arm toward it. Same thing happens when you're swinging your arm. Try it."

Brandon nodded. "Okay." With a thought, he willed the blade's retraction mechanism to life. His suit translated the winch into a sensation like something crawling along his forearm. It was weird.

Once the lethal-looking blade was back into its locked position in his forearm, Brandon said, "Okay, here we go, again." He pulled his arm back, leaning backward. The targeting circle was red again.

"You're not throwing the first pitch," the team technician said. "More like a punch."

Brandon adjusted his stance, then whipped his arm around. The moment the targeting reticle blinked green, he triggered the blade's release.

The trimetal blade leaped out of his forearm to sail across the street, slamming into the movie theater's remaining wall.

"Yes!"

"Very cool, *amigo*," Paco said, his suit nodding his head.

Before Brandon could reply, the squad channel came to life. "New contacts! Sector five!" It was Delta Two.

Bravo Team turned toward sector five and broke into a run.

THE THREE SUITS made it about four hundred feet when a Category 2 megafauna pushed through a thicket of alien plant life nearby.

"Woah!" Brandon shouted as the beast lunged, closing the gap between it and him.

"Contact! Contact!" Lucy shouted on the ground force's channel. "Sector three north. Category 2." Valiant Azure dropped into a crouch, her particle cannons whining as they built a charge.

"Are you okay to engage?" Commander Tanner asked. This was Bravo's first real world encounter with a monster.

"We got this!" Paco shouted, moving to Midnight Tango's side.

The beast—a scaly thing about thirty feet tall with two thick legs and at least a dozen wriggling tentacles instead of arms—roared and tackled Brandon to the ground.

Midnight Tango struck the parched ground hard enough to cause cracks to spiderweb outward. The monster sprawled across the dark suit's chest, tentacles flailing and lashing the armored body beneath it. "Maverick, little help?"

Crusher Maverick reached down, massive hands grasping the screeching creature. Pistons in the shoulder fins strained, the powerful arms pulling the creature away from Midnight Tango and hefting it into the air over his head.

"Yee-haw!" Paco shouted as he turned and tossed the creature away.

The moment the creature landed, Lucy opened fire,

sending twin particle beams into it. Flesh and scales and tentacles melted under the onslaught.

When the twin beams of high energy shut down, Midnight Tango moved in, one of his BFG-9000s in hand. The weapon barked, sending a high velocity armor-piercing round into the wounded creature's torso. The monster twitched, roaring. Its remaining tentacles lashed out, trying to grasp Tango.

Another round tore into the creature, sending bright neon colored gore splattering everywhere.

"Ew, you got it on me!" Paco said, Maverick taking a step back.

"GOOD JOB, Bravo. That one wasn't on our screens," Commander Tanner said. "Congrats on your first field kill. Now get your asses over to sector five."

"Copy that!" Brandon answered, turning away from the remains of the creature that had attacked him.

The *Saratoga*'s ground forces were still at three quarters strength while the new Charlie Team pilots drilled in the simulator with Stacy and their new suits.

Overhead, the *Saratoga* rumbled, her station keeping engines burning to fight the breeze that was picking up. Brandon couldn't help smiling. This was everything he'd hoped it would be. The team faced its first monster and killed it without anyone taking damage.

Better yet, the team had followed his lead. It wasn't much—he'd been pinned, but Paco had answered his call and tossed the creature so he could get to his feet and send two kaiju-killing rounds into it.

"I need backup. Like now!" someone shouted on the squad channel, bringing Brandon back to the present.

All three Bravo suits spun. Paco pulled up the local area map that *Saratoga*'s combat information center beamed to all the ground units. The pale blue image floated in his mind's eye like a projection. With a thought, he rotated the image, zooming in.

Three megafauna—Category 3s, all of them—surrounded one of Delta Team's suits. The other two Delta suits were rushing across town as fast as forty-foot-tall, multiton war machines could run, but they were still a few minutes away. Brandon and Bravo Team were closer.

His grin was huge as he said, "Bravo Team's on the—"

Commander Tanner interrupted him. "Stand down, Bravo. Alpha is close enough."

Brandon pulled up his own tactical map. Alpha Team was moving in from sector six, approaching the brawl from the side. All three Alpha units were already moving toward the Delta suit and its attackers.

"Copy," he groaned.

Tanner must have sensed Brandon's disappointment. "It's not personal, Bravo. Three Cat 3s are no joke. Alpha and Delta have the experience. Secure your immediate area and be ready if called."

On the tactical map, Delta One and Three swept in, flanking Delta Two and his trio of attackers. Alpha Team arrived at the same time. Even just watching the tactical map, seeing dots of multiple colors move around, it looked like a savage battle. Two of the three megafauna were eliminated, their red icons fading away; the other was surrounded by six suits.

Brandon and Bravo watched as the final megafauna met a grisly end.

Lucy switched to the Bravo Team channel. "Stop trying so hard."

Midnight Tango slammed a fist into his open hand, sounding like metallic thunder. "This is crap. We could've helped. We just took down that tentacle thing." The forty-foot mech jabbed a finger northward.

Lucy turned her enhanced optics toward the fight, watching as Delta Two Coyote Zulu's suit stood over the last creature. The suit was damaged but operational. Alpha Three also looked like he had taken damage. Both suit icons were orange rather than green. But at least not red.

She zoomed back out. "The optics on this bad girl are incredible."

Paco chuckled over the comm. "You are our long-range gun, after all." Maverick turned and stopped dead. "Hey, guys. Look." Crusher Maverick was pointing a thick finger toward what looked like a water tank.

A water tank made of reinforced concrete three feet thick. A bunker. The building's door swung outward. A man stepped out, his gaze moving up and up and up until, to Brandon, it looked like the man was looking him in the eye.

"Command," Lucy called. "We've got survivors." She brought Valiant Azure over to the bunker. People were spreading out from the opening, shielding their eyes as they came up the ramp to ground level.

Brandon activated Midnight Tango's loudspeakers. "Help is on the way. Please stay put."

In the beginning, the NAC encouraged cities and towns on the verge of being overrun to evacuate, helping transport people to nearby cities.

At first, cities and towns welcomed the refugees with open arms, assuming the alien menace would be dealt with swiftly. In short order, it became the tenth abandoned city and millionth refugee, and cities ran out of room and sympathy.

As more and more mayors and governors began turning refugees away, the NAC turned to helping people stay in place. They used bunkers, walls, and smaller computer-controlled suits that were good for keeping Category 1 and below megafauna away but had no chance against anything larger.

Walls like the one in the distance had proven ineffective, even when lined with battleship grade guns. Eventually the megafauna burrowed, clawed, battered their way under, over, or through the walls.

The ruins of walls littered much of the world near the Impact Zones.

Several breaches and ruined cannons were visible under the vines and jungle growth that was slowly pulling the wall apart.

"Copy that, Bravo Team. Stand by," Commander Tanner replied.

The three Bravo Team suits took up protective positions near the bunker's entrance.

Over the squad channel, Alpha One said, "Command, two of these Cat 3s, they're..."

"What is it?" the officer in Command and Control pressed.

"They're weird, sir." Molly sounded shaken to Brandon.

"I'M REALLY glad these things don't have noses," Brandon said. He was nudging a dead megafauna with Tango's left foot. The suit's left thigh armor slid apart to reveal a holster that extended out beyond the two armor panels. All three fire teams surrounded the corpses of two creatures that Alpha Team had engaged. "I should learn to spin this thing like an Old West gunslinger," Brandon said, dropping the BFG-9000 into its holster. The gun retracted and the metal panels locked in place over it.

Crusher Maverick slammed his hands together, dusting them off and flinging monster gunk everywhere. Paco said, "Me too! They're gross when they're alive, but this is super gross."

The remains of the other megafauna that Alpha Team engaged was trussed up in a harness, slowly rising into the waiting cargo hold on the *Saratoga*'s underside.

The three mech's heads looked up as the massive monster vanished into the ship, the cargo doors grinding closed under the beast.

The last two days, the *Saratoga* has been helping the people of Piedras Negras repair as much of the town as possible. It was slow going. The rampaging megafauna had done a lot of damage before the *Saratoga* and her suits arrived.

Alpha Team's Void Romeo strode across the town square, twisting to avoid a miraculously intact gazebo.

"Hey, new guys," the pilot broadcast.

Brandon was glad that shells didn't mimic the facial expressions of their pilots. "Yes, sir?"

"You've been on deck for ten hours. Get some rack time."

Lucy guided Valiant Azure in front of Midnight Tango. "We're good, sir. We can keep helping."

Void Romeo shook his head. "We haven't seen another megafauna in thirty-six hours. I think we're good." The shiny black mech pointed at the air carrier overhead.

Crusher Maverick put a massive three fingered hand on the shoulder of each of his teammate's mechs. "I could eat."

Brandon sent the request to the ship for extraction, and less than five minutes later, three thick cables were dangling before them. After hooking each other up and ensuring secure connections, the three suits rose into the air.

"Pretty damn exciting, right?" Paco asked.

Brandon looked up at the *Saratoga*, the drop chutes looming overhead. "Yeah. First kill, you guys! We're officially not rookies!"

Lucy shook her head, Valiant Azure doing the same. "That monster they brought aboard. It was weird, right?"

"They're all weird," Paco said. "I mean, killer whale aardvarks aren't normal."

Lucy shrugged, at least in her mind. Azure did nothing, lacking the specific actuators for the gesture. "I dunno. It was the last one standing and did a fair bit of damage before it fell."

Brandon wasn't really paying attention. "They all die the same."

CAPTAIN BARTELL ENTERED BIO-LAB ONE. Labs One through Four were closest to the cargo hold where the carcass of the unusual megafauna was being held.

Even after a six-on-one fight, the thing was more intact than not, and clearly different from any other Category 3 megafauna the captain had seen. He took in the scene. The creature filled almost the entirety of the cargo hold. Bright orange blood had pooled around the creature, likely dribbling out between the massive cargo doors that made up the floor. "Well, this is super gross. The ensigns are not going to be happy when they get called in to clean that hold."

A woman in a white lab coat, the VarTech logo stretched across the back, cleared her throat. "Captain. Thank you for coming." She turned to a worktable, grabbing a tablet.

"You said you had something, Doc?" He turned and nodded to a pile of gore on a nearby table. "Megafauna related?"

Dr. Andrews nodded, holding out her tablet. "This is

definitely a new evolution." No point in waiting to deliver the worst of the bad news.

The captain took the tablet, looked at the screen, and immediately handed it back. "Not my field."

The VarTech scientist smiled, accepting the tablet back. She gestured to a wall display. She tapped her tablet screen a few times, then pointed as the screen came to life.

"Jesus!" Bartell took an involuntary step back. "Is that a—"

"Brain? Yes," Andrews said. Bloody gray matter filled the screen. She worked the tablet, zooming in. "See this?"

Bartell nodded. "Gross brains, yes." He didn't step closer to the display.

The scientist shook her head. "These ridges."

The captain nodded.

"We've never seen a megafauna with ridges like this."

Bartell squinted. It looked like a brain to him. Admittedly, he hadn't seen all that many of them, but other than its size and neon colored goo, it looked like every other brain he had seen. "Meaning what?"

The woman cocked her head. VarTech was a scientific research company. Military weaponry, while immensely lucrative, was a new endeavor for the company. They were first and foremost scientists.

She took a breath. "They're smarter. This many ridges likely increases the creature's intelligence by at least twenty percent."

Captain Bartell was silent. Smarter monsters? These things were dangerous enough as it was. Something the size of a small office building with enough strength to rip through steel didn't need to be getting smarter by the year.

He looked at the screen. "Like, human, smarter?"

She shook her head. "No, not even close." She shrugged. "I don't know where they fall. Maybe cows?" She shrugged. "Maybe koalas?"

Holding his cap in one hand, Bartell rubbed his forehead before running his other hand over his close-cropped salt and pepper hair. He put the cap back on, squaring it up just right, then nodded. "Okay. So, smarter monsters is definitely bad, but also expected, right? We've seen evolutionary jumps in these things, what—two or three times since they started showing up?"

Andrews nodded. "You're right, of course." She tapped her tablet a few times. "But then there's this."

The screen on the wall updated. Seeing the captain's blank look, she said, "These protein markers are new as well." The captain was still giving her a blank look. "So far, we've seen these evolutionary leaps in small stages. This creature has two unique..." She rubbed her chin with her free hand. "Actually, three."

"Three markers?"

"Three." She tapped her trusty tablet again. The wall screen updated, and the captain turned away from it.

"You gotta warn a guy, Doc," he said. He glanced at the screen. "Is that stomach contents?"

She smiled. "Sorry. Yeah." She pointed to the screen. "This. I'm not one hundred percent certain, but this is a new megaflora strain. I've requested a drone. It'll be here in a few hours. The VarTech labs, of course, have more resources, but I'm pretty sure."

Bartell took a deep breath. "Doc, please. This is interesting and all. Well, actually it's not, but can you give me the stupid military officer version?"

The doctor stared at him for a moment. Most of the time, the science division and Command didn't interact that much. VarTech was close to passengers aboard NACAF vessels. When the NACAF was formed, VarTech offered its amazing technology on the condition that every air carrier had a VarTech science division aboard. Dr. Andrews was the *Saratoga*'s head of xeno-biology.

She tapped her tablet again, causing the wall display to show a collage of everything she'd shown the captain. "Taken together, this is concerning."

He nodded. "How concerning?"

Her expression told him everything he needed to know, but she said, "Very."

CHAPTER EIGHT

THE *SARATOGA* WAS STILL on station over Piedras Negras, having launched several recon drones to fan out southward in search of information about these weird new megafauna.

Brandon, Lucy, and Paco entered the pilot's lounge. Their technician, Jennifer Morris, was doing an overhaul on Crusher Maverick and Midnight Tango while patrols were on hold. Not that it mattered. Nothing even as interesting as a Category 1 had shown itself since that seemingly coordinated attack the previous day.

The pilot's lounge was the only place on the massive air carrier that was exclusive to the pilots. Much like on the ocean-going aircraft carriers, pilots were the royalty of the boat.

The room was dim as they entered.

"Uh..." Brandon drawled.

The lights in the room snapped to full as the three other fire teams all applauded.

"What...?" Lucy looked around the room. It looked much the same as it did the last time the three of them were there, except for a few crepe paper streamers taped here and there.

Sophie Belanger stepped forward, three beer cans clutched in her hands. "Here you go, rooks." She grinned. "Well, not rooks now, are you? First kill under your belts. Congrats."

The rest of the teams rushed to surround Bravo team, clapping them on the back, offering high-fives, and raising their own drinks for toasting.

Brandon was the first of the three to find his voice. "Thanks, everyone."

The two new Charlie Team pilots were standing off to one side. Brandon caught the eyes of one of them— Bradley or something—and nodded. The stocky surfer returned the gesture, then turned back to his teammate. Brandon had seen little of the new pilots since they'd come aboard. One of them had seniority, which forced Stacy to remain Charlie Two. Whichever one was Charlie One, he'd demanded as much time in the sims as possible to get a feel for their new suits and each other as a fire team.

It was rare to end up with suit-less senior pilots, but when it happened, there was always a learning period. Brandon had no idea why, but VarTech insisted on making each suit unique in some way. As far as he could tell, the only benefit was that it kept pilots from swapping suits once paired, whatever value that offered the mega-corp that built the suits.

"How's it feel?" Grace Abumwe asked, clasping Brandon on the shoulder, clinking her drink against his.

Brandon beamed. "Pretty awesome. I thought it'd be weeks or even months before we got a chance to show what we can do."

She smiled. "Don't get cocky now. You're still green."

Lucy edged in. "Oh, I'm sure he's already telling himself he's an ace."

Brandon knew his cheeks were red; he could feel the heat rising on them. He turned, glaring at her. She was ruining his moment. This was his chance to shine, get noticed.

He steered Grace away from Lucy, Paco, and the rest of the teams.

Paco watched Brandon and Grace head off and shook his head. He knew how much it meant to Brandon to move up the ranks. He wished his friend didn't try so hard though. Shaking his head, he turned to Jacob Parsell. "*Amigo*, tell me about your first kill."

ONCE THE EXCITEMENT around Bravo's new status died down, the pilots all broke into smaller groups, spreading out around the lounge, having smaller conversations.

Delta Team were in the far corner, huddled around a tablet sitting on a low coffee table. Brandon looked at his friends and nodded toward the much more senior trio of pilots. "Mind if we join?" he called out.

Grace Abumwe, Delta One, looked up. "Sure, new kids. Come on over." One of her pilots gave her a playful shove, saying something low enough that Brandon and the others couldn't hear. The two new Charlie Team guys were with them. They heard what was said and laughed. Brandon frowned.

Pulling extra chairs over, Lucy asked, "Reviewing that last engagement?"

Jacob Parsell, Delta Three, looked up at her. "Yeah. Seeing if Alec did anything wrong."

Alec Lefebvre leaned across the table, punching Jacob in the shoulder. "I did nothing wrong!" he said in a thick French-Canadian drawl. "I am without flaw."

Brandon and Lucy dropped into chairs between Grace and Jacob. Lucy said, "That was a gnarly fight." She looked at Jacob. "You were amazing."

The Delta pilot grinned. "Well, yes. I am pretty amazing."

Grace rolled her eyes. "Lord help us." She nodded to the two Charlie Team members nearby. "Met the new guys?" Head shakes all around. She made eye contact with the red-haired one and waved them over. Brandon glanced around the room for Stacy and spotted her leaning against a table, chatting with Alpha Team.

The two Charlie men brought chairs over and introduced themselves. Malcom Taggart looked around at the gathered pilots, toying with the beer bottle in his hand.

Grace made the introductions, then asked, "How're you settling in? Things got pretty hectic after you came aboard."

Brady Davidson ran a hand over his tightly curled

blonde hair. Brandon figured him for a surfer. The Hawaiian shirts he seemed to wear helped with that impression. "I think we're getting pretty comfortable with our suits. Older models than we had aboard the *Detroit*."

Jacob—Brandon had learned he did not like "Jake"—leaned forward. "Heard your suits got trashed?"

The redheaded pilot nodded. "Yeah. Lost our third, and another entire team." His free hand was balled into a white-knuckled fist. "Ugly bastards were waiting for us when we deployed to help some wildcatters that thought they could still live in Orlando." He shook his head.

"Bigger and uglier and stronger than anything we'd seen before," Brady added before tipping his beer back, finishing it. "We didn't stand a chance."

"Christ," Alec swore. Everyone nodded.

Grace raised her bottle. "Well, welcome to the *Saratoga*."

The two Charlie pilots smiled. Malcolm leaned back in his chair and looked at Bravo Team. "So tell us, what brings you youngsters to the NACAF?"

Jacob looked at the two Bravo pilots, smiling. He leaned back in his chair, hands behind his head. His expression faltered when Alec slipped a foot under the upraised front legs of his chair, threatening to tip his teammate over. "Asshole," he growled.

Ignoring the two Delta pilots, Brandon gestured to Paco to go first. His friend looked like a deer in headlights; all eyes were on him. "Oh, well." He swore under his breath in Spanish. "Not a lot of options down here," he said to start. Which was true. While the NAC covered Mexico, the United States, and Canada, one of those members was very much the minority member: Mexico. "I hate dirt and vegetables, so farming is out."

"Don't look at the menu in the mess," Jacob said in a low voice, chuckling.

Paco went on. "NACAF was really the only way to get out of my hometown. When it turned out I was the right height to be a pilot, I figured, what the hell? You know?"

Nods all around the table. Because of limited space inside a suit, the height limit for pilots was five foot ten. The crèche was a specific size, and while short pilots could make it work, a pilot taller than six feet wouldn't fit.

It was probably the only time in human society that being on the shorter side was considered a blessing, outside of horse and motorcycle racing.

When Paco didn't continue, Lucy added, "What else is there to do? Monsters keep coming. We keep losing ground. It's us or them."

Abumwe held her fist out toward Lucy. "Hell yeah, sister." Lucy bumped her fist against Delta One's fist, grinning. She turned her attention to Brandon and Lucy. "What about you two?"

Lucy looked at Brandon. He could tell from her to look what she was about to say. He opened his mouth, but she beat him to it. "He's from Vail."

Brandon coughed. All three Delta Team pilots looked at him. Damn Lucy. He cleared his throat. "Yeah." He drew out the syllable, hoping the collective gaze of the group would shift from him to Lucy.

"No shit. Vail?" Jacob asked.

Malcolm Taggert squinted. "They kick you out or something?"

Brandon nodded at Jacob, then shook his head at Malcolm. He took a deep breath. "I don't know what to say. Vail is Vail. They think the problems of the world don't apply to them. A giant wall helps with that thinking, I guess." He shrugged. "I couldn't sit back and have a cookie cutter life in a cookie cutter town and ignore what's going on in the world." He looked around. "Plus. Fuck snow."

Everyone at the table laughed.

"GOOD MORNING," Becca Otinabe said as Dr. Andrews walked into the lab followed by an older man: Dr. Thorin Erasmus, head of the VarTech contingent aboard the *Saratoga*.

The senior most of the pair smiled. "I've read your preliminary report, Becca. Quite the adventure."

The young biologist nodded. "I hate fieldwork, but you knew that." Her boss smiled. She continued, "I've finished going through the data we brought up from San Antonio." She looked at her colleagues. "Did either of you know what they were up to?" Head shakes from both. "Before a base fell, they found what they first thought was a Category 1 megafauna wandering around near the city."

She tapped her tablet a few times, causing a nearby bulkhead-mounted display to come to life, showing several images of dissected megafauna. "Turns out it was an infant. A Category 3 infant." She watched that information sink into her colleagues' faces. "Once I went through all the data, I realized it had several similar protein markers to Leslie's find."

Erasmus reached out to the display, swiping between the images and charts Becca was casting from her tablet. "Interesting. So that wasn't a one-off."

Andrews shook her head. "We knew it wasn't."

Erasmus nodded, running a hand over his hairless head. "I know, but I did hold out a little hope. These evolutionary changes are coming faster and faster."

"Was the base attacked because the infant was there?" Andrews asked.

"That's a disturbing notion," Erasmus said. He looked to Otinabe. "Anything to indicate that?"

She shook her head. "Not in the VarTech files. The base commander purged the rest of the facility's servers, so if he thought so, or any of his officers did, that died with them." She cocked her head. "Honestly, it would make sense. Plenty of terrestrial animals will follow the scent of their young for miles if they've wandered off or been taken."

Erasmus blew out a breath, shaking his head. "Add this to the fact that those little ones dug their way under and into the base, and it can only mean one thing. Coordination."

The two women exchanged a look. The one thing humanity had going for it against the alien plants and animals was just that: they were still animals, mindlessly going about whatever their natural inclinations dictated.

Coordination meant intelligence. Planning. Nothing good.

Becca updated the screen. "There may be a silver lining." She nodded to the screen. "A month or two before the infant showed up, the base's fire team found this." On the screen, a large scale was lying on an examination table. "Harder than anything we've found yet. Unfortunately, wherever this sample was in the base, it was lost in the attack, but if we can find another creature with scales like this, it could improve suit and ship armor." She brought up a page of notes on her tablet. "Almost half as light as the last sample we used to create armor and thirty percent stronger."

The other two scientists smiled. "That is good news," Andrews said. "We just need to find it again."

"Maybe our contractors will have a lead on it?" Erasmus said. He jotted a note on his own tablet. "I'll send this back to corporate and they can reach out." He looked around the room. "Good work, Becca."

"CAPTAIN. I've got NACAF Command on a secure channel," a young ensign at the communications station announced.

Bartell and Willis were at the bridge's midsection, standing around the massive map table. The older man looked up, taking his ball cap off to scratch at his head. "Thank you, Ensign Jones. Patch it through to my ready room."

"Yes, sir."

"Bridge is yours," he said, looking at Willis before heading for the hatch to his private office off the side of the command deck.

Taking a seat, he tapped the console on his desk. The display came to life, flashing the NACAF logo briefly before changing to the face of Admiral Janice Lancaster. A ticker along the top of the screen read, "SECURE TRANSMISSION."

"You've been having quite the adventure, Tommy." She smiled.

He shook his head. "You could say that. I take it you've had a chance to review my updates?"

The admiral nodded. "And the updates from your VarTech contingent. The unencrypted parts, anyway."

"I take it that wasn't much."

She shook her head. "Of course not. But I got enough to know that something is happening down there. Something they're being cagey about."

He nodded his agreement. "How's all this been happening down here, Jan?" Bartell shuddered, thinking about the brain and other gunk that Dr. Andrews had shown him. "You read about the proteins and brain folds and shit?"

Rubbing her temples, she said, "Yeah. In graphic detail. Add to that the work they were doing in San Antonio and you're right. Something is going on down there. What, I can't even guess at. I'm not even sure VarTech could say right now—which in and of itself is a bit terrifying."

Bartell nodded. VarTech not knowing something wasn't a thing he thought anyone was familiar with.

Despite having worked with VarTech for going on fifteen years, it was still jarring. In his previous career in the United States Navy, private contractors all answered to the Navy. None had the kind of carte blanche that VarTech enjoyed.

Bartell leaned back in his chair, looking out the window. New, smarter megafauna. New plant growths. "So, what's next?"

The admiral ran both hands over her forehead and through her close-cropped hair. She exhaled. "We've been planning to send a survey mission south to the Impact Zone. Supposed to be a coordinated effort world-wide. See what's been going on at each site. We've been building a new scout class craft. This would've been the new ship's test flight." She shrugged. "Doesn't look like we have time for that. It's not due to be completed for another year. Add in that VarTech corporate is urging us to pull you back to the border. I think it's even more warranted."

Bartell smiled. "You know I like a challenge. And, yeah, seems prudent." He chuckled. "Erasmus is gonna be pissed."

"Okay then. Those are your orders. Survey the Exclusion Zone down to the Impact Zone, see what's going on."

Bartell sat upright in his chair, pulling down his captain's jacket in a quick tug to straighten it out. "Copy that, Admiral. We'll get it done."

"I've no doubt, Captain. Godspeed." The screen went blank.

The captain leaned back in his seat once again to

stare at the ceiling of his ready room. The cold gray metal was unmarred, reminding him that unlike his time in the wet navy, air carriers didn't have to fight a never-ending war against rust. Monsters, yes, but not rust. He chuckled as he got to his feet.

Exiting his ready room, Captain Bartell called out, "Commander, we've got new orders."

Willis stood up from the command chair in the center of the bridge's forward command center. "Sir?"

Bartell walked past the map table, running a hand along it. Reaching the command section, he looked around. "We've got new orders."

"Back home, sir?" Willis asked.

Bartell smiled as he shook his head. "Actually, we're staying put."

Willis, walking to stand near the helm station, stopped and turned. "Really?"

Bartell smiled. "Command has ordered a full survey of Impact Zone Five."

Several bridge officers turned from their stations. Several mouths were hanging open.

"A survey, sir?" the officer at the navigator console asked.

Bartell dropped into his command chair, smiling. He tapped the 1MC control and waited a second for the announcement tone to finish. "Attention all decks. This is the bridge. The Saratoga has been given orders to complete a survey of Impact Zone Five and the surrounding area. From this point forward, we'll be at Condition Two." He tapped the control to close the channel.

Turning to his helm and navigator, he said, "Start working out a survey route."

The light strips that lined the ceiling and floor of the bridge and every other deck of the *Saratoga* shifted from white to orange.

Willis looked up from his console. "Condition Two, ship wide."

CHAPTER NINE

IT TOOK the piloting team an hour to work out the optimal survey route from their current location. Once Commander Willis signed off on it, the *Saratoga* headed off east across the remains of Mexico.

"This should be exciting," Willis said as the mighty ship made its turn, engines roaring to full power.

Captain Bartell adjusted his cap as he looked over the flight plan. "Certainly something new."

The lift at the rear of deck 1 slid open to release a harried looking man in a white lab coat smeared with what could only be monster blood or something worse. He stormed around the map table toward the forward stations.

Bartell looked up at Willis with a smirk. "I expected him five minutes ago."

"Captain! Captain Bartell!" Dr. Thorin Erasmus said. The face of the head of VarTech's science division aboard the ship was beet red. "We're still in the Impact Zone," he growled.

Bartell guided his seat around to face the angry scientist. "Yes, we are, Doctor."

Dr. Erasmus frowned. "Why? We have important work to do back in the states."

The captain nodded slowly. "I'm sure you do, Doc. You're just going to have to do it on the fly. We've got orders to do a full survey pass of Impact Zone Five."

"Why?"

Bartell gave the other man a look. "Because a lot of weird shit's been happening out here and Command would like to know why." He raised an eyebrow. "You can't deny something is...different down here."

The other man nodded. "Of course, Captain, which is why we'd like to return to NAC airspace so we can more easily confer with colleagues in corporate."

"I understand, Doctor. For now, you're just going to have to work with what you've got aboard the *Saratoga*."

The doctor's own eyebrow quirked upward. "With what we've got here. Not remotely with our colleagues?"

Bartell gave a slight shrug. "Afraid so. While we're at Condition Two, all nonessential communications are restricted."

"Captain, please."

"Sorry, Doc. Rules are rules. Until we're sure there aren't any other new threats to be discovered, we're at Condition Two." His expression made it clear the issue wasn't up for further discussion.

Dr. Erasmus inhaled. "Understood, Captain. Perhaps we'll find more interesting new developments on this little tour for my team to bring back."

"God, I hope not, Doctor."

Erasmus said nothing. He turned and strode back to the aft lift.

Commander Willis stepped up next to his captain. "You know he's just going to be annoying until we get back, right?"

Bartell nodded. "Yeah, can't be helped. We have our orders, and," he lowered his voice, "they're partly informed by VarTech corporate's reluctance to share with command what they were up to in San Antonio."

Willis straightened. "I see." He glanced up in time to watch the lift doors at the back of the bridge slide closed on the sour countenance of Dr. Erasmus.

Turning back to his console next to the captain's chair, Willis smiled. "Interesting times."

Bartell, facing the panoramic window at the front of the bridge, said, "We'll reach the gulf in two days. Command is sending some additional supplies, since we'll be out of pocket for a while." He turned to his first officer, who nodded his understanding.

Most air carriers operated within or at the edges of their territory, always within reach of resupply. *Saratoga* was already several hundred kilometers beyond the current southern border of the NAC and moving further away by the hour. They'd need to be fully self sufficient.

BY THE TIME the *Saratoga* reached the eastern shores of the Gulf of Mexico, Command had cargo transport en route. In the last few years, the entire gulf had become almost unreachable, the alien plant life choking the shores. While the carrier waited for its cargo transport, the captain ordered a complete survey of the nearby area.

Alpha and Charlie Teams were on the ground, with the latter team getting its first chance to work together in their actual suits instead of the simulators. The six mechs were cutting through the brightly colored alien plants. Somewhere nearby, according to their maps, was a small village. The village was surely deserted, but it provided a good exercise for the newly formed team.

Aboard the *Saratoga*, Captain Bartell was making his way to the science labs that occupied the lower decks of the ship. After saluting a junior officer he passed in the corridor, he took a right heading deeper into the ship.

Air carriers were constructed with a revolutionary alloy: a blend of titanium and elements VarTech was closed lipped about the source of. The rumors were that the mystery material was somehow derived from megafauna.

Two more turns and a walk past one of the cargo holds and he was at Science Lab One. He took a deep breath and walked in.

Science Lab One was a massive space filled with long metal tables littered with all sorts of things that the captain had no idea the function of, and occasionally random bits of alien plant and animal gunk. He turned away from a table covered in bright orange offal. Shuddering, he turned to Dr. Erasmus' office.

"Thank you for coming, Captain," the gray-haired man said, gesturing to the seat opposite his desk.

"What's up, Doc?" Bartell asked, easing his frame into the chair. Dr. Erasmus' office was just off the main lab space. One wall was entirely glass, allowing the scientist to see what his subordinates were doing.

The research department about the *Saratoga,* and every other carrier in the NACAF fleet, was run by a VarTech senior researcher. The company had exclusive rights to anything the ships came across in the field. While they had no official rank in the NACAF, heads of research often dictated a carrier's course of action. Bartell did his best to resist that dynamic at every turn.

Dr. Erasmus activated a display on the wall behind him. "You're aware of our recent discoveries." The captain nodded. "Well, they were the tip of the iceberg." He was beaming.

"See, and you were worried you wouldn't have anything to do while we were out here," the captain smiled. Erasmus pursed his lips but said nothing. Captain Bartell nodded. "Okay. So, this is bigger than the brain thing I saw earlier?"

"So much," Erasmus said, forgetting the captain's little barb. He gestured over his shoulder as the screen updated.

The captain squeezed his eyes shut as fast as he could.

"What're you doing?" The lead researcher leaned forward.

The captain waved a hand toward the doctor. "The screen's full of brains and shit, isn't it?"

Erasmus looked over his shoulder. "No."

The captain opened one eye. The other opened. "Oh. What is that?"

The doctor shook his head. "Mashed up plant matter."

The captain shrugged. "Okay. Less gross." He moved his gaze back to the doctor. "Why's it special? I mean, we're already looking at the possibility of smarter monsters, but..." He didn't understand at all where the other man was going with this.

"Not possibility. Near certainty," Erasmus corrected.

Bartell nodded. "Okay, near certainly smarter monsters." He pointed to the screen. "And this? Smarter trees?"

Erasmus chuckled. "Thankfully, no."

"Okay?"

"We found this plant matter in the footpads of that Category 3 we brought aboard. Wherever it came from, this plant is growing." The doctor's excitement was palpable. The screen behind him updated. A chemical composition 3D model, slowly rotating.

"This protein is unlike any we've seen in other megaflora samples," Erasmus said, leaning forward again. He tapped a screen on his desk, and the display behind him updated, a grid of various goops. "Andrews has looked at the stomach contents of every megafauna we have killed recently." He hitched a thumb over his shoulder. "None had even the slightest trace of this plant in them. We know they're omnivorous. They clearly stopped for a bite more than once, but avoided this plant, even though it was present enough to be trampled."

Bartell nodded along. "Like I asked Andrews, can you explain this to me like I'm five?"

Erasmus had forgotten how much the captain didn't

enjoy dealing with—what did he call them? "Squints." The captain preferred towering mecha and air-carrier-mounted rail guns. He tolerated the science types but wasn't interested in what they did. "Andrews was the one to suggest it. We tested the protein found in this plant against samples we've got aboard ship." He took a deep breath. "Every sample we tested this protein against caused acute necropathy within an hour."

The captain stared at Erasmus. "Do you even know any five-year-olds?"

After releasing a whole-body sigh, Erasmus said, "I believe that this plant kills monsters."

This time it was Captain Bartell who leaned forward in his seat. "Are you saying—"

"That this plant could wipe these things off the face of the planet?" Erasmus nodded. "Yes."

A HEAVY CARGO shuttle roared into the *Saratoga*'s main hangar. Brandon and Stacy Decker, Charlie Two, were sitting on Midnight Tango's foot. The well tanned blonde from San Diego watched the shuttle land on the deck with a clang.

She turned to Brandon. "That's the third one."

He nodded. The two of them had been spending time together the last few days. Once Charlie and Alpha Teams returned to the ship, he'd mustered the nerve to ask her to dinner. She said yes. Fraternization between pilots was neither against nor within regulations. It was just something that happened, and everyone ignored it so long as both parties did their jobs. He wasn't sure if it would go anywhere but was keen to see.

"How's the new team going? Looked like you were getting on pretty well down there." He kept his gaze on the shuttles near the aft end of the hangar.

She shrugged. "It's going. Davidson and Taggart are alright. Hearing their voices come from Peterson and Mduba's mechs is tough."

He nodded. He didn't quite understand but thought he might. Even though he, Paco, and Lucy had only had their suits for a few weeks, already he was used to seeing their suits and hearing their voices.

Stacy nudged him, nodding to the shuttle. "All VarTech nerds too. From the Chihuahua NACAF Base, I think."

They watched the shuttle's rear hatch lower to the ground. *Saratoga* crewmembers moved in to begin offloading the crates that filled the smaller craft's hold.

"I heard it had something to do with those monsters we tangled with the other day when we first got here," Brandon said. He added, "Like that big one we brought aboard."

She smiled. "Yeah, yeah. First kill." His grin was enormous. She shook her head.

From the nearest shuttle, a quartet of technicians rolled something that looked heavy and expensive onto the deck. Another technician approached from the hatch all this new equipment and personnel had been going through and pointed behind her, saying things Brandon and Stacy couldn't hear.

She watched the piece of equipment vanish, then

said, "They took over a lot of the midship space one deck down. Unused labs and store rooms. All filled up."

"Think you'll get used to your new teammates?" Brandon asked. Another shuttle was on final approach, its lift engines screaming as it slowed down before entering the hangar.

"I have teammates. No need of new ones." She didn't turn to look at him.

Fire teams came together in the academy and it was rare to break them up. Brandon had heard about the injuries to the other two members of Charlie Team. He was surprised to learn that Charlie Two remained aboard the *Saratoga* when he and his team arrived.

He was glad Stacy had stayed aboard, of course. She was an excellent trainer, and he enjoyed her company.

He nodded. "Of course."

She didn't say anything, instead standing up and walking away. Brandon watched her leave through the hatch that connected to the pilot's lounge.

From behind him, Bravo Team technician Morris said, "Smooth."

Brandon did his best not to leap out of his skin. He was only partially successful. Had Jennifer been there the whole time? Turning, his cheeks red, he said, "Creep much?"

Morris shrugged. "Unlike you, I've got work to do, and you're in my workspace." She pointed to Crusher Maverick. "Your boy Paco keeps fucking up the left hip." Looking up, she shouted at another technician who was working on Midnight Tango from the scaffolding that surrounded the rear section of the mech. "Don't disconnect the—damnit." She looked at Brandon. "Duty calls, lover boy."

He made a face. "Have fun, J-Dawg." He drew out the last syllable as he hopped up and stepped outside her reach.

DESPITE HIS EXCITEMENT about the possibly game changing megaflora, Dr. Erasmus had been unable to give Captain Bartell any useable detail on where to find the mystery plant.

After the last supply shuttle left, the *Saratoga* turned to begin her survey of Impact Zone Five at the southern tip of Mexico.

Once the crew sorted all the new cargo and personnel and cleared the hangar, they rolled the simulators back out so that the fire teams could stay sharp. Despite what the press would have most people think, the Impact Zones weren't packed with monsters, shoulder to shoulder.

The larger megafauna seemed to be solitary in their nature. Spotting one that wasn't actively trying to attack was often difficult, especially in the denser, more heavily jungle covered regions where the alien plants had been growing for years and reached ten to twenty stories tall.

While the truly big ones were hard to spot, the more common Category 2 creatures—what many called monster cows—were easy to spot, moving in giant herds grazing on alien shrubs as big as a house.

Not every megafauna was out to destroy life on this

planet. Many seemed to fill other niches in the alien ecosystem that was slowly taking root on Earth.

"WATCH YOUR LEFT!" Brandon warned Crusher Maverick.

The warning was a split second too late as Viridian Slammer came in with a one-two punch to the thicker mech's head and torso. Paco swore in Spanish as he staggered backward, reeling from the attack.

Midnight Tango moved in with a forward kick aimed at the green tinted suit's torso. A quick move by his opponent meant that the kick hit Slammer's hip, where the impact was far less severe. There was still enough power to send the other suit stumbling. Brandon didn't wait, leaning in to deliver a right hook that reverberated through the pilot's crèche.

"Damn!" Malcolm Taggart shouted from Audacious Thunder. "I think I felt that over here."

"Lucky shot," Stacy Decker growled, moving Slammer back to put some space between herself and Midnight Tango.

"More warning next time, *si*?" Paco said over the team channel. "Leader."

"Sorry. I got distracted," Brandon admitted. He'd turned his attention briefly to Valor Ascendant and Valiant Azure grappling and missed Viridian Slammer breaking off to attack Paco.

"Big picture, *amigo*. Team leader's gotta see the big picture," Paco said.

Brandon bit back a retort. His friend was right. If he was going to show that he could be Bravo One, he had to act like it. A blow from behind derailed his train of thought and sent him sprawling to the ground.

"Watch your back," Malcolm Taggart drawled as Audacious Thunder clapped his hands together.

"Okay, that's it," a voice called over the simulation channel. "This round is over."

Without warning, the sensorium input that filled Brandon's senses faded to nothing. His eyes refocused, and he saw the blank wall of the simulation crèche a split second before the device split down the middle to let him step out.

The hangar was as busy as usual. Several of the smaller scout craft that the *Saratoga* carried were laid out near the massive rear hatch, parts and technicians strewn around them.

Malcolm Taggart walked up to Brandon. "No hard feelings?" he asked in his southern drawl.

Brandon forced a smile. "All good, man. Rather learn these lessons in there," he patted the side of the simulator pod, "than down there."

The other pilot nodded, running a hand through his sweat-soaked red hair. "Truer words." He nodded toward the hatch that led to the pilot's lounge and locker room. "Come on. First round is on me."

Brandon's smile turned sincere. "Deal."

PART 2

CHAPTER TEN

"OKAY, okay. Sit down and shut up," Commander Steven Tanner said from the lectern. He looked out on all twelve suit pilots scattered around the small briefing auditorium as they slowly took their seats. He noticed that none of the fire teams sat exclusively together; Brandon was with Charlie Two, the two new Charlie guys were with Delta One and Three, etc. He smiled. It was good for the teams to comingle.

Much like the Air Wing Commander aboard the old wet navy aircraft carriers, the Commander Ground Forces was in charge of all suit deployments and operations. Even having only recently met almost half of his team, he already felt like he knew every one of them. He looked out on his new Bravo Team. The greenest pilots onboard. They'd already gotten their first combat kill, which was unusual, but still hadn't fully meshed as a fire team. Having no clear pecking order didn't help.

Brandon Sinclair so desperately wanted to be the team leader but couldn't keep the entire battle space in mind. Several times in the simulators, he moved to help a teammate, only to be attacked from behind when his guard was down.

Lucy, cool and collected, seemed to have the opposite issue: she worried as much about what her teammates were doing as she did about what she was supposed to be doing, often leaving herself open to attack by focusing on the tactical display and not what was right outside her own suit.

Paco Rosales, Tanner had figured out from the day the team came aboard. The young man wanted to make a difference, to get away from what he saw as a dead-end life, and interestingly, didn't want to lead.

Focusing on the task at hand, Tanner activated the screen behind him. A map appeared on the screen with three concentric red circles marked with a five, a ten, and a fifteen. "As I'm sure you're all aware, we're still south of the border." The ship's rumor network had been running amok for two days, so he knew they knew. After the beach exercises and the supply shuttles, it seemed like the whole ship was vibrating with excitement. He pressed a control on the lectern, and the ship's position blinked to life.

"We've been ordered to survey what's left of Mexico all the way south to Impact Zone Five." He watched the reactions of everyone in the room, then continued. "We'll be walking patrols on and off as we go. This is, well, a first for any air carrier in recent history."

"What's the point, sir?" Grace Abumwe asked from the middle row.

Tanner gave her a minute shrug. "You're all aware

that at least one of the creatures we tangled with back in that little town was different." He watched as all the pilots nodded. "It seems it was really different. Between that and the attack on FOB San Antonio, Command is concerned that something is happening down here that we don't understand."

"Uh...isn't understanding these things the job of VarTech?" Sophie Belanger, Alpha One, asked. She leaned forward, brushing a lock of chestnut colored hair out of her face.

Tanner nodded. "Yeah, and they seem as in the dark as Command. Which, as you might guess, is disconcerting to those back home."

As he expected, that garnered a few looks of surprise. "I'm told the onboard VarTech teams are working with what we brought aboard. You obviously know we brought on supplies and personnel. They'll keep working while we're here and sync up with their folks back home once we're done."

Brandon raised a hand. "Sir, what do we hope to accomplish down here?"

Tanner gave the younger man a look, glad someone asked that question. "To learn. No one's been to Impact Five in at least ten years. Our satellite coverage is spotty, especially over the Impact Zones, with all the dust and radiation still hanging in the air even after all this time."

The briefing went on for another few minutes before Tanner released the pilots to their various duties.

"WE ARE NOW HALFWAY between the Impact plus fifteen and ten exclusion boundaries," the helmsman announced. The *Saratoga* had been cruising for almost two days after taking on more scientists than she'd ever carried, not to mention a ton of supplies.

The landscape below was a mix of terrestrial vegetation that had yet to give up the fight against the aggressive alien plant life that was creeping inexorably forward. The ground went from brown and green to too-bright oranges, purples, and blues.

Smaller Category 1 creatures, not worthy of the term "megafauna," roamed the landscape. Despite being relatively small—most were the size of an elephant—ninety percent were carnivorous and made quick work of local fauna.

Captain Bartell was staring out the forward bridge windows. The expanse of the *Saratoga* lay before him. Her massive top-mounted big guns at the forward edge of the ship matched a pair mounted on the lower section of the ship. He never understood why air carriers had top-mounted weapons, but VarTech had insisted they were needed and NACAF Command had not argued. Military leaders always liked more guns over less.

He nodded. "ETA to the ten-year exclusion boundary?"

"Five hours," the woman said. She reached forward and adjusted a control.

Commander Willis took a breath. "To boldly go where no—" The Captain gave him a look. "Sorry. Just... you know. No one's come this far south through the Exclusion Zone in, well, ever."

"Not a milestone I'm overjoyed to be setting." He turned back to the window, leaning on a nearby console, sighing.

Commander Willis pointed to one of the larger displays lining the upper edge of the bridge. "A town." He turned to an officer nearby. "Zoom in."

The screen updated showing a town a little more than a kilometer in diameter; hard packed dirt roads formed concentric circles. In the center was a church or town hall, maybe both. Homes and businesses fanned out from the center. None looked to be in great shape.

"Do we know what this town's called?" the captain asked loud enough for most of the bridge staff to hear.

A lieutenant manning one of the bridge's aft computer stations answered, "No, sir. Nothing on file. Granted, few, if any, of these wildcat towns are known to the NAC." It was the officer who'd been born in San Antonio. She continued, "Folks move out to these towns when they have nowhere else to go. They've either been turned away at the border or even if they got in, there was nothing for them in the NAC, so they left."

It boggled Bartell's mind that anyone would choose to be out here so far from humanity, surrounded by literal alien monsters. But he couldn't argue with the young woman. The NAC was getting more and more crowded as it retreated north. Space and opportunities were limited.

The town was passing underneath the ship.

"Looks deserted," Commander Willis said. He turned to the junior officer. "Zoom in?" She nodded. He whistled. "Damn." The town was in shambles; the town hall in the center was cleaved in two. There was a clear path from one side of the town through the center and out the other side. Something big had come through and it hadn't let something like buildings, or people, get in its way.

"Think that was caused by one of our friends from up north?" Captain Bartell asked, again loud enough to invite an answer from anyone on the bridge.

The woman at the console said, "I'm not seeing any signs of life. Guessing this town's been abandoned for a while. No heat signatures."

Bartell nodded. "Onward, then."

In a low voice, Commander Willis asked, "Wonder where the survivors ended up?"

The display zoomed back out, the town with no name passing behind the *Saratoga*.

DOWN IN THE MAIN HANGAR, everyone watched as three suits circled one another.

"What ya think of 'em?" Paco asked his two friends. The three of them were standing off to the side of the gathered pilots and technicians watching Charlie Team melee in the simulator.

In the middle of the hangar, like last time, three large metal spheres were arrayed in a row, surrounded by computer equipment and large displays angled so anyone in the hangar could watch the show. On the screens, Charlie Team engaged in hand-to-hand combat. The new Charlie Team members were officially acquainted with their rigs and Stacy, but with nothing else to do, the simulators were always busy.

Brandon felt for Stacy. She still hadn't fully gelled with her two new teammates. The red-haired guy was a bit egotistical, but the black dude was okay as far as Brandon could tell from their infrequent interactions.

The problem was that Stacy, like every other member of a fire team, had bonded with her two teammates in the academy. So had Taggart and Davidson. Making a new team from the remains of two others was rumored to never go that well. During school Brandon assumed that was just hyperbole, but seeing it now and thinking about what it'd mean if he lost Lucy or Paco, he thought he understood.

Audacious Thunder leaned forward, arms outstretched, hands in fists. With a whoosh of igniting rockets, both fists separated from the mech's forearms.

Paco whistled. "I don't think I knew Thunder could do that."

"I did," Lucy offered. Both men rolled their eyes. Of course she did.

Viridian Slammer dodged to the right, letting one fist fly past. The other struck the suit in the side, a metallic clang echoing from the speakers mounted on the displays.

"Ouch," Paco said.

Thick cables groaned as both fists reeled back in. Slammer moved to stomp on the cables but was knocked aside by Valor Ascendant's fist.

"Double ouch," Lucy said.

Slammer staggered backward, Stacy doing her best to keep her balance. Thinking her still off balance, Valor

Ascendant moved in to deliver a right hook, only to see the deep green suit twist, bringing its arm up to grab onto the white and gold mech's chest, pulling it off balance to crash to the ground.

"Nice!" Brandon shouted. He looked across the gathered crew and pilots to Alpha Team. Grace nodded her agreement.

Without looking up from the skirmish, currently one on one, as Slammer stood atop Valor Ascendant, Lucy said, "You hear? We'll be passing over Mexico City soon."

"Oh good. Massive graveyard. At night. My favorite," Brandon quipped.

A tone sounded and the displays around the simulators when dark. The three pods hissed as they powered down and cracked open. The overhead speakers whooped twice before the captain came on. "Attention all hands. We'll be passing over Mexico City in approximately twenty minutes. If you'd like to observe, all nonessential video screens will carry the feeds from the ventral cameras. That is all."

The three Bravo Team members exchanged a look. "Lounge?" Paco asked.

Brandon nodded, pointing across the hangar. Alpha Team was already on the move. "Let's go. I want to get a good seat." The three of them headed for the hatch to the pilots' lounge.

By the time Charlie Team entered the pilots' lounge, the lights were dim, and the main display, taking up most of the wall opposite the door, was showing a tiled view of camera feeds from the ship's underside.

Stacy joined Bravo Team, her new teammates having moved off to the side of the room, grabbing barstools.

Brandon leaned over. "Still not getting along?"

She glared at him through narrowed eyes. "We're getting there. They're nice enough guys, but they have a shorthand I don't know, and they don't know mine."

Lucy looked over. "I guess that makes some sense." She waved a hand to her friends. "I hadn't really thought about it, but yeah, we've got a rhythm that would be hard to teach to someone new."

"Not to mention, you're trying to teach them, and they're trying to teach you," Paco said.

Stacy nodded. "Yeah." She brightened. "Wait. That's it!"

Paco beamed. "I'm a genius. What do you got?"

Brandon rolled his eyes. Stacy said, "Trying to make them fit my style, or me theirs, won't work. We need to come up with our own thing." She rose from her chair and headed toward the two new pilots.

Someone made a shushing sound. One of the camera tiles expanded to fill the screen. The remains of Mexico City filled the screen in ghostly night vision. The city fell in the tenth year after impact. Megaflora had been choking the entire region, meter by meter. The Mexican government, with the help of the United States and several South American nations, spent years and billions attempting to eradicate the alien plant life.

Then the first megafauna appeared.

CHAPTER ELEVEN

MEXICO CITY LAY SPRAWLED beneath the *Saratoga*. High-rise office and residential towers were scattered; some leaned on their neighbors, others had crashed down to the ground, crushing whatever was in their path.

Scattered throughout the city, suits. Dozens of first-generation suits. It took years to figure out that the only way to defeat the alien monsters was with metal monsters. The armed forces of Earth had tried conventional weapons, even nuclear weapons. Tanks, jets, bombers—all caused either too much collateral damage or did nothing against the rampaging monsters.

The only thing that didn't end in the mutual destruction of humanity were the suits. The first generation of suits were nothing more than human scaled machines with no weapons other than the fighting skills of the pilot. Then the suits got weapons; tanks with legs, most called them. Finally, someone came up with the current generation of suits, blending the pilot's fighting prowess with weapons designed to inflict the most damage on thick skinned alien monsters.

"Look. Omega Foxtrot." Lucy pointed at the screen. The ruined suit was sprawled out in what was once a mall parking lot. Its right arm was a mechanical ruin, its left gone at the shoulder. The center of the torso was a caved in mess of wiring, glass, and other equipment.

The old suits had the pilot in the front of the torso behind armored glass. Mexico City showed the world's armies how flawed that design was.

"Damn," Brandon whispered. Omega Foxtrot was lying between two megafauna, Category 2s, which, at the time, was as high as the scale went. Both creatures were beaten and broken. "Took those two with 'em."

"Plus three more," Lucy said. She'd always scored higher in military history than Brandon—a fact she never let him forget. She smirked.

Someone in the room swore. "Look. At. That," they said.

The wall screen had switched to another view. Ten wrecked suits and nearly three dozen megafauna corpses littered the remains of Arena CDMX.

"The final battle," Lucy said in a hushed voice. "I never thought I'd see it."

Grace hung her head. "Rest in peace."

Paco nodded, crossing himself like a good Catholic.

Grace looked up at the screen. "Worst defeat in history. Twice as many suits lost in one go as Aswan."

"And they managed to hold the dam at Aswan," Brandon said. Turning to Lucy, he added, "I did read the material, you know." She rolled her eyes.

The ruins slid by underneath; the pilots' lounge fell silent.

Paco rubbed his neck. "Well, we've got combat watch first thing in the morning. I'm turning in."

Lucy rose, following his lead. She looked at Brandon, still sitting. "Coming?"

He pursed his lips. "Yeah."

UP ON THE BRIDGE, Commander Willis took his eyes off one of the displays, the same view as the pilots' lounge. "This place gives me the creeps."

Captain Bartell nodded. "Same. They couldn't even get back in to recover the pilots' remains."

As if to prove the captain's point, a Category 3 megafauna lumbered out of the neon-colored jungle growth that was covering most of the arena. It looked around the ruins, then turned its four-eyed gaze skyward, directly at the *Saratoga*.

On the screen, the thing that looked like a scaly penguin with two tails opened its mouth to emit a scream that shook the bridge windows.

"Should we target the megafauna, sir?" the senior tactical officer asked.

Bartell should his head. "No. Not the mission." He looked at his executive officer. "I'm turning in. The bridge is yours."

"Aye, sir," Willis said.

Captain Bartell closed the hatch to his ready room. The lights came on gently, illuminating his desk and workspace. He continued past them to the hatch that opened into his ready quarters. The wall display opposite his bed came to life, showing the view from one of the forward cameras. With civilization more or less over in this part of the world, the view was pitch black. Anyone living this far south wouldn't be giving themselves away with lights at night.

"Captain, sorry to interrupt. You have a call from NACAF Command," the communications watch stander announced over the intercom.

"Put 'em through." He moved back to his desk, sitting as the screen across from him came to life.

"Captain Bartell," the man on the screen said by way of greeting.

"Admiral Leera." He inclined his head.

"I thought you'd like to know, the Coalition Council is debating another wall." The other man was younger than Bartell, one of the youngest people to be promoted to admiral in the NACAF's short history. Most, including Bartell, felt the promotion was undeserved, but since Leera was the NACAF rep to the Coalition, he was harmless. Mostly.

Bartell shook his head. After Mexico City, the governments of the world thought a wall would keep their regions safe. Most of the projects were never even finished. The United States and Mexico worked together to build the Cancer Wall that followed the Tropic of Cancer. The wall, complete with battleship grade guns and specially formulated concrete and titanium rebar, lasted thirty minutes.

The wall in New Delhi fared slightly better.

Repelling the first attack, the massive guns mounted every twenty-five meters, ripping the first wave of monsters apart. The second wave, however, proved too much for the wall. It was breached in under two hours.

"Because walls worked so well the first time," Bartell said.

The admiral reached up, pushing his fingers through his jet-black hair. Admirals should be gray, Bartell thought. "No argument. I'm working with the admiralty of the other coalitions to put together proposals, but," he shrugged, "the recent elections here and abroad have opened the door for several conservative factions to think it's their time." He gave another slight shrug. "I'm just passing things on."

The *Saratoga's* captain rubbed his chin. "Of course. Guess my little scavenger hunt just got more important."

The admiral quirked the faintest smile. "Guess so."

THE MEGAFLORA JUNGLE south of Mexico City was an impenetrable thicket. Neon colored trees soared hundreds of feet into the air, wrapped in thorned vines that sprayed concentrated acid as a defense mechanism—against what, no one had ever figured out. Most of the megafauna seemed impervious. The plants decimated the landscape, paving the way for the animals. Perfectly symbiotic in an evil, world-destroying way.

Megafauna didn't register on most sensors other than radar, which meant to complete the survey, the *Saratoga* had to fly low enough to detect them. It made for slow going as the ship crisscrossed the Mexican peninsula, slowly moving south toward the Impact Zone.

After La Paz and a few close calls in the Gulf of Mexico and Red Sea, air carriers stayed over land. Both bodies of water were now nearly devoid of terrestrial life and unsafe to travel in or over.

Commander Willis consulted a nearby screen, a tactical view with the carrier in the middle of the screen. The ship was passing over the narrowest and most densely infested section of Mexico. The remains of Villa-hermosa were a few hundred kilometers ahead.

"Captain, Commander. You should look at this," someone from the sensor section called out.

Both senior officers moved to the center of the bridge, looking at the situation table. The table's top updated to show a tactical overview, with the air carrier in the center over an outline of the part of Mexico they were cruising over. The table marked several towns and cities in red, adding the date of their fall next to each name.

A section of the map was glowing orange, bracketed in a pulsing red square.

Captain Bartell looked up from the table. "What am I looking at?"

The senior sensor officer joined them. She double tapped the orange section, zooming in. "Honestly, sirs, not sure. I've never seen a heat signature this large."

Willis tilted his head toward the table. "We're just checking off new boxes left and right." He double tapped the table top, restoring the zoomed-out view. Drawing a line with his finger from the ship to the heat signature, he looked at the distance. "Fifty kilometers."

Bartell looked over to the section of the bridge where tactical and field ops were located. "Drop the watch." The officer at field ops nodded and spoke into his headset, letting Lieutenant Commander Tanner know.

Down in the main hangar, the lighting dimmed and orange warning lights began to strobe. "Attention. Attention. Bravo Team, prepare for drop."

Inside Midnight Tango's secure crèche, Brandon shouted, "About time!" The glossy black suit stepped from its docking and repair cradle. "Let's do this," Brandon said. Bravo Team had been on standby watch for several hours, and he was bored out of his mind.

Valiant Azure and Crusher Maverick followed, stepping up to their drop chutes in the hangar floor. From the ceiling, the drop cables lowered into position.

Brandon reached up to grab the thick cable, stepping over to Valiant Azure to connect it. Each suit connected a teammate to the tether, then took its place.

Over the team channel, Commander Tanner in field ops said, "Drop in five."

Lucy turned her head, scanners taking in her two teammates.

"Four."

The ship was still fifteen kilometers from the mysterious heat signature.

"Three."

She flexed her hands, making fists. Rather, her mind sent commands to her hands to make fists, and her pilot suit and thinking cap intercepted those impulses and sent them to Valiant Azure's fists.

"Two."

Alpha Team's suits were moving into position to follow Bravo down if needed.

"One. Drop."

The locking mechanism on the cable winches released, sending all three Bravo suits plummeting to the ground below, the winch brakes slowing their descent at the last second. With a meter or two to go, the powerful magnets released, letting the multiton mechs fall to the ground with a deafening thud.

"Bravo on the ground," Lucy announced.

Midnight Tango turned his head to look at Valiant Azure, who returned the look for a moment before turning toward the mystery heat signature. Her shoulder-mounted particle cannons deployed.

Paco brought Maverick up next to Azure. His suit's reinforced hands reached out for two massive alien tree trunks. The thick pistons in the suit's shoulders whined until the thick purple truck split. Reddish-blue sap spilled out of the trunk as Paco heaved it away.

Brandon deployed blades from each arm. "This will make quicker work of these damn tree things." He slid Tango in between Azure and Maverick, arms raised. Two quick slashes felled a thick pink trunk with meter-long thorns.

As another enormous trunk slid to the ground to topple out of their way, Brandon said, "This is fun!"

Lucy shook her head. Her suit wasn't designed for close-quarters combat. Other than brute mechanical strength, she had little to offer in clearing the invasive jungle. Maybe a pair of high intensity particle beams could burn through the canopy. She was about to ask the two men to step aside when something in the jungle released an ear-piercing scream.

"Uh oh," Brandon said, taking a step back from the thick alien plants.

THE ONLY WARNING Bravo Team or the *Saratoga* got was the one bestial scream. From half a kilometer ahead, three massive megafauna leaped out of the jungle into the air, wings spreading out more than ten meters across as they flapped to close the distance with the mighty air carrier hovering nearby.

On the ground, six Category 3 monsters rumbled out of the jungle directly in front of Bravo Team. Before the three pilots could react, the nearest monster backhanded Midnight Tango, sending the mech flying through the air. Paco ducked Crusher Maverick just in time to avoid being knocked over by his airborne team member.

Brandon crashed into a thick alien tree, splitting it.

The field ops commander shouted over the squad channel, "Alpha Team dropping!"

Overhead, the *Saratoga*'s ventral guns opened fire. Alpha Team dropped, weapons deployed. Brandon got Midnight Tango to his feet as one of the monsters approached; it looked like a crawfish mixed with a cat and a llama. The massive claws clacked as they opened and closed. The creature lunged.

"Oh, no you don't!" Brandon slashed his arm and its deployed blade upward, cleanly severing one of the claws at the elbow. The creature reared back, its lower legs flailing. He leaned back and planted a kick square in the creature's midsection, sending it staggering back from Tango.

"Coming through!" Paco shouted right before Crusher Maverick barreled into the creature, his massive fists hammering at the hard exoskeleton. The creature bellowed as its shell splintered and cracked under the onslaught.

"On your six," Alpha One announced as the three Alpha suits ran into the fray. The creature wrestling with Crusher Maverick flipped the heavy mech, tossing Paco deeper into the thick alien jungle. As the creature turned, Stalwart Rook swung her right-hand-turned-war-hammer in a savage overhand blow that caved in the creature's head. The beast twitched a few times on the way to the ground, then fell still.

Two of the creatures, a matching pair of koala-slug-spiders, tackled Tacit Ronin, bringing the dark gray suit to the ground in a thrashing pile of articulated limbs ending in claws and pincers. Molly Chen grunted over the team channel. "Little help here?" She was twisting and turning under the mass of limbs, but the suit's arm blades were pinned and she couldn't get a good angle.

"I got you!" Lucy said. She ducked behind Midnight Tango and brought both of her shoulder-mounted particle cannons to bear on the writhing mass of furry slug creature. She planted her feet, the whine of both cannons building to full power. "Brace!"

Each cannon glowed a moment before a pale blue shaft of light appeared, stabbing into the body of one of the koala-slug-spiders. The thing shrieked, its skin bubbling and burning away. It fell off Tacit Ronin, a smoking ruin.

The other creature was stabbing at Chen's suit with ferocious intensity. Lucy was lining up for another shot when a pair of two-meter bonded titanium blades erupted from the slime covered back of the monster. The blades turned ninety degrees and sliced laterally, cleaving the monster nearly in two.

Overhead, the *Saratoga* lurched, smoke billowing out of a large wound on her side.

THE THREE WINGED megafauna soared up out of the jungle, all wings and sharp-looking spines. All three were nearly identical, something like a pteranodon with scales and razor-sharp claws at the ends of the wings.

"The hell is this?" Captain Bartell demanded, eyes wide. In all his years, as far as anyone on Earth knew, megafauna didn't fly.

The three creatures rose over the top of the ship, each roaring as they gained altitude.

After a beat, Commander Willis turned to the tactical officer. "Target those things!"

The young man turned to his subordinates. "Lock on targets!"

"Targets locked," one of the gunnery officers announced.

The tactical officer looked to Commander Willis, who nodded.

"Forward batteries, open fire!"

The two main batteries at the fore of the ship swiveled, their three barrels lining up on the nearest of three inbound monsters. The six snub barrels whined a moment before pale blue beams of light lanced out of each to stab into the target. It screamed, skin bubbling as its insides boiled. As the six beams faded, the ruined remains of the winged creature plummeted to the ground, trailing greasy smoke.

Before the guns could lock onto the remaining two airborne monsters, they swooped, diving erratically, to close the gap between them and their attacker as quickly as they could. Captain Bartell watched, eyes wide and glued to the forward windows as the two creatures dropped onto the *Saratoga*'s upper hull. Talons as long as a grown man dug into the titanium composite hull armor, securing them to the air carrier.

One of the creatures turned to the portside big gun, its thick arms grasping the cannon as it attempted to rotate towards the target. The monster gave two quick twists and a tug. The cannon ripped free of its anchor point, leaving a gaping hole in the ship's armor and trailing sparks as thick power cables tore apart.

The added weight of the two beasts forced the ship's bow to dip several degrees. Warnings appeared on the navigation consoles as well as the engineering consoles near the rear of the bridge. The forward anti-grav system was straining under the additional weight. Air carriers remained aloft thanks to a careful balancing of forces from fore-and-aft systems. Now the forward motors were overloading as they attempted to push the ship's bow back up to level.

"Disable safeties on gun one," the tactical officer barked. "Get it into firing position!" Safeties kept the big guns from rotating into position where they might fire on the ship's conn tower.

Gun one rotated, turning past its safeties, ready to fire on one of the attackers. It stopped short when the monster got to it first, slamming its fists onto the number three barrel, deforming it and jamming the turret in place.

"Gun one is offline!" a helpful junior tactical officer called out, adding, "Gun two has taken significant damage. Barrel three damaged."

"Get some suits up there, now!" Commander Willis shouted.

The field ops section acknowledged the order and repeated it down to the hangar.

While the two main guns were being rendered inoperative by the surviving megafauna, several smaller weapons' emplacements deployed and swung into position. These smaller weapons primarily served to repel attacks from human forces such as pirates—a task that occurred more often than Captain Bartell preferred. Given that it was humanity versus monsters, humans fighting humans felt wrong.

Captain Bartell leaned on the railing, looking out the forward window. Rail guns, distant cousins of the phalanx weapon systems on wet navy ships, opened fire. The window blocked all sounds, but Bartell knew that outside the bridge, the roar of those guns was deafening. Hundreds, then thousands, of armor-piercing rounds struck the two beasts. They shifted under the withering fire, protecting their faces. With each step they took, the ship rocked and tilted, its grav systems straining to keep the ship and this new additional weight balanced in the air.

One of the creatures' wings was shredded to nothing as railgun rounds tore through it.

Two heavily armored panels at the midship slid open. Each covered a heavy lift meant to bring equipment from the hangar to the topside. Now, however, each brought two suits ready for battle.

"Charlie and Delta Teams arriving topside," the field ops watch stander shouted, looking up from his station.

Delta Team's Coyote Zulu was missing along with Charlie's Valor Ascendant. The lifts could only fit two suits at one time, and only barely. The third suit from each team would arrive once their teammates stepped off the lifts.

Delta Team's two suits wasted no time, rushing toward the nearest creature. Spotting their attackers, and shrugging off the annoying stings of the antiaircraft rounds, the creature roared and dropped to all fours to charge.

Spectacular Zephyr led Delta's charge, her ruby red armor glinting in the sun. The suit's forearm-mounted plasma cannons, lighter versions of Valiant Azure's shoulder-mounted models, lit up the distance between the suit and the monster with brilliant blue light.

Scales and muscle boiled away as supercharged plasma splashed against the creature. It screamed, ducking low as it continued its charge.

Sierra Slammer was right behind Zephyr, blades deployed, ready to lunge in when his teammate dodged.

Charlie Team's suits rushed the remaining monster, the one with the shredded wing. Charlie Two, Viridian Slammer, took the lead. That is until Audacious Thunder edged in just before reaching the monster. He brought both hands together, creating a massive sonic wave that rocked the monster in front of him off balance.

Charlie Two used that momentary distraction to come in from the side to unleash four rapid strikes with her spiked knuckles. When she made a fist, meter-long spikes deployed like brass knuckles. The spikes tore into the creature's side, causing it to scream and stagger towards the front of the ship away from the attack. Each step left giant holes in the hull, exposing the equipment and personnel inside. Smoke was issuing from several of the wounds the creature's talons were ripping open.

The ship's captain and commander watched the battle unfold, unable to do anything else; the smaller weapons' batteries had proven ineffective, so Bartell ordered them deactivated. Armor-piercing rounds wouldn't do much against the suits either, but they didn't need the distraction.

The ship lurched. Willis pointed. "Oh, shit!"

The creature engaging Charlie Team had latched onto Audacious Thunder and was taking flight, dragging the big mech off the *Saratoga*'s hull. The shift in weight was throwing the ship's bow upwards as the straining grav-motors now had less weight to lift.

CHAPTER TWELVE

AUDACIOUS THUNDER SLAMMED to the ground ten meters from where Void Romeo was standing. The force of the impact mangled the thickly armored suit. The winged creature circled overhead before dropping like a stone, forcing the wounded mech deeper into the soil with a sickening crunch.

Romeo's pilot, Victor Isaacson, took an involuntary step back before regaining his composure and leaping to the defense of his fallen comrade-in-arms. The shoulder-mounted slug thrower pivoted to take aim on the winged monstrosity that was bouncing atop the fallen Audacious Thunder, tearing into its torso with each landing.

Romeo's weapon fired with an ear-shattering bark. The megafauna staggered, the first impact not penetrating its thick hide but doing tremendous damage all the same. The second shot penetrated, eliciting an enraged shriek from the creature as it leaped into the air.

Unlike the much faster moving railgun rounds the

Saratoga's point defense guns fired, Romeo's slugs were specially designed to kill monsters.

The wind kicked up by the massive flying creature's wings was almost enough to knock Void Romeo over. His shoulder-mounted gun adjusted and fired again. The creature dove toward its attacker, bright blue blood and entrails trailing behind it. Victor was standing his ground, both arms upraised, forearm particle beams flashing to brilliant and destructive life between suit and monster, boiling away more of the creature with each shot. A second before impact, Midnight Tango tackled the other suit, the two barely escaping the raking claws as the creature swooped past as it crashed to the ground.

"Thanks," Victor said over the squad channel. He added, "Thunder is down, repeat, Audacious Thunder is down hard."

Brandon could hear the sadness in his voice. Pushing himself up and off the other suit, Brandon just said, "Yeah." He extended a hand to Void Romeo to help the other suit up as he glanced over at Audacious Thunder, motionless, half pushed into the loose soil forming a crater around the fallen mech.

From deeper in the neon-colored jungle, a five-meter diameter rock shot up toward the *Saratoga*. The already listing air carrier brought its underside-mounted guns to bear, but the rock hit first, crumpling the ship's armored skin. A fourth winged creature swooped under the ship, trying its best to grapple one of the underside big guns.

"What the hell was that?" Brandon asked.

Void Romeo raised an arm. "Came from that direction. Let's go." Victor didn't wait. His suit took off at a run.

BRANDON SCANNED the tactical display floating in the corner of his vision. The other suits on the ground were engaged with megafauna all around him. He spied Valiant Azure and said, "Lucy, come on!"

"Kinda busy," she replied. On his display, she was standing off from the various melees, firing in whichever direction presented itself to her long-range particle beams. "Stalwart Rook, juke left!" she barked.

Brandon rolled his eyes. "Need you more." He sent her the coordinates he was following Void Romeo toward. The pair had already covered a quarter kilometer. He glimpsed another boulder sailing overhead. He heard Lucy release an annoyed breath. Her dot on his display headed his direction.

"You're not Bravo One, just so you know," she said.

"Not yet, you mean," he corrected.

Pushing aside a blue scaled trunk a meter thick, he saw the source of the boulders. "What. The. Fuck."

From fifty meters to the right, Void Romeo sent, "We go on my mark." Brandon spied the glossy black and red suit crouched beside an alien plant that looked like melted wax.

The creature they were going to attack was nearly as long as two suits lying end to end and nearly as tall. It sat hunched low on eight multi-jointed legs, by far the most insect-like megafauna Brandon had ever seen. The creature leaned forward, grabbing a massive mouthful of ground. The creature swallowed and took two more bites, leaving a hole that matched others nearby.

Lucy pushed her way through a thicket of ropy yellow trunks that bent more than broke as she pushed through. "Oh, my—" She was ten meters to Brandon's left.

The creature's abdomen pulsed and curled up and over its head. A final convulsion wracked the beast as a boulder like the others shot out of the creature, sailing straight for the *Saratoga*.

Midnight Tango glanced over to Void Romeo again. Victor was likely feeling the same wonder. No one had ever encountered megafauna that seemed to have such a specific function besides ripping things apart and stomping on things.

The glossy black head of Void Romeo turned toward Midnight Tango. "We go on my mark."

Brandon held up a hand to point toward Lucy. "We can use her particle beams to keep it busy while we move in for the kill."

Romeo nodded his head, side-stepping further around the creature that seemed oblivious as it shifted to begin chewing its next salvo. The thick tail began to pulse again. Brandon's audio sensors picked up a loud grinding noise coming from the creature.

"Go!" Victor shouted. Romeo and Tango bolted straight at the beast while Azure unleashed twin particle beams, aimed at the pulsating abdomen. The creature released a bone shaking scream as its flesh boiled.

Romeo's shoulder-mounted slug thrower barked as

Victor fired on one of the creature's legs, hoping to destabilize it. The joint exploded in a splash of orange ichor and exoskeleton, sending it staggering.

Brandon pulled back his right arm like he was on the pitcher's mound. The triblade locked into its ready position. He told himself he could do this. With a powerful forward throwing motion, he sent the blade slicing through the air to embed in the neck of the artillery creature.

Valiant Azure stepped closer to the creature, her powerful particle beams cycling in and out of existence to burn holes into the creature's softer tissues.

The creature stumbled, its abdomen quivering as it tried to create another boulder while internal organs spilled out of numerous steaming wounds.

"Single-minded, isn't it?" Victor said as Void Romeo moved to target another leg.

Brandon grasped the thick cable running from his other arm to the blade penetrating the monster's neck. With a yank he pulled the behemoth to the ground. It shrieked something between pain and rage, turning toward its attacker.

"Uh oh," Brandon said.

One of the creature's remaining legs reached up and grabbed the cable.

"Brandon, watch your—" Lucy started.

"Oh bo—" Midnight Tango took flight, sailing toward the creature. The claw clutching the cable swung to intercept the airborne mech, sending it hurdling off in another direction. The trimetal blade tore free, following its owner.

"Brandon!" Lucy shouted. She turned her cannons on the creature's face. One half melted instantly under the twin particle beams.

The creature screamed again as Void Romeo leaped onto its back, blades slapping repeatedly into the creature's back. Legs spasmed as the creature thrashed.

"Go for the head!" Lucy said, coming closer to the creature to fire. One of the creature's remaining legs lashed out, knocking Valiant Azure to the ground.

With a final lurch, the creature collapsed to the ground, its orange life blood bubbling out of multiple stab wounds on its back and even more seared and smoking holes along the massive abdomen.

Midnight Tango walked up and offered a hand, hauling Valiant Azure up to her feet. Dirt and grime covered both suits.

Void Romeo slid off the dead creature's back. "That was fun."

The other two mechs turned to look at the glossy black mech, cocking their heads.

Something back where they'd come from roared.

STALWART ROOK SPUN IN A CIRCLE, her right hand in the powerful war hammer configuration. The face of a massive scaled creature with scythe-like hooks for hands exploded in a flash of bright blue gore and brain matter. The spasming corpse fell to the ground, the momentum imparted by the hammer carrying it several meters. The heavy suit was limping, fluids pouring from her left knee and hip. Sophie Belanger winced, her pilot suit passing on the damage as nerve impulses.

Paco's Crusher Maverick had his back up against Molly Chen's Tacit Ronin. The two suits were slowly rotating, trading blows with a matched pair of megafauna that looked like they were based on what a gorilla and a platypus might look like if they were to breed.

"These ugly *putas* are tough," Paco said, bringing up an arm to block a blow that might have dented Maverick's head if it connected. He brought his other hand up to grab the monster's arm. Thick metal fingers squeezed. The creature wailed as its limb was turned to pulp. Paco leaned back, planting a kick to the creature's midsection.

Overhead, one of the *Saratoga's* large underside-mounted guns opened fire. One of the gorilla-platypus creatures was torn apart by the trio of particle beams that slammed into it repeatedly in the span of seconds. It wailed, gurgled, then exploded in a flash of super heated gore that covered both Crusher Maverick and Stalwart Rook.

The two suits turned to face the remaining creature with the ruined arm.

"Better odds," Paco said, taking a step towards it.

The wounded creature looked from suit to suit, growling and mewling.

"Agreed," Molly said, deploying the jagged chainsaw like blades her suit kept in its forearms. Once in their locked positions, the ultra dense chains roared into motion. As the blade spun, the links started to glow and throw off sparks. "Let's finish this!" She lunged for the creature, arms moving in a fluid motion, blades screaming. The beast pivoted, narrowly avoiding one of the dark gray suit's blades.

It didn't avoid Crusher Maverick's left hook or the right cross that followed. The dazed creature staggered backward until it stopped. Two glowing chainsaws erupted from its chest, the spinning teeth sending gore splattering all over Maverick's orange and blue chest and face.

In the secure crèche, Paco winced as the thing's guts covered his suit's optic sensors. "Gross." He brought a thick metal hand up to Maverick's head, but neither hand nor head was designed for wiping goo off. He switched over to infrared, leveraging the suit's sensor suite.

ABOARD THE *SARATOGA,* things were going less well.

"Sir, we're losing the number two thruster," one of the officers near the engineering station announced. The ship had already lost the number three thruster. Losing another would effectively cut the ship's top forward speed in half.

"Forward grav-motor two is fluctuating and midship eight is out altogether," another engineering officer announced, panic lacing her words. Air carriers had twelve grav-motors that kept the enormous war machines aloft. A ship could make it on eight, seven in a pinch, if it had to, but VarTech did not recommend it.

Commander Willis watched as the two remaining members of Charlie Team, their suits back-to-back, severed the right wing of one of the attacking creatures. Gore spilled across the ruined upper hull of the ship. Not out of the fight, the beast swung its remaining limb, clipping Viridian Slammer, crumpling the side of the suit's head. The green armored mech stumbled to the side, dropping to one knee. The optical mesh that served as the suit's face, covering the sensors and cameras, was in tatters, emitting sparks. Without the sensors and cameras in the head, the pilot was close to blind. Suits had redundant sensors in their torsos, but they were limited to LiDAR and RADAR.

In her secure crèche, Stacy said, "Viridian Slammer." She took a deep breath to clear her head. "No longer combat effective."

Nearly half a kilometer away, Brandon looked up from the finally dead rock launching creature. He couldn't see the *Saratoga*'s topside but could see the thick black smoke that was coming from several places along the ship's top and sides. The mighty air carrier was visibly listing to one side.

Atop the *Saratoga*, Valor Ascendant's shoulder-mounted rocket launchers clicked as they reloaded. "Fire in the hole!" he announced as both launchers locked in place. The right side roared as the meter-long ordnance shot from the launcher on target for the one-armed monster moving toward Viridian Slammer's kneeling form.

The missile lifted the creature off its feet as the explosion ripped most of its torso to neon-colored shreds. "Splash one," Brady Davidson said.

"All units, stand down," Commander Tanner

announced to all suits. "Bridge reports no megafauna on scopes."

Coyote Zulu and Valor Ascendant helped Viridian Slammer to her feet. "We got you," Brady Davidson said.

The trio made its way to one of the topside lifts as the armored panel slid out of the way.

CHAPTER THIRTEEN

ONCE ALL THE fire teams were back aboard the *Saratoga,* the ship's company got started assessing the damage, attending to the wounded, and mourning the dead. The ship wide funeral took place the next day, giving everyone time to rest and get cleaned up.

All the training in the world couldn't have prepared Brandon for the loss of a fellow pilot. Thankfully Paco and Lucy came through the megafauna ambush, mostly unscathed, though Crusher Maverick would be down for repairs for a while.

Charlie Team had been less fortunate. Stacy's Viridian Slammer was down for the count, the head damaged beyond repair, which rendered the entire suit useless. Her new teammate Malcolm Taggart had been killed when Audacious Thunder slammed into the ground from a kilometer up. The repeated blows after that as the winged creature tore at the suit's chest armor while slamming the machine up and down on the ground hadn't helped. Taggart was dead by the time they recovered the suit and got it opened up.

With all attention on Audacious Thunder, it was a while before anyone realized Sierra Slammer was down and his pilot, Alec Lefebvre, was barely hanging on. The blue and black armored mech was the last to come down from the upper hull. He stumbled off the lift, nearly taking out Spectacular Zephyr. The EMTs had rushed him to the *Saratoga*'s sick bay. His status was still listed as critical the last time one of the pilots went to check.

In their shared quarters, Brandon adjusted his dress uniform. "So scratchy." His jacket was at least a size too large.

"Better than the alternative," Lucy growled, pulling at the neck of her own uniform. "But yeah. Did they design these as punishment?" Her slacks appeared to be one size smaller than she would normally wear.

Paco walked in from his small room. "I dunno, *amigos*. I think they look nice." He did a slow spin. Somehow his dress grays looked good on him, and seemed to be perfectly tailored.

Brandon's mouth fell open. "Did...did you have your dress uniform tailored?"

Paco affected a stricken look. "What? No. My *abuelita* was a seamstress. Taught me everything she knew." He shrugged, his jacket moving in just the right ways with the gesture. "You know, in case the academy didn't work out."

"And you never offered your services to us?" Lucy demanded.

He shrugged again. "I am not a seamstress." He gestured to the hatch. "Ready?"

Brandon shook his head. "No. But that doesn't matter." His two friends nodded their agreement.

The walk to the main hangar took longer than normal; several corridors were closed off for damage repair. The upper decks of the ship had taken a beating, and many corridors had been ripped open or collapsed. Several vital systems in those areas were damaged.

The ship was still listing nearly ten degrees to port, but engineering was confident that they could get the ship back shape to continue their mission.

Every member of the crew not engaged in repairs was in the hangar. The massive forward doors were open; ten squat, lozenge-shaped coffins containing deceased *Saratoga* crewers were lined up in a row. The captain was standing at a lectern to the right of the line of coffins. The bodies would be stored until the *Saratoga* returned to port.

WHILE CAPTAIN BARTELL led the funeral service, Commander Willis oversaw repairs. The view from the forward bridge windows was bleak. The *Saratoga*'s dorsal was a shredded mess all along the ship's kilometer-long hull. It was unclear if the winged megafauna had somehow known what to do or just followed whatever instincts drove the alien monsters, but the result was the same, regardless. Both dorsal forward big guns were wrecked, as were several smaller weapons emplacements —none of which could be repaired in situ.

In addition to the ship's weapons, power junctions and data network nodes had been damaged or destroyed as well, forcing the engineering department to reroute more systems than would normally be allowed on an air carrier in the field.

A young man approached, data tablet in hand. "Latest report from engineering, sir." He offered the tablet.

"Thank you, Ensign." Willis took the tablet and immediately regretted looking at the screen. There was more red and yellow on it than there had been two hours ago. Not a good sign. Tapping his commset, he said, "XO to engineering." The ship's computer, even at its currently reduced processing capacity, routed the call to the chief engineer's commset.

The call connected, and after an audible sigh, the *Saratoga*'s chief engineer said, "Engineering here. Go ahead, sir."

"Gomez, there's more red and yellow on this repair status report than before," he accused.

Sonia Gomez, the ship's chief engineer, sighed again. "Yes, sir. I'm not color blind. Those damn monsters really fucked us. The AG systems are still throwing errors across seven of twelve nodes."

"Can you fix them?" Seven nodes being damaged was not good.

It took twelve AG field generators—six starboard, six port—to keep the massive air carrier aloft. In an emergency, the ship could operate on eight if they were in perfect working order and ideally evenly spaced. With seven showing intermittent faults, the odds weren't in their favor for staying in the air.

"While we're in the air? Not likely. We're doing what we can, but, well..." She let the end of her sentence hang there in the silence. Both of them were aware that NACAF Command wouldn't be sending a repair ship this far south, especially now that Captain Bartell reported not only the existence of megafauna capable of flight and of hurdling multiton boulders into the sky, but also that they seemed to be coordinating their attacks.

"What do you need?" Willis was certain he knew the answer, more certain he wasn't going to like her answer.

"We need to set down. I'm pretty sure we can get all of the nodes repaired if we can take them offline, reset them, maybe beat a few with a hammer. I'm very certain we can get at least eight of them reliably online."

"And if we don't?"

Another pregnant pause, then a sigh. "We're gonna end up on the ground one way or another, Linc." She rarely used his nickname. Doing so now ensured he knew how serious she was.

"Okay. The captain should be wrapping up the funeral service shortly. I'll confirm with him, but let's assume we'll be setting down in the next few hours."

"Copy that." The channel clicked closed.

Willis turned to the navigation officer. "Find us a place to set down."

The senior pilot turned. "Sir?"

"*Saratoga* is landing or crashing. I'd prefer the former."

"Aye, sir."

Turning a slow circle, the commander watched the bridge officers go about their duties. This survey mission was going off the rails quickly. They were still a few hundred kilometers from Impact Zone Five. He reached out and pulled up the ship's inventory on his console.

"Hmm," he continued, pulling up menus and inventories. "That could work." He tapped his commset. "Commander Tanner. I've got something I want to run by you."

THE *SARATOGA* FOUND a place to set down five kilometers from where the ambush occurred. As far as the sensors could tell, the area was clear of megafauna. How long that would remain true was anyone's guess.

Despite the relatively short distance, the ship had been sailing for three hours and had another hour to go before reaching the designated clearing, the thought being that going slowly with failing AG nodes was safer than going flank speed.

Everyone aboard was holding their breath as the ship groaned and creaked with every meter traveled.

While the *Saratoga* made its way, the main hangar was a scene of barely controlled chaos. Technicians were running between suits, making repairs where they could and scavenging parts where they couldn't.

The main lift between the forward and aft hangar never stopped moving as techs not involved in suit repairs were prepping the carrier's ground vehicles for the upcoming mission continuation over ground. Equipment was moving back and forth at a frenetic pace.

The aft hangar had a powerful crane that was able to bring Audacious Thunder back aboard. The inoperable suit lay sprawled out near the midship hangar lift, as out of the way as possible for something forty feet tall and weighing tens of tons.

Despite the urgency, only VarTech technicians were allowed to work on the ship's complement of suits. With Charlie Team back to just one suit, the team's technicians were scattered to other teams, helping where they could.

Bravo Team technician Jennifer Morris was shouting at a borrowed tech about their lack of attention to detail after a section of Crusher Maverick's hip armor clattered to the deck. "You gotta watch out. That crushed a toolbox!"

"Sorry, Jen!" the other woman replied as she confirmed the chains holding another piece of armor in place were secure. From inside the damaged hip joint, blue-tinted goo pumped and oozed from several damaged tubes.

Brandon and Stacy threaded their way between rushing technicians and stray bits of suit armor. They watched as someone drove a cart past them at breakneck speed with a severed forearm on the flatbed. "That's mine."

It took Brandon a moment to realize what she meant. It was Viridian Slammer's arm. He put a hand on her shoulder, squeezing. "I'm sure they need it."

She nodded. "Yeah. Just sucks."

He thought he understood what she meant. The idea of losing Midnight Tango was weird to consider.

"Make a hole!" someone shouted, forcing the pair to duck to the right toward the remains of Audacious Thunder. They looked up at the ruined suit. The damage was extreme; the impact with the ground and the subsequent attack by the winged megafauna had left the armored mech tattered and torn.

Several technicians were walking along the forty-meter body looking for parts to pull. Brandon shook his head. "I know it needs to happen, but it sucks to see."

Stacy grunted but said nothing. She nodded toward the massive lift. "Let's go see the ground prep."

Brandon nodded, and they jogged over to jump on the lift a moment before it began its next trip down to deck eight. The lift platform was crammed with wheeled carts full of power cells and equipment neither pilot recognized.

As the lift platform cleared shaft and opened out into the forward hangar, the pair realized how big the mobilization truly was.

"Woah," Brandon breathed. He'd actually never ventured into the forward hangar. It wasn't where suits were kept or launched from, so he hadn't been interested. The space was less than half as big as the suit hangar. The entire hangar deck was covered in ground vehicles and equipment.

AS THE *SARATOGA* descended toward the clearing the sensor team found earlier, thick landing struts deployed from almost two dozen panels along the ship's underside. The attack damaged several armored landing strut covers. One fell off halfway through retracting.

The ship's remaining dorsal weapons systems had been deployed as a precaution, tracking back and forth. The low thrum of the AG field nodes grew as the ship lowered to the ground. Several of the nodes were throwing critical errors now. One had already failed, causing one corner of the ship to dip.

"Ten meters to ground," the helmsman announced, his hand slowly pulling the power lever for the AG systems closer and closer to himself. "All functional landing struts locked," he added. Next to him, another member of the pilot team was adjusting the maneuvering thrusters as best they could to try to compensate for the failing AG nodes.

Captain Bartell had his eyes glued to the tactical display. Once they were on the ground and the suits and science teams departed, he would deploy their remaining shuttles in a makeshift air patrol.

Commander Willis' idea of sending out the ground forces with a science team, while beyond dangerous, was the only realistic way they'd be able to complete their mission. The *Saratoga* was likely to be grounded for a week at least, according to Chief Engineer Gomez. Less, if Command sent help, which wasn't likely this far south.

"Five meters to ground," the helmsman announced.

The most shocking development had turned out to be the insistence of the VarTech science division that they accompany the team going over ground to the Impact Zone. Dr. Erasmus, despite his earlier protests about this mission, had changed his tune. Bartell wasn't sure why, and despite his best efforts, had been unsuccessful at deterring the scientist and his people from joining the ground mission.

After the attack, members of the science division searched the ground for their mysterious new plant. They'd come up dry. No sign of the plant other than a few bits and pieces like before.

In the end, as always, VarTech won. The remaining combat capable suits would accompany a ground team to Impact Zone Five to complete their survey as well as help the science team find the plant that Erasmus swore would tip the scales in the war against the alien megafauna.

"One meter."

The captain's attention turned back to the displays around him. The tactical display was now clear, as was the hastily added sky scan, that airborne megafauna were a thing. Why had there been so many and now there were none? He shook his head.

A thud announced the ship's touching down as the landing struts absorbed the weight of the ship, hydraulics hissing as tons of air carrier settled on them. After a moment of slight tilting as the computer adjusted the individual landing struts to bring the ship level from its ten-degree tilt, the helmsman announced, "We're down."

"Kill AG systems," Commander Willis ordered.

The low-level thrum that was a part of daily life aboard the *Saratoga* fell silent. "AG systems, offline," the engineering watch stander announced. She cocked her head, listening to reports from her department. "Engines now at standby, Captain."

Bartell nodded. "Very good. Let Chief Gomez know that she's clear to begin repair operations." He turned to Willis. "Commander, let the away team know they're clear to depart."

CHAPTER FOURTEEN

FOR THE FIRST time in a long time, the activity in the forward hangar matched that of the rear. The smaller of the two hangar complexes on the ship, connected by a massive lift the width of the two cavernous spaces, it provided storage for ground vehicles and air support craft when not in use.

While the remaining functional suits were being repaired or scavenged by the VarTech technicians, NACAF crew members were busy prepping the ground mission. Four armored transports measuring ten meters each were being loaded with food, water, scientific equipment, and weapons.

Each transport sat on six thick all-terrain wheels two meters in diameter. The wheels were a thick rubber composite all the way through; flat tires in no-man's-land were a death sentence. The forward section of each vehicle had a pair of articulated arms with circular saw blades at the end. Getting through the alien jungle ahead would not be easy.

Watching from an observation lounge, Commander Willis couldn't recall ever hearing about a time a carrier had deployed ground forces outside of disaster recovery. He turned to Lieutenant Commander Tanner. "You ready for this?"

The other man shook his head. "How could I be? We don't even drill for things like this. Sending transports into the wild without carrier support?" He blew out a breath. "Undiscovered country, my friend, undiscovered country."

Willis nodded and clapped his friend on the shoulder as he turned to leave.

In addition to the ground transports, four small, one-seat Wasp assault fliers were being prepped alongside the starboard bulkhead. In the beginning, air carriers had several dozens of the small quad rotor vehicles. As megafauna grew in size and toughness, their effectiveness diminished until most carriers stopped carrying more than a single wing of four craft.

Despite drones taking over the job of airborne scout, there was still a place for the nimble craft from time to time. *Saratoga* carried twelve. The remaining eight would patrol the ship's landing zone.

"Transport One is ready to roll!" a NACAF deck-hand shouted. In response, several nervous looking scientists in jumpsuits boarded the vehicle. The whine of its power plant spinning up filled the space. Another transport rumbled to life, followed by the remaining two. The combined rumbles filled the forward hangar with a drone that had folks on the deck covering their ears.

Lieutenant Commander Tanner had moved down to

the hangar deck and was standing off to the side, trying to keep out of the way of the busy crewers. He turned to the man next to him. "Bring as many as you can back."

Major Nick Thompson nodded. "That's the plan, sir." Thompson was Tanner's second in command of the field ops command center, so leading the ground mission had seemed like a natural fit to Captain Bartell. Thompson wasn't as sure, but orders were orders. "At least we don't have too far to go."

"Still about nine hundred clicks," the commander replied, adding, "without much air cover." He nodded toward the row of Wasp assault fliers. "Those aren't that effective, unfortunately."

Thompson frowned. "You're welcome to take the lead on this, since you're doing such a great job of selling it. Sir."

Willis chuckled and looked at his friend. The two of them had been a year apart at the academy in Chicago. "Just be careful." He nodded to the four gigantic machines idling two abreast at the forward hangar door. "Those things don't get a lot of field testing."

"That's not something I needed to be reminded of," Thompson said. He saluted his friend and commanding officer. "Better get going. They're waiting for me."

A siren sounded twice before the large forward hangar doors split at the middle and slid apart. Orange strobes in the corners of the entryway twirled to warn all present that the door was open. The dusty landscape beyond didn't look very welcoming.

Willis returned the salute and watched his friend jog over to Transport One. As he entered, the rear hatch closed and the boarding ladder folded up to create a protective barrier over the hatch. Every little bit would help where those vehicles were going.

The four Wasps lifted off, their miniature versions of the AG pods that kept the *Saratoga* aloft humming. Each craft shot out of the hangar ahead of the rumbling transports that took their turn, rolling down the boarding ramp that had extended out from the ship before dropping the leading edge to the ground.

While ground missions were a rarity, NACAF was always prepared. At least that was the theory.

Commander Willis watched the final transport descend the ramp before he turned to leave the hangar. The sound of the thick armored doors grinding closed drowned everything else out.

IN ADDITION to the ground transports and Wasps, Alpha and Bravo Team escorted the scientific mission. The remaining suits from Charlie and Delta Team stayed with the *Saratoga* to protect the ship while it was on the ground.

Alpha took point while Bravo brought up the rear, each in a triangle formation. After some cajoling, Brandon convinced Molly Chen to have the two teams trade places each day. As Alpha One, she was the most senior pilot and thus in charge of the six-suit unit when they were on the move.

The transports, while designed to cut through the alien plant life and push through the jungles, tried to stick to long abandoned roads and highways. By now, both were also overgrown, but to a lesser degree.

After a few hours of silent marching, Paco said, "It's so weird how interchangeable suit parts are." Crusher Maverick's thick hand reached up to pat his chest plate. It was no longer blue with orange highlights, instead sporting the much-scuffed paint job of Viridian Slammer. Stacy had been happy to donate her suit's armor, hoping Paco could deliver some payback on her behalf. Viridian Slammer's crushed head ensured it was out of the fight until the *Saratoga* reached a NACAF base.

The huge claw mark cutting diagonally across the armor hadn't penetrated, so it was deemed more functional than Maverick's own armor, which had ended up punctured in more than one place.

"Weird that we had to leave the hangar while the techs worked," he said.

Midnight Tango's head bobbed up and down. "Yeah, that was kinda strange. I mean, they're always a little secretive when they have the suits opened up, but you woulda thought it would be an all-hands-on-deck type of situation."

Valiant Azure's head shook. "VarTech proprietary technology." Lucy's disdain was obvious. "No one can steal their tech if they make it illegal to learn about it."

Molly Chen in Tacit Ronin cut through on the squad channel. "Contact bearing thirty, two hundred out."

Bravo Team slowed and put some distance between each other, creating three distinct targets. Ahead of them, the four transports rumbled to a stop. The Wasps, riding on the back of the transports to save power, rose into the air.

Brandon zoomed in the tactical display floating in the corner of his vision. Sure enough, a pulsing orange dot was two hundred meters off to the right of their direction of travel. Two of the Wasps zipped overhead, green dots on Brandon's display. He watched as the two small craft converged on the orange dot, Alpha Three right behind them as fast as he could go. The dot would turn red or green once the Wasps got a visual on the target.

The dot went away.

"Alpha Three? Report," Alpha One called out. Molly's voice was laced with stress. On Brandon's display, Alpha Three had reached the location of the dot and was standing right where it had been. The two Wasps orbited overhead at fifty meters' distance from the lone suit.

"Uh, yeah. Sorry, Alpha One. All good. We're clear." Victor cleared his throat. "No threat." He sent a video feed access link to the entire ground element.

In Transport One, Major Thompson said, "What're we looking at?"

"Holy," Lucy whispered over the channel.

Brandon's mouth fell open. Standing like some kind of metal scarecrow was a rust- and moss-covered suit in the middle of a clearing.

"I don't recognize it," Sophie Belanger, Alpha Two, said.

"I think it's Astral Pioneer," Paco offered. Of the three of them, the Hispanic suit pilot was the biggest history buff. Brandon wasn't sure about Alpha Team.

Grace made a noise, then said, "I think you're right."

The mystery suit was taller and thicker than the suits of Alpha and Bravo Teams, built when armor composites weren't as refined. To get as much protection as modern armor, suits had to have a lot more room for the thicker plate. Its cylindrical body and blocky limbs looked like it would be a beast to operate. Moss hung from the machine's outstretched arms and rust speckled the entire body. Several jagged holes marred the mech's torso. One of them was surely the blow that killed the pilot.

"Why's it here?" Lucy asked.

"Not our mission," Major Thompson said over the squad channel. "Let's get back on track."

"Wait! Look!" Victor shouted. The shared video feed shifted to something near the rusted old mech's feet. Its right hand was pointing at something.

"What is that?" Grace asked.

Void Romeo kneeled down to pull something out of the underbrush near Astral Pioneer's feet. On the video feed, a pair of glossy black metal hands, with red outlines, pulled up a battered metal sign five meters across.

"What's Libertad?" Victor asked.

Over the squad channel, Major Thompson said, "Whatever it is, it's one hundred kilometers in the direction we're heading." He cleared his throat. "Let's roll."

"Copy that," Victor said, dropping the metal sign with "Libertad" burned into it along with an arrow, to the ground.

Brandon watched Alpha Three's dot on his tactical sensor display move back into position. The Wasps headed back to their mother vehicles.

ONE HUNDRED AND ten kilometers passed without incident, to everyone on the ground mission's surprise. Other than a few Category 1s that gave the six mechs and four rumbling ground transports a wide berth, they saw very little in the way of alien life.

It was Bravo Team's turn to walk point. Lucy was the first to see what she assumed must be Libertad. "Woah," was all she said, barely loud enough for the comm system to pick up. Regaining her composure, she shared access to her suit's video feed. All three Bravo suits could see what she did, but the transports and Alpha Team were still far enough back on the road.

Brandon, walking a few hundred meters to Lucy's right, watched as she approached a suit-sized arch with "Libertad" in two-foot-tall letters across the top. A low wall, barely three meters in height, ran from each side of the massive arch to encircle a sprawling and, by the look of it, well-populated town.

On the shared video feed, a man emerged from a house near the gate. He was a man in his mid-fifties with shoulder-length, jet-black hair pulled into a ponytail. He motioned toward Valiant Azure to step through the gate. When the big suit didn't move, he exaggerated the movement.

"Uh, sir?" Lucy asked.

Behind Azure, Crusher Maverick and Midnight Tango were moving to stand behind and on either side of their friend. Lucy watched as several dozen townspeople joined the first man, all staring up at the three modern war machines, hands up to shield their eyes from the afternoon sun.

Major Thompson sighed. "Anything hinky?"

"I'm not picking up any weapons," Lucy offered. She mentally toggled another scan of the crowd and nearby buildings. "Well, not anything big anyway." Several people had pistols in tucked into their belts.

Now that he and Paco were next to Valiant Azure, Brandon zoomed in with his own sensors and cameras. He could see that the first man who greeted them was unarmed. Several other people had pistols, and a few were packing rifles. Nothing that would threaten a suit or even a person with combat armor.

The four transports rumbled up behind the suits, fanning out around them. The man inside the massive gate motioned at the three suits again. Brandon motioned for his friends to follow him as he guided Midnight Tango through the suit-sized gate. The other two suits followed, taking up positions on either side of the entry.

Brandon guided Midnight Tango a few steps further into the village before dropping the powerful suit to one knee. Valiant Azure and Crusher Maverick followed suit.

"Be careful," Major Thompson cautioned from Transport One.

Brandon looked around one more time, his sensors keen for anything that might be a threat. Hundreds of buildings made up the village, several were two stories tall, which seemed to be the maximum. "How is this even possible?" he asked out loud in the confines of his pilot's crèche. He could see hundreds of people going about their lives, ignoring or otherwise not caring that three NACAF suits had just walked into town.

"We'll find out," Thompson said. On his sensor display, Brandon saw Transport One's boarding hatch open.

How a town could exist this deep in the alien wilds was beyond him. It was true they had encountered nothing bigger than a Category 1 megafauna on their way to Libertad, which defied conventional wisdom. As far as the NAC and other alliances around the world knew, the territory taken by the monsters was crawling with megafauna.

But for a town this size to exist, with nothing more than a few meters tall wall, in plain sight, with no armaments along the walls or in the town...Brandon sent the mental commands to put the suit into standby mode. The steady thrum of the mighty machine's power plant faded to nothing.

With a thought, the armored panels in the suit's back that covered the pilot's crèche slid apart amid a series of clanks and groans, followed by the inner hatch splitting down the middle to open up.

Light flooded in around Brandon, temporarily blinding him. One by one, the data connections across his body disengaged, freeing him from the body-shaped socket he was in. He leaned back, enjoying the feel of sunshine on his face as he pulled off his helmet.

He eased himself around to see the armored panels on Valiant Azure opening. Reaching over to a panel just inside the crèche, he activated the emergency access system. Small rungs extended out of Midnight Tango's lower back, down its backside and leg. The suit's computer knew which knee was on the ground and extended rungs just in that leg. It wasn't the most graceful way to get in and out of a suit, but it was the only way to do it outside a NACAF air carrier or VarTech facility.

Outside of town, Alpha Team's suits were kneeling to the ground around the parked ground transports.

Brandon hit the ground just as Major Thompson was approaching the man who'd first waved to Lucy. The man said, "*Hola*. I'm Miguel." He held out his hand for the major.

"Major Nick Thompson, NACAF," he said as he took Miguel's hand.

"Welcome to Libertad," Miguel said, beaming.

CHAPTER FIFTEEN

AFTER SETTING up a guard rotation and Wasp patrol schedule, Major Thompson told the entire ground team they could take the afternoon and evening to explore the village. He made it clear that they'd be leaving first thing in the morning and anyone not on a transport would be left behind.

Miguel, who turned out to be the village's mayor, escorted Major Thompson, Alpha Team, and several senior scientists and technicians on a tour of Libertad. Several dozen villagers had come out to ogle the new arrivals. "We don't get many visitors, as you can imagine," Miguel explained as he guided the major and the others off into town.

The rest of the expedition watched the senior officers and VarTech folks walk off into town, then broke into their own groups to explore the town. Paco led Bravo Team and a few of the technicians from the transports toward a small group of young men and women.

"*Hola*," Paco greeted the group.

As Paco spoke to the group in Spanish, Lucy leaned over to Brandon. "How the hell is there a town this close to Impact Zero?"

He shook his head. "Alpha Team went with the major."

"What?" Lucy stopped walking. Brandon stopped too, a sour look on his face. "Are you serious?"

He shrugged. "We found this place. We should—"

"I found this place," she interrupted, a smirk on her face.

He held up both hands. "Okay, fine. You found it. Either way, we should be with the major on the VIP tour."

She shook her head. "Alpha Team is senior most between us. It makes sense for them to accompany the major and science folks." She clapped a hand on his shoulder. "Look at it this way. We get shore leave, Alpha gets..." she shrugged, "...whatever they're doing."

Brandon took a breath. She was right, he knew, but it still felt like a slight. He looked around as Paco continued to chat up the locals. "I feel so exposed." She nodded. They both hustled to catch up to Paco.

Their friend turned to them. "Good news, *amigos*." His face split by an ear-to-ear grin.

Brandon knew that look. "Bar?"

Nodding, Paco said, "*Sí*." He waved to the locals. "They've agreed to show us around."

"Don't worry. We speak English," a young woman said, approaching Brandon. "Angela. Angela Ruiz-Aguilar."

"Bran—uh—Bra—," he stammered. Angela was beautiful. She smiled, running a hand through her jet-black hair. Her other hand found the necklace at her throat, a series of adamite stones bound in hemp cord. "Brandon…"

Lucy sighed. "He's Brandon Sinclair. I'm Lucy Jones." She offered her hand. Angela took it with a smile.

Brandon regained his composure, his cheeks returning to their normal hue. He turned to Paco. "You mentioned a bar?"

Angela smiled. "Come with us."

Following Angela and her people, Lucy leaned over to Paco. "Where do you think they get the beer?" Brandon had sidled up to walk next to their guide.

He shook his head. "Don't think too hard on it." He knew full well how small towns got by in the way of alcohol and many other things. He was actually looking forward to some small-town homebrew.

Walking through town, Brandon marveled at the meticulous upkeep of every home and business. They were hundreds of kilometers from any other human civilization, and as far as he could see, completely unprotected. Yet, the buildings could have easily fit into any NAC town.

After seeing so many abandoned and ravaged towns, seeing one intact and occupied was jarring. He had so many questions.

MAJOR THOMPSON, Dr. Erasmus, and Alpha Team

followed Miguel down a wide dirt road that led from the town's main gate toward the center of town.

Major Thomson elbowed Erasmus. "You know this place existed, Doc?" The older man shook his head. "Did VarTech?" Another shake.

"Mr. Mayor, how long—" Thompson called.

"Miguel, please," the man leading the procession said, turning to smile at his guests.

Thompson inclined his head. "Miguel. How long has Libertad been here?"

The group reached an intersection with a road that seemed to bend as it went in each direction. Molly Chen, bringing up the rear of the procession, looked both ways, thinking the road must form a rough circle. Maybe most of the major roads formed concentric circles. She smiled. Would make sense. Up ahead, the major and mayor were talking about the town's history. She was paying only partial attention.

Sophie Belanger fell back next to her. "This place has been here since before impact. Can you believe that?"

Molly shook her head. "How?"

The other woman shrugged.

A saloon, a general store, and two two-story apartment buildings framed the intersection. Next to the saloon was a building with a hand painted sign that read, *Administración*. "My office."

"Looks...cozy," Dr. Erasmus said. "You said you'd tell us about your town?"

The Hispanic man smiled. "Of course. But first, tequila." He gestured to the saloon. "Come."

The inside of the saloon looked like a set piece from

an Old West drama. Tables littered the first floor; about half were occupied. A pair of bartenders worked the bar.

Victor Isaacson looked up at the second-floor railing. "Think that's a brothel?" He wiggled his eyebrows at Sophie, who punched him in the shoulder.

Miguel smiled. "Meeting room." He gestured to the stairs.

True to his word, the second floor of the saloon with —as far as Molly Chen could tell—no name, was meeting rooms. Three, by the looks of it. Saloon and conference center, deep in the middle of alien plant- and animal-infested southern Mexico. Sure, of course.

Once everyone was seated, Miguel announced, "Officially, welcome to Libertad."

"On behalf of the North American Alliance, thank you," Major Thompson said.

One of the bartenders from downstairs came up, a tray loaded with shot glasses balanced on one hand.

Taking a glass, Miguel asked, "What brings you to our humble little town?"

The bartender made his way around the room. Dr. Erasmus accepted a mug. "We're looking for some new megaflora."

When the town's mayor made a face, Major Thompson said, "Plants. We discovered evidence of some new plants. We don't know where they're growing."

The other man cocked his head. "You think they grow here?"

Thompson shook his head. "No...well, we don't know. Some of our folks are looking around outside town to see." He pulled his comm out of a thigh pocket and slid it over. On the screen was an image of the plant they'd found mashed up in the footpads of a kaiju, plus a DNA analysis.

The other man took the device and looked at it. "Not the greatest picture." The NAC members at the table nodded. "I don't recall seeing anything that looks like these." He pushed the comm back toward Thompson. "I can ask, though."

"We'd appreciate it," Dr. Erasmus said. He took a sip of drink. "Now. Forgive me, but how has this town survived the last ten years?"

Miguel leaned forward. "Libertad—not the original name, by the way—is here because we have friends and we don't attract attention."

"Friends?" Thompson asked.

"Attract attention?" Sophie repeated. The three Alpha Team pilots were sitting side by side opposite Major Thompson.

Miguel nodded. "As you no doubt noticed, the town isn't very flashy, doesn't stand very tall, or sport any color beyond green and brown." He shrugged. "When a monster comes around, we don't start shooting at it. We don't have the means to, for one thing, but we find it easier to not draw their attention. They don't just attack randomly. They don't attack without reason. No more than a grizzly bear or lion would. More often than not, they wander off on their own."

Victor tapped his shot glass on the table absently. "Bears and lions aren't forty meters tall and capable of knocking down buildings."

"And when they don't wander off?" Thompson pressed.

Miguel smiled. "True, of course." He leaned back in his chair, the front feet leaving the floor. "That's when our friends in the Syndicate usually step in to help."

"The Syndicate?" Major Thompson leaned forward.

THE SALOON ANGELA brought Brandon and the others to had no name. The group had walked down a wide dirt road to the town's center, then swung right down another spoke road, stopping at an intersection with a general store, laundromat, the saloon, and maybe someone's home on the corners.

Once everyone had a cold beer in hand, one of the VarTech people asked for the name of the bar.

"No name," was all Angela said.

"Come again?" the confused technician said. She raised an eyebrow as she took another sip of beer.

Angela smiled. "This place," she gestured to the noisy room, "doesn't have a name because most places in Libertad don't." When everyone just stared at her, she continued. "It's because nothing is permanent," their guide explained. "Nothing in Libertad is. Nothing out here can be." She turned to her friends, who all nodded their agreement.

One of Angela's friends, Ricardo, added, "Why name something if it might be gone tomorrow?" He took a sip of his drink and leaned over to the VarTech technician next to him. "Life's short, *mi encantadoro*. Don't you think?"

The young man blushed but nodded his agreement. His beer glass had just become incredibly interesting.

Brandon rolled his eyes, then glanced at Angela and felt his own cheeks warming. She was beautiful. With her jet-black hair pulled back, the dim lighting of the bar accentuated her cheekbones. Without warning, Stacy Decker's face popped up in his vision. He almost spit out his beer. Paco side-eyed him as the corner of Angela's mouth quirked upward.

Lucy leaned forward on the table. "How often is the town attacked?"

Angela gave a shrug. "'Attacked' wouldn't be the right word." She looked around the table at her friends.

Another woman, Cecile, shrugged as she took a sip of her drink. After licking her lips while making direct eye contact with Paco, she said, "It's like accidentally stepping on an anthill. You didn't do it intentionally. It was just in the way, maybe you didn't even it see it. *Sí?*"

Lucy looked at Brandon, then Paco, who was doing his best to not look at the woman who was still intently staring at him. "So, they just come through? Accidentally stepping on the town?" The idea of living in a place that at any minute could be attacked by megafauna made her skin crawl, especially after seeing them in action when they attacked the *Saratoga*.

Angela shook her head, wobbling her free hand. "Sort of. It's been several years now since one came through and did any real damage. The Syndicate tends to intercept them and guide them around the town."

The bar's sound system came to life with a bass track that shook the beer glasses on the table.

Cecile's gaze roamed the table before settling on Paco. "So, why are you here?"

"Come again?"

She ran her fingers through her close-cropped hair. "You didn't come to see me." She ran her tongue over her teeth, her eyes locked on Paco's. "Did you?"

Brandon choked on his beer and turned away from his friend.

Paco did his best to not look like he was about to die. After a calming sip of his drink, he shook his head. "No, *señorita*, but only because I didn't know you were here." He smiled a toothy smile. "We're doing a survey of the state of the continent around Impact Zone Five."

Cecile took a long sip of her of drink, her eyes never leaving Paco's. "So you're not here to see the big flower thing?"

Brandon, Lucy, and the VarTech technician all turned to the petite Hispanic woman, who finally tore her gaze from Paco. "What?"

Brandon was the first to speak. "What do you mean? Flower thing?"

She shrugged. "I don't know, it's what the one of the Syndicate men called it. Said it was like an avocado pit split in two. Said this enormous..." She looked at Angela. "*Cómo se dice, tallo?*"

"Stalk?" Angela offered.

Cecile nodded. "*Sí*. Stalk. This enormous stalk rose straight up out of the rock thing that brought the monsters. Right up into the sky."

Lucy leaned forward. "So, it came out of the original asteroid?"

After the impacts, the world tried to study original asteroids, but they emitted so much radiation scientists gave up.

Cecile nodded. "That's what Rosario said."

Lucy leaned over to Brandon. "That's gotta be important."

He nodded.

Cecile stood, offering her hand to Paco.

He downed the rest of his beer and followed her. He turned back to his friends and winked and shouted, "Don't wait up!"

RICARDO WATCHED Cecile and Paco reach the dance floor, then turned and offered his hand to the VarTech technician he'd been flirting with. The man smiled and accepted the hand, letting Ricardo lead him out onto the dance floor.

"So, uh, what's the Syndicate?" Brandon asked.

Watching the dancers, Angela took a long sip of her drink, then turned to Lucy and Brandon and the remaining VarTech technician. Brandon thought her name was Abigail. "Libertad was founded by refugees from several nearby cities and towns shortly after the first monsters started showing up. The town was originally called Tepetitán.

"The government back then, they didn't give folks in this area much notice. Several towns woke up one morning on the wrong side of makeshift barricades and fortifications with alien monsters roaming the countryside."

She took a drink and continued. "At the start, it was little more than a few huts on the outskirts of town. The refugees started to build, doing their best to not get noticed by the creatures." She turned to the bar, flagging the bartender for another round. "The government had already abandoned trying to do anything at the Impact Zone. The radiation killed hundreds of townspeople pressed into service to help with excavation."

Brandon remembered the stories from *Impact History* 101. The Mexican and American governments tried for years to dig up the meteorite.

Human rights organizations screamed bloody murder. Governments were burning through people with nothing to show for it. Not a single meteorite around the world had been excavated.

The trio sat silently for a moment until Brandon asked, "And what? The megafauna just don't bother you? Because of this—what was it?"

"Syndicate," Lucy offered.

Angela nodded. "More or less. They help keep the beasts away when they wander too close. Generally, we try to make sure they don't notice us. It's not like the Syndicate is here all the time."

"But they attack humans whenever they see us," Lucy said. She took a sip of her beer, squinting at the woman opposite her.

"This is riveting, but I think I'm gonna find a dance partner," Abigail, the VarTech technician, said as she stood. She gave an exaggerated wink to Lucy and strode off into the thrashing crowd of dancers.

Watching Abigail depart, Angela ran a hand through her hair, pulling her hair out of the ponytail in order to gather it and secure it back where it was. The bartender arrived, tray balanced on one hand, loaded with frosted pint glasses. Not a one had a logo that matched another, and many were so faded they were closer to plain unprinted glass. More than one was chipped.

Angela smiled at the bartender, saying something to him in Spanish, before turning to Brandon and Lucy. "Maybe they attack because giant metal monsters look threatening to them?" She leveled her gaze at Brandon. At nearly a head taller than the pilots, she cut a fairly imposing figure. Life in Libertad was clearly a life of hard work.

Setting his glass down, Brandon said, "The suit program is the only thing that's kept the megafauna—and flora, for that matter—at bay. The monsters attacked before we had suits."

Their host took a sip of her drink, leaning back in her chair looking at the two pilots. "We seem to do all right."

CHAPTER SIXTEEN

MIGUEL NODDED. "The Syndicate operates out here and keeps us safe in exchange for a place to rest from time to time."

Major Thompson opened his mouth but closed it as the mayor motioned one of the bartenders from downstairs. He came up the steps balancing a large platter loaded with plates. "Ah! Dinner is served."

As the bartender deposited plates, the mayor said, "*Tlayuda* with *chapulines*."

"Lay what now?" Sophie asked, poking at the pile of shredded meat, cheese, and beans atop a homemade tortilla.

"Chappy who?" Victor added, nudging the contents of the bowl next to his plate around. He looked up. "Are these—"

"Grasshoppers. *Si*," Miguel said, scooping several spiced critters and dropping them on to his *tlayuda*. "The seasoning comes from a local family on the fifth road." He took a bite, his eyes twinkling as he watched his guests all take experimental bites of their meals with and without grasshoppers.

"Quite good," Dr. Erasmus said, scooping more seasoned grasshoppers onto his plate to mix into the shredded meat and cheese. He looked up. "What's the meat?"

"*Monstruo pequeño.*"

Everyone but Dr. Erasmus stopped chewing. Molly discreetly spit her mouthful out into a napkin. Thompson struggled to swallow. Victor opened his mouth and let the chewed-up mass roll off his tongue.

Erasmus noticed. Around a mouthful, he asked, "What?"

Major Thompson pursed his lips. "Megafauna."

The other man paled as he swallowed.

Miguel looked at his guests. "Something wrong?" He sat his fork down and took a drink, eyes moving from one northerner to the other.

Thompson pushed his plate toward the center of the table. "Is that even safe?"

He turned to Erasmus, who shrugged, holding a forkful of spiced monster meat with grasshoppers and cheese. He took a bite. "Hasn't killed them," the scientist said before taking another.

Victor looked at his teammates and said, "Any chance the kitchen has anything I wouldn't try to kill in my suit?" Molly and Sophie nodded.

Miguel rubbed his chin and called out in Spanish. One of the servers came up to stand next to Miguel. The mayor whispered to him and sent him back downstairs. "*Pollo* on the way."

Molly raised a hand. "Uh, can I have no meat, please?" The mayor nodded and said something to the server, who was almost out of sight. The man turned and smiled at Molly before he headed down the steps.

"Thank you," Thompson said. Then he said, "So, this Syndicate. How do they protect the town?"

"Robots. Like yours."

Thompson was taking a sip of his drink and almost choked. "I'm sorry. They have suits?"

The other man nodded, taking another bite of his meal. "Not as nice and shiny as yours, of course."

The three suit pilots looked at their commanding officer, who gave the tiniest of shrugs. He asked, "Where did they get them? Where do they keep them?"

Miguel shook his head. "I don't know. They don't live in Libertad."

"Where do they live?"

Miguel shrugged.

"But suits show up here?"

"Sometimes."

Thompson looked at Erasmus. The latter made a face as he ate another bite of his meal.

The bartender arrived, balancing four plates like those already on the table but presumably made with chicken.

Thompson wasn't ready to let the matter go. An unknown faction, with suits, was operating in the alien wilds of southern Mexico, and as far as he knew, the NACAF was none the wiser.

"Okay, this is good!" Victor said, stabbing a pile of shredded chicken covered in cheese and spices. He even stabbed a few crunchy grasshoppers to top it off. His fellow pilots nodded their agreement.

"What kind of suits?" Thompson asked.

The mayor of Libertad shook his head. "I'm sorry, I don't know. We rarely see them." He took a bite of his meal, then added, "Like I said. They don't live here. They come and go as they please. Their machines, like yours, can't come closer than the entry gate."

"How many suits do they have?" Molly asked. She was thoroughly enjoying her meal. The beans, cheese, and whatever they substituted for the grasshoppers were delicious.

Miguel smiled at his guests. "I'm sorry. I don't know." He grinned. "Who would like flan?"

AFTER THE SALOON, Angela urged Lucy and Brandon to follow her to what she called the "night market." The rest of the original group were happy to stay with their dance partners. Paco had waved and told them to have fun.

In the time between their entering the saloon and exiting, the town center they'd skirted the edge of had become packed with townspeople and makeshift tents and stalls. Someone in the crowd was strumming a guitar while someone sang along.

"Woah," was all Brandon could get out.

Angela draped an arm around his shoulders, nodding. "You picked a great time to visit."

"Oh? Why is that?" Lucy asked as the trio made its

way into the bustling maze of people buying, selling, and bartering.

"The night market only happens once a month. Some of our trade partners were just in town. Probably brought all kinds of stuff." She pointed to a ramshackle stall that was lined on the three sides, ground to tent top, with NAC rations and other foodstuffs.

The two NACAF pilots exchanged a look but chose to say nothing, following their guide further into the market. They passed a mariachi band that was serenading the crowd.

Angela stopped at a stall where a woman was frying something in a massive shallow skillet over an open flame. Spying Angela, she smiled and handed her a grease spotted paper bag. The younger woman returned the smile and handed the vendor a slip of paper from her pocket.

She handed the bag to Brandon. "Try one."

"What did you pay with?" Lucy asked as Brandon opened the bag, peering inside. He fished out a crunchy little morsel of unknown origin. "NAC scrip?"

Angela watched Brandon sniff the fried nugget before popping it into his mouth. She took the bag, holding it out for Lucy. "No. We don't use much actual currency here. We've got pesos, of course, but they're used rarely. NAC scrip has even less value. Libertad operates on barter. I gave Griselda an hour of my time."

"A what?" Brandon asked. He held his hand out to Lucy.

Lucy handed the bag to Angela, giving Brandon side-eye. "These are good. What are they?"

"*Chapulines.*" She didn't offer anything further. She took a few and handed the bag back to Lucy. She gestured further down the walkway. "The easiest thing to barter with is your time if you don't make things." She turned to look over her shoulder. "I tried knitting and managed to stab my *abuelita*. I can more easily help someone in exchange for something than trade my things for theirs." She motioned for them to follow, handing Brandon the bag.

Brandon looked around as they walked, munching on another whatever-they-were. The market was impressive, to say the least. It filled a central square with dozens of stalls in two concentric circles. Vendors sold and traded everything from produce to cured meats to bits of what looked like salvaged technology. Not to mention the NAC ration packs they'd seen before.

He spied several other *Saratoga* crewmembers from the ground expedition moving through the market, many with arms loaded full of goods. He wondered how they'd paid for all those things. It wasn't like they could offer their time like Angela did. He noticed that several of the crewers were lacking rank insignias and other uniform decorations. Angela motioned them down the next lane.

"Where do you get all this produce?" Lucy asked as the much smaller group made its way through the inner ring of the market. "Is this all that Syndicate you mentioned? Surely they can't bring in this much fresh produce all the time."

The local woman shrugged. "Do you ask the places that you buy produce from where they get it?"

Lucy gave a one shoulder shrug. "Fair."

Angela accepted a fistful of sticks with some kind of charred meat on the ends from a vendor as they passed. Thanking him, she turned to the group, offering Lucy and Brandon each a stick.

"What's this?"

"I think you call them megafauna." She took a bite of the charred meat.

Both pilots held their sticks at arm's length. Their guide chuckled and took the sticks back. "Come on. There's some seats over here."

The trio sat and watched the market live and breathe; townspeople bartered, laughed, caught up on gossip, and carried on business. The guitar player they'd heard earlier passed by, strumming an aimless tune.

Finally, Lucy asked, "How does the Syndicate get around? It's gotta be too dangerous to drive overland."

"Robots," Angela answered. "Like yours."

Brandon looked at Lucy, who made a face back at him.

Angela laughed. "What? You thought only your American military had robots?"

"Suits," Brandon corrected absently. "And, yeah, kinda. I mean, not just America or the NAC, but suit technology is classified." As far as he knew, VarTech suits were considered military hardware. Even police and security forces didn't have suits. VarTech kept a tight grip on that technology.

Angela smiled. "We don't care what they're called or where they get them, only that the Syndicate uses theirs to help and protect the people in this area. They encourage the beasts to not get too close to town. They help farmers move boulders from their fields. Guard shipments. Whatever is needed."

"Do you know what they look like? Their robots?" Lucy asked. Maybe if Angela could give them descriptions, they could report back to Major Thompson. He could look into it.

Angela gave a shrug and said, "I've seen them. Their robots. Once when I was a kid." She waved her arms. "Big. Metal. Like yours." She tapped her chin. "Well, mostly. They were less...robot looking...than the ones you came in. I think they were green."

"What's that mean?" Brandon asked.

Angela wiggled one hand in the air. "*No sé.* Softer? Less robot-like." She looked around. "Once you've seen them, it gets old. I've never really paid much attention when they come around."

The crowd in the market had thinned considerably while they'd been sitting.

Angela looked around the crowd before standing up. "You know it's getting quite late." She mocked a yawn.

Lucy pursed her lips and gave Brandon a look. It was difficult to stifle the laughter she felt rising when he realized what was going on. His eyes grew to the size of saucers, and a flush began its way up from his collar.

"Oh...uh. We should get you get to bed, then," he stammered, standing up.

Angela's eyebrows arched. She looked at him, offering her his hand, then looked at Lucy, who gave a knowing smirk followed by a shrug. Accepting Brandon's hand, she said, "I was thinking I could show you my place."

Lucy turned so Brandon wouldn't see her fighting back a chuckle.

"Oh," was all Brandon got out. "I...uh."

Angela took a step closer to Brandon, who released a small noise. Lucy looked over her shoulder. It was like watching a slow-motion car crash. She cleared her throat. "We, uh, we have to get back to the transports. We're due to leave in the morning and need to rest up. Suits are hard enough to operate when we're rested." She gave the other woman a look.

"Oh, of course." Angela smiled. "Come. I'll walk you to your robots."

"Suits," Brandon corrected absently.

She mumbled something in Spanish.

"I SHOULDN'T HAVE DRUNK SO MUCH," Paco said from across the portable table set up outside Transport Three. Several similar tables were set up, filled with ground mission personnel.

Lucy made a clucking noise. She and Brandon had been forced to wander around the town until they'd found someone that knew Angela. They'd woken her and gotten her to guide them to Cecile's apartment.

"At least you slept in a real bed," Brandon replied. He and Lucy had been forced to get what few hours sleep they could in what the transport teams called the cheap seats. Crash bunks were little more than thin shelves that folded down. A thin memory foam pad with a slightly thicker memory foam pillow was all there was on each shelf. No one slept on them if they could avoid it.

Victor and Sophie approached, trays in hand. "Hey, you three," the latter said as they joined Bravo Team.

Victor looked at Paco. "You look like hell."

"*Sí*. I feel like hell," Paco said. He took a sip of coffee and winced.

Molly turned to Brandon. "You all have a good time? We heard Lydecker and Agame are both in what passes for an infirmary in this town. Something about eating bugs that didn't agree with them."

"Monster meat isn't for everyone," Victor said knowingly.

Brandon raised an eyebrow. "Huh?"

Molly shook her head. "Bugs aren't the only things on the menu in Libertad." When the three Bravo pilots didn't respond, she said, "These folks have figured out how to eat megafauna." At the looks from the rest of the table, she nodded. "Yeah." She gave a half shrug. "Erasmus loved it."

"They eat megafauna?" Paco asked. He rubbed his temple with one hand, the other clutching his coffee.

Victor nodded. "You know, kinda tasted like chicken."

Brandon made a face. "Nope." Paco nodded, then pinched his eyes closed in pain. "You guys hear about the Syndicate?" Brandon asked.

Molly nodded. "Yeah. Crazy right?"

"Unauthorized suits roaming around out here playing Lone Ranger? Crazy isn't the right word," Lucy said. She reached over and stabbed a sausage link off of Paco's plate. "How is it even possible?"

"What about the giant flower thing coming out of the Impact Five meteorite?" Brandon added. "Crazy, right?"

All three Alpha pilots turned to him. "The what?" Sophie asked. She sat her fork down, rehydrated eggs still on the tines.

"Giant plant tower?" Victor asked.

Brandon looked at them, then his friends. "Guess that wasn't at the VIP dinner."

Lucy gave him a look, then said, "According to the locals, a big space asparagus split the Impact Five meteorite in half. Apparently, it's a few hundred feet tall."

"And growing," Brandon added.

Molly leaned forward. "What's it doing?"

Brandon and Lucy both shrugged.

"Pilots."

Everyone scrambled to their feet. Lucy snapped off a crisp, "Sir."

Major Thompson and Dr. Erasmus were standing side by side, each holding a tray piled with rehydrated food just like the pilots were eating.

"As you were," the senior NACAF officer said, motioning for his pilots to sit back down. He and Erasmus joined them at the long folding table. "So, what're we talking about?" he asked the table.

"Sir?" Brandon asked.

Thompson smiled. "Looked serious."

Molly cleared her throat. "Sir, Bravo was telling us about...well." She looked to Lucy, then Brandon.

Before Lucy could react, Brandon jumped in. "Sir,

something is growing out of the meteorite at Impact Five."

"Nothing can grow there, the radiation is too severe," Dr. Erasmus said without looking up from the sausage link he was moving through syrup on his plate.

Lucy gave Brandon a look but said nothing, inclining her head. He continued, "According to the local woman we met last night, the meteorite split in two a month or two ago and a big alien asparagus rose up out of it."

"Alien asparagus?" Thompson repeated.

Dr. Erasmus looked up, his syrup covered sausage forgotten. "It came out of the meteorite?"

"That's what she said."

"How did she know?" The senior VarTech researcher was leaning forward, and his plate slid toward the center of the table.

Brandon licked his lips. "Well." He looked around at Lucy and Paco.

Lucy shook her head. "She is, uh, popular." Thompson looked confused. "She's seeing one of their suit pilots."

"Ah," Thompson said, nodding slowly.

He looked at Paco, who blushed and said, "They're not married."

Dr. Erasmus looked at the assorted pilots. "What else did this woman say?"

Brandon shook his head. "Sorry, Doctor, that was really it. Just a big weird plant split the meteorite like an avocado pit, right in two."

The VarTech researcher turned to Major Thompson.

"We must go there." Thompson opened his mouth, but Erasmus continued, "Immediately."

"Doc, we'll be there in a few weeks. Our survey grid covers Impact Zone Five."

"Major, if something has happened to the meteorite, and it's a giant plant, tower, thing...We must investigate now. Not later." He cocked his head. "This, whatever it is, could be the source of the new protein markers and plant matter."

Thompson took a bite of sausage. "Okay, then."

"ALL UNITS, CHECK IN," Major Thompson called out over the squad channel.

"Alpha Team, ready," Molly Chen called.

"Bra—" Brandon started.

"Bravo Team, ready," Lucy interrupted.

Brandon scowled but said nothing. He was too tired to argue with her. Once Thompson gave the order, breakfast was over and the camp went into action. It was a scramble to pack up the ground transports, barter with Libertad for additional foodstuffs, and allow time for the crew to say their goodbyes.

Miguel came out to wish the exploration team well. "Major, Doctor. I hope you find what you're looking for."

Erasmus nodded. "As do I. If we're successful, we will finally solve the megafauna problem."

Brandon watched the mayor walk back into town, then pushed Midnight Tango to its feet. Lucy hadn't been exaggerating when she told Angela how difficult operating a suit was when a pilot was tired. He watched the ground team load the transports from high above.

Now that he knew there were—if not hostile—not directly friendly suits out roaming the countryside, he panned left and right every few seconds, his sensors primed.

"All units, move out," Thompson ordered as the cargo hatch on Transport Four slid closed. Alpha Team would be walking point today, so Bravo watched as the three Alpha Team suits strode away from the village, the transports rolling to fall in behind them.

Midnight Tango turned to look over his shoulder. "Hard to believe there's a town that big out here just... existing."

"Maybe that means there's still hope," Paco offered.

"Nice thought," Lucy said. "Think we'll pass through on our way back?"

"I hope so," Paco replied.

"Of course you do, Romeo," she quipped. "Better hope her other pilot of interest isn't in town if and when we come back through." She heard Paco's chuckle over the channel.

TWO DAYS LATER, aboard Transport One, Major Thompson was sitting in the small conference room near the vehicle's rear. Across the table, Dr. Thorin Erasmus was practically vibrating. "Major. Don't you understand?"

"Honestly, Doc. Only a little. You think the plant stuff we're looking for came from the big asparagus?" The VarTech technicians that searched the area immediately surrounding Libertad had turned up nothing as far as the mysterious new plant was concerned. He tapped his fingers on the table absently. "Wouldn't that mean the megafauna we fought up north came all the way from down here?"

The other man nodded. "It would."

"To our knowledge, they don't typically travel that far."

"To our knowledge—which is limited. You know that."

The major inclined his head. The doctor had a point. The total sum of human knowledge about the megaflora and fauna that was choking the planet could fit on a single data card.

"Between this and whatever this...Syndicate is..." He shook his head. "How'd this happen?"

Dr. Erasmus stared at the man opposite him, wishing he could be more forthcoming. He didn't know the answer to the major's first question but was fairly certain the Syndicate must be the contractors he knew VarTech got much of the material from. He shook his head. He didn't always agree with his employer's decisions and tactics, but at the end of the day, you didn't piss off the world's largest employer of scientists.

He was about to attempt to change the topic when the loudspeaker crackled. "Megafauna spotted." It was Alpha Three. "I think there's a vehicle out there, too."

The two men looked at each other. Thompson stood. "Of course."

Erasmus watched the man leave, thankful that he didn't have to lie to him.

CHAPTER SEVENTEEN

AS ONE, Alpha Team strode forward. Up ahead, a pair of small transports were surrounded by a dozen megafauna—Category 1 and 2.

"That's new," Molly said on the mission channel. "Ones and 2s, working as one?"

"Wasps launching," Major Thompson announced.

From the rearguard position, Brandon watched the tactical overlay update. Twelve red dots were moving around two yellow triangles.

An icon appeared in Brandon's vision: video feeds from the Wasps. With a thought, he brought all four feeds up in a small tiled array. The two vehicles were makeshift ground transports. Possibly they started life as school buses but now sported wide all terrain tires that wouldn't flatten. Metal panels layered the sides, covering the windows.

Each vehicle had a gun mount on the top. Both gunners were tracking the monsters but not firing.

The Wasps swept in overhead. "Ground vehicles,

ground vehicles. This is NACAF Wasp Zero Zero One overflying now. Please respond."

A Category 2 creature with a multitude of tentacles coming from its back, all waving rhythmically, lunged toward the lead transport, its tentacles lashing forward.

Two of the Wasps sprang into action, pivoting in midflight, their double-barrel, under-nose blasters roaring. The creature staggered under the barrage.

Brandon was itching to jump into the fray. Bravo was a quarter kilometer behind the four transports arrayed in a triangle. Until ordered to engage, Bravo Team were spectators. He mentally pulled the tactical view front and center, enlarging it in his vision.

The dot representing the attacking Category 2 with the tentacles was fading. The Wasps had killed the creature.

"Thank God!" someone shouted over the channel. "We thought we were done for!"

"Caravan, what're you doing out here?" the Wasp pilot asked.

"We're en route to Libertad from Bogotá. There were four vehicles when we started. Normally, the Syndicate provides escorts, but they didn't show up, so we came on our own."

"Stupid idea," Brandon said under his breath.

"Stay put, Caravan," the Wasp ordered.

"Alpha, move in. Bravo, forward to cover the transports," Major Thompson ordered.

Midnight Tango made a fist and pumped it in the air once. "Copy that," Brandon said. He sent the tactical view back to its default size in his field of vision. He took a look around, making sure nothing looked amiss before pushing the massive mechanical body that surrounded him into action.

The three suits strode toward the four transports to take up position around the ground vehicles.

The remaining eleven megafauna surged toward the civilian transports. The person on comms screamed.

Brandon watched the four Wasps make attack runs, hoping to push the attacking beasts back. Some fell back; others did not.

Alpha Two and Three moved as a pair into the fray.

Brandon engaged all of Midnight Tango's weapons, ready to spring into action if ordered. He looked to his left, spying Valiant Azure deploying her own weapons: shoulder-mounted particle cannons lowering, forearm beam cannons deploying from their recessed positions.

Stalwart Rook and Void Romeo waded into the mass of monsters; blades and a massive war hammer began slicing and smashing through hide, scales, and chitin.

"This is weird," Lucy said over the Bravo channel.

Crusher Maverick nodded his blocky head. "Yeah, this is the second time we've seen the little ones coordinate like this."

Before Brandon or Lucy could reply, a loud tearing sound came from somewhere. All three suits crouched, heads moving side to side.

"Movement, sector one-oh-eight!" someone in Transport One announced. Bravo Team's tactical overlay updated with an orange triangle in the indicated sector, moving toward them. Brandon and Paco were closest.

Lucy watched them move in, her attention on the two

Bravo suits charging toward the new contact. She didn't notice the thick bodied Category 3 lumbering up out of a hole in the ground a hundred meters from her. It was on her before she turned.

ALARMS POPPED up in Lucy's field of vision; the monster had both of her arms pinned, its face less than a meter from Valiant Azure's.

"I can smell your breath!" she growled, tilting her head back, then slamming it forward into the beast's face. Bright orange blood sprayed from the creature's snout. It roared, releasing Valiant Azure from the bear hug.

Brandon turned to see Lucy stagger backward, putting distance between herself and the creature. "Stay on mission. I got this!" she ordered.

"You sure?" Midnight Tango slowed, Crusher Maverick putting distance between the two.

"Go." A pair of blades slid into position in Valiant Azure's forearms. "I got this. No one sneaks up on Lucy Jones and gets away with it."

Midnight Tango turned to follow Crusher Maverick. Their own orange dot was now a bright red one with four arms and a split mandible mouth full of half-meter-long teeth.

"Damn, this thing is ugly," Paco said as he reached the creature. He stepped in close, drawing back for a right hook. The creature tilted to the side, pivoting. "Woah!"

Midnight Tango tackled the creature before it could get ahold of the surprised Crusher Maverick. The two tumbled to the ground in a heap. The black mech rained blows on the creature as all four arms grappled for purchase. Brandon mentally triggered the trimetal blade and used it to stab the monster's top left shoulder. The arm spasmed before going limp. The scream the monster released shook Brandon in his pilot's crèche.

He rolled off the creature, dodging the remaining arms as he drove a knee into the creature's side.

"That thing anticipated my blow," Paco said, bringing Maverick around behind the monster as it scrambled to its feet, its damaged left arm dangling uselessly. A massive armored fist slammed right into the creature's head, staggering it.

Lucy lunged for her opponent, slashing first with her right, then left, arm. "These things are learning to fight," she said over the shared team channel. The creature ducked her swipe and thrust a scale covered fist into Azure's chest, ringing the suit like a bell.

Midnight Tango readied the trimetal blade, but the stunned creature turned away, shielding its head.

Midnight Tango cocked his head. "What the—?" Brandon said, momentarily confused. Before he could ready his weapon, the now three-armed creature ducked into a crouch and tackled him. The blow reverberated through Tango's frame, rattling Brandon's teeth.

The blows rained down on him as Brandon struggled to get his arms up in defense. Warnings popped up in his vision.

Before he could get his arms free, the creature rose up off him, hoisted into the air by Crusher Maverick. "This. *Puta*. Is. Heavy."

"Hold him!" Brandon ordered as he brought Tango to his feet. Panels in each thigh slid open, revealing the BFG-9000 suit-size pistols. In the top right of his field of vision, two floating counters appeared, both showing a six.

"Hurry up," Paco urged. Maverick was straining. The monster was thrashing its many arms and legs. The orange and blue suit wobbled underneath, feet shuffling to keep balance.

Brandon lined up his shot and pulled each trigger. The powerful specially designed rounds tore into the thing's thick hide. One severed the lower right arm; the other ripped up its torso.

Maverick staggered backwards, dropping the wounded megafauna.

Midnight Tango strode up to it before it could get to its feet and sent another round into its skull.

"I want one of those," Paco said, Maverick's head nodding slowly as it looked at the carcass.

Brandon spun each pistol on a finger before sliding them into their docks. In his field of vision, the two floating counters flashed, five and four, before fading away as the thigh panels closed.

The two suits slammed their fists together, turning to find Lucy.

Lucy staggered away from the creature. It had blocked two punches in a row before landing a raking swipe across her chest. Several alarms sprang to life in her field of vision. "Okay, screw this." With a mental command, she dismissed the alerts and commanded her blades to slide back into their storage location as forearm-mounted beam cannons locked into position. Before the monster could close the gap, she rose both arms and sent two piercing blue energy beams stabbing into the beast. Flesh and scales sizzled.

The megafauna roared and fell to the side, trying to dodge the coherent energy superheating its insides.

The ground shook as two suits charged in from either side of her. "We got you, Luce!" Brandon shouted.

"I don't need it!" she growled, cutting off her beam cannons.

The creature shuddered as it got its feet under it. It noticed the two metal attackers and roared a challenge.

"Damn Lucy! You got the big one!" Brandon said. He had one of his BFG-9000s in hand.

"Just lucky like that," she replied, slipping between the suits. Her shoulder-mounted cannons locked in firing position. Bright purple particle beams stabbed into the monster's hide. The skin bubbled. The previous wounds from Valiant Azure's smaller weapons erupted as internal organs and other offal superheated.

"She's gonna blow!" Paco warned a moment before the enormous beast exploded, sending neon colored blood and gore in all directions.

"BRAVO TEAM, ALL THREATS CLEAR," Brandon announced.

"Copy that Bravo. Return to Caravan," Major Thompson ordered.

"Alpha, you all good?" Brandon asked over the suits-only channel.

"Copy, Bravo. We're good," Molly answered. "Never seen so many of these things all in one place."

"Because that's never happened before," Victor said from Void Romeo. "Coordinating like this. It's getting creepy."

The three Alpha Team suits surrounded the two dilapidated transports.

Major Thompson strode out of Transport One after the six suits were arrayed around the two civilian and four military transports.

The leader of the caravan was a woman in her mid fifties. She extended her hand. "Thank you."

Thompson shook her hand. "You're very welcome. I'm Major Nick Thompson, NACAF."

"Graciela. Graciela Sandoval."

"From Bogotá." He smiled. "Long way from home."

She inclined her head. "We got held up passing through Guatemala. The *putestas monstruosas* are different. I've made this trip twice a year, sometimes three times, and avoiding the things—not easy, but doable." She shook her head. "This time...This time, they moved in packs, and were, I dunno, systematic. It was like we were being hunted."

Thompson nodded slowly. "That seems to be going around." He looked over her shoulder. "Your transports are both still functional?" She nodded. He tapped the commset in his ear. "Alpha One, take your team and escort the caravan back to Libertad. Catch up with us after."

"Copy that, sir," Molly replied.

He turned to Graciela. "Alpha Team," he pointed at the three suits, "will escort you back to Libertad. We just left there a few days ago."

Graciela smiled. "Thank you. I appreciate it."

Thompson nodded. "Of course." He tapped his commset again. "Ground mission. We move out in ten."

Brandon watched the two dilapidated transports roll off towards Libertad, surrounded by three towering war machines.

"Midnight Tango, you take right. Crusher Maverick, point. Valiant Azure, you're on the left. Let's roll out," Major Thompson ordered as Transport One got moving.

Thompson looked at the woman next to him monitoring the sensor feeds from the three suits as well as the transports. "Never woulda guessed there'd be so much...I dunno. Life? Activity? After all this time." He didn't know what else to say. With the flood of north-bound refugees over the year as the alien infection spread, it was assumed the same thing happened southward. The South American Alliance wasn't one of the more collaborative world alliances, but they did share information from time to time.

The woman looked up at her senior officer. "Guess it's to be expected. Not everyone can run, and even when they can, the NAC is a lot less welcoming than it was ten years ago. I don't know that the SA wasn't ever welcoming."

Thompson nodded. "True." He stood. "Holler if anything shows up. Maybe we'll find a roving band of performers."

The woman chuckled as she nodded.

Thompson entered what passed for the communication center on the transport, a small corridor with two workstations, one on each side. "Gentlemen. Anything new?"

"Afraid not, sir. This deep into the Impact Zone, reliable comms are a non-starter. We were able to get a burst transmission out to the *Saratoga*. No reply yet."

He took a deep breath. They were only a few more days from the Impact Zone. He didn't like the idea of this Syndicate being out there somewhere, not to mention the alien tower thing they were heading straight for. It'd be nice to check in with the ship. The alien plant life emitted a type of radiation that human science could only partially quantify. VarTech knew it was there mostly by its side effects; satellite sensors and imagery of the Impact Zones were always a garbled mess that got worse the closer to each Impact Zone you got. Communications suffered a similar fate, getting worse the deeper into the zone you went.

Those factors were a large part of why most assumed the Impact Zones and their spreading infection areas were deserted.

"TRANSPORT ONE, TAKE A LOOK AT THIS," Lucy called out. It was Valiant Azure's turn walking point. The big blue and white suit was on a small rise looking down into a wide ravine filled with suit-knee-high flowers.

"Flowers?" the major asked from the transport.

"Sure looks like it, sir." Valiant Azure panned around, taking in the area. The flower stalks were a half meter thick, at least. Hundreds, if not thousands, of bright yellow and pink flora filled the ravine.

"If I remember my megaflora classes," Paco offered, "megaflora is always vines and tree analogs. Right?"

Midnight Tango nodded. "Yeah. I didn't think they did shrubs."

Aboard Transport One, Dr. Erasmus chimed in, "We need to get a sample. Maybe this is the plant we're looking for."

Thompson nodded, not taking his eyes off the video feed from Valiant Azure. "Looks like there's a clearing." He tapped the screen. "Azure, look to your right. Ten degrees down." The image shifted.

"You're right," Erasmus said. He leaned closer to the screen, squinting.

Thompson tapped a control, opening the comm system to the entire ground mission. "All forces, we're gonna set up camp here. We'll wait for Alpha Team and let the science folks look around."

Bravo escorted the four transports to the clearing on the edge of the ravine. It was just big enough for the four-wheeled vehicles to pull in and arrange themselves in a rough square shape.

Once each vehicle was stopped, thick struts deployed to hold the vehicle in place. From Transport Four, a gaggle of environment-suit-clad VarTech researchers swarmed out into the ravine to take samples.

Dr. Erasmus followed Major Thompson out of the transport. "I'll never get used to the smell."

Thompson grunted. "Yeah. Pickles and sulfur, not a great combo." He looked at the older man. "You all still don't know why? The smell, I mean."

The other man shook his head. Dealing with the military could be exhausting. "Actually, yes." When Thompson turned to him, he smiled. "We believe it to be part of the terraforming process."

Thompson cocked his head. "Terraforming?"

"The theory, as far as we can determine, is that the plants don't just provide a ground cover for the creatures. That smell is them releasing toxins into the air."

"Toxins?" Thompson paled.

Erasmus chuckled. "We're safe. VarTech believes even this deep it'll be a decade or two at least before concentrations get to a point where they would be dangerous for humans." He chuckled mirthlessly. "These things play the long game."

"Not good news for Libertad," Thompson said.

"Indeed," Erasmus agreed.

The pair reached the edge of the clearing. Beyond, a half dozen researchers were visibly moving between the enormous flowers that dwarfed them. Erasmus sighed. "I've been researching these things since they emerged. A flower patch is the last thing I expected to see."

"Maybe these are the plants you're looking for?" the major offered.

"That'd be nice."

"DR. ERASMUS! DR. ERASMUS!"

"Yes, Toby?" the senior researcher said, wiping sleep from his eyes. Privacy was something that didn't exist aboard the transports. It was one of the things Thorin Erasmus missed. He sat up.

The young lab tech was shifting his weight from foot to foot. "It's a match," he blurted.

The elder scientist sat bolt upright. "You're certain?"

"Yes, sir." The other man's head bobbed up and down.

Erasmus waved Toby away. "I'll be right there."

Toby left the doorway of the small compartment. Erasmus found his lab coat and shoes.

Transport Two was the main lab facility of the convey. The rear two-thirds were the lab space. The doors that closed off the lab section from the bunks and a small kitchenette slid open.

"Talk to me," Erasmus demanded.

Toby and another technician were hunched over a microscope. Both looked up, the former saying, "We just double checked, sir. Protein markers are a match."

Erasmus joined the pair at the workstation, moving to look at the microscope as the junior researchers stepped aside. Toby was right. The sample on the slide looked just like the sample he had collected a few weeks ago.

He held out a hand, fingers snapping. A tablet dropped into his hand. Glancing from the microscope's eyepiece to the tablet, he pulled up the data on the more recent flower sample.

Standing, he tapped a control on the side of the

microscope. One of the wall-mounted displays came to life showing the sample under the microscope.

"You're right." He nodded to the display and then the tablet in his hands. "We've found it." The two junior researchers beamed. "This can change the tide of this war." Setting the tablet aside, he reached for the comm in his lab coat pocket. Before he could open a channel to Major Thompson in Transport One, the lighting in the lab dimmed and turned red.

"All transports, general alert," a voice called out.

PART 3

CHAPTER EIGHTEEN

"I'VE GOT FOUR—NO—FIVE contacts. Category 3, at least," Brandon announced. Out of nowhere, multiple megafauna appeared around the edge of the ravine.

"Cat 3?" Major Thompson confirmed.

"*Sí*, definitely Cat 3," Paco answered. Crusher Maverick had waded out into the knee-high flowers. He slammed metal fists together. "Lots of 'em."

Four Wasps leaped into the air. One of the pilots called out. "What're they doing?"

The five megafauna weren't moving. Three of them were the same family or species or whatever: thick bodied with long arms that ended in hooked claws and short legs. Razor sharp plates protruded from their backs from hip to top of head. Brandon thought of them as what the child of a stegosaurus and sloth might look like.

The other two were shaggy things Brandon couldn't readily apply a description to beyond scruffy, bug-eyed nightmares; each was as tall as any other Category 3 but lanky and thin. Normally, megafauna were heavily muscled. These looked like they wouldn't stand up to a stiff breeze.

"It's unnerving that they're just watching us," Lucy said. One of the bug-eyed things turned to look right at Valiant Azure. "Ew," she said.

The three dino-sloth things charged.

Valiant Azure opened fire. Her particle beams popped in and out of existence to stab into the rushing monsters. The closest creature staggered, the flesh of its right shoulder a ragged, smoking ruin.

"Tango, take the one I've marked Target 3," Lucy barked as she fired another salvo at Target 1. She zoomed her tactical view in. "Maverick—" Target 2 tackled Valiant Azure.

Brandon drew both of his pistols and rushed to the tumbling mass of spiky sloth creature and Valiant Azure. His first shot shattered several of the serrated plates on the creature's back. The second shot tore up a chunk of the creature's side. It screamed as a claw slammed into the ground feet from Azure's head.

Target 3, the creature Lucy thought Brandon should take out, rushed in to tackle him. Paco stormed in, knocking aside the monster wrestling with Lucy. As it rolled off of Valiant Azure, he caught one arm in Maverick's thick, armored hand. The three massive fingers tightened until the arm turned to pulp, splattering Azure with gore. Paco tossed the limb aside and kicked the wailing creature.

"Incoming!" someone shouted over the mission channel. A second later, all four Wasps buzzed overhead, raining supercharged plasma on the attacking creatures.

"Thanks, sky guys," Lucy said as she got Azure's feet under it. She turned to the creature trying to rip Midnight Tango's arms off. The dino-sloth thing was too close to Tango for Lucy to get a clean shot with her particle beams.

Her forearm beam cannons wouldn't do much but scratch Tango's paint, but they'd hurt the creature enough to drive it off, maybe. She raised both arms. At the same instant that she mentally triggered the cannons, something knocked her to the ground. It was Crusher Maverick. Before the two suits hit the ground, destroying a wide swatch of alien flowers, a massive shadow passed overhead.

"I didn't know they could move that fast," Lucy breathed.

Maverick nodded, as he pulled Azure to her feet.

"Anyone call the cavalry?" came over the mission channel. It was Victor Isaacson. Void Romeo cleared the top of the ravine, his shoulder-mounted version of Midnight Tango's pistols barking as armor—or in this case, thick alien hide—piercing rounds tore into the creature that attempted to tackle Lucy.

The remaining members of Alpha Team came over the edge of the ravine, weapons blazing. "What the hell are those things?" Sophie Belanger said, Stalwart Rook pointing at the big-eyed creatures that had not yet moved a step from where they were when the creatures attacked.

"No idea," Brandon replied. "They've just been standing there watching."

"Monster Peeping Toms. Excellent," Sophie said.

Lucy turned toward the nearest of the observers and

fired a pair of particle beams. The creature shuddered, its chest erupting as superheated viscera exploded in all directions. "Not very tough."

The other two observer creatures turned and walked out of view. The surviving dino-sloth creature bellowed as it withdrew.

"Uh..." Victor said. Void Romeo was looking left and right.

"Stay sharp, everyone," Molly Chen urged. She guided Tacit Ronin into the middle of the now mostly ruined flower patch. "These things don't retreat."

"Guess they do now," Brandon said.

"I can't imagine how that's a good thing," Lucy said as Valiant Azure made a slow circle of the field, scanners at full power. The creatures were nowhere in sight.

ONCE THE VARTECH team collected as much of the alien flower as the transports could hold, the mission packed up. Dr. Erasmus was annoyed that the bug-eyed "observer" creature had been so thoroughly destroyed by Valiant Azure's particle beams, but there was nothing to do about it.

The convoy continued on until they turned northeast and saw their destination.

"All units. Full stop," Major Thompson ordered from Transport One. No one had set eyes on Impact Zone Five in at least eight to ten years. At least no one official. Now it was less than a kilometer away, in plain view, in the center of the Yucatán Peninsula.

The tower, whatever it was, was clearly visible in the center of the impact crater, the last piece of the planet-killing asteroid that would have killed Earth. Whatever the outer material of the meteorite was, years of weather had eroded it away to reveal what might be the galaxy's largest avocado pit. No one knew what the material was because up until now, nothing had been able to penetrate it.

The giant alien stalk rose straight up out of the massive brown and blue pit, which had been split in half. There weren't any visible roots. The two halves of the meteorite's core were more shell-like. Whatever had been inside had been used to grow the flower tower thing.

Midnight Tango looked up. The tower structure was nearly two kilometers tall. The top had unfolded to resemble a monstrous moonflower. The surrounding area was clear of foliage, alien or otherwise, save a few tough, scraggly alien shrubs.

"Each petal has to be thirty meters long," Lucy said. The underside of the petals glittered even though no sunlight was touching them.

"I bet the pollen is the size of golf balls," Paco said.

"That's...weird," Brandon said.

"We'll set up camp here," Thompson said over the comms. "Suits establish a one-kilometer perimeter. Wasps, two kilometers."

In Transport One, Thompson was eyeing the tactical display as it updated with each step the suits took. He looked at one of the officers next to him. "Send teams out to set up sensor poles."

"Yes, sir," the woman replied before turning to exit the command section.

One by one the transports lumbered into position, forming a square a quarter kilometer from the base of the tower.

"Radiation is off the charts," one of the junior officers in the command center on Transport One reported.

Thompson nodded. "Hard suits from here on out."

A series of loud clangs echoed through the transport as sturdy stabilizing struts deployed and locked into position. Once locked in place, the transports could withstand a Category 5 hurricane. The transports weren't going anywhere.

Thompson watched on the command center's monitors as several prefab structures were unloaded from Transport Two. The vehicle's side was open, exposing the large cargo hold where Transport One's command center was.

The four large transports contained everything the expedition needed. At least that was the theory. They'd packed everything that the science team thought they would need for the mission in the four vehicles' holds. Much of the project's planned cargo remained on the *Saratoga*. Thompson briefly wondered how the air carrier was doing. With the ground radiation from the megaflora, he hadn't heard from the *Saratoga* in over a week.

On one of the screens, he watched the four Wasps fly lazy two-kilometer-wide patrols, keeping their distance from the tower until ordered otherwise.

"SET up the electron scan array over there, please," Dr. Erasmus said, pointing toward a swath of cleared ground next to Transport Three. He was clad in a bright orange "hard suit," a VarTech-designed suit that could protect its wearer from all manner of radiation, at least for a while. Every few hours, they needed to be recharged.

"Yes, sir," one of the techs replied. The trio moved off, each in a similar bright orange hard suit.

Major Thompson approached the senior VarTech scientist. "This thing is creepier up close." His own hard suit was a mottled digital camouflage pattern. He looked up at the tower.

Erasmus nodded without looking away from the massive plant. The thing was at least twenty meters in diameter and covered in blue-green scales like a monstrous artichoke. "I can't wait to get samples. If this is anything like the flowers we discovered..." He shook his head. "Could save the planet."

A young NACAF officer approached. "Excuse me, sir?" Thompson turned. "Where would you like the floodlights?"

"Set them up in a twenty meters' perimeter."

The young woman nodded and turned back to the group gathered around the waiting flood lights.

Turning back to the elder VarTech researcher, Thompson asked, "You really think it's forcing some type of accelerated evolution or something?"

"Honestly, I don't know. But what other reason would there be for these new megafauna? You saw the analysis of those bug-eyed creatures. They stood and watched the last attack, then withdrew. Something is going on."

Thompson nodded, his helmet bobbing up and down.

"Speaking of," Erasmus continued, "I'd like you to send a team out to get one of them."

Thompson nodded once, then stopped. He slowly turned his head to the other man. "Get one?"

"Yes," Erasmus said.

"One what?"

Erasmus turned. "One of those—what is everyone calling them? Observers? Yes, observers."

"The bug-eyed ones?"

"Yes."

"Why, exactly?" Thompson turned his back to the massive alien structure.

Thorin Erasmus looked the young major in the eyes. It was easy to forget that the NACAF was not interested in scientific discovery. "If that creature is somehow tied to that," he hitched a thumb over his shoulder, "seeing what makes it tick could be incredibly valuable."

Thompson thought it over. With the transports locked down, the camp was in a good defensive position. Not to mention they hadn't seen a megafauna since arriving at the flower tower thing. He reached up to run a hand through his hair but stopped short.

"Okay, sure. I can send a few suits to bag you a monster." He shook his head. "Now we're trying to capture the damn things."

IN THE SMALL bunk space assigned to their fire team aboard Transport Three, Brandon, Lucy, and Paco huddled together. It was a far cry from their shared living quarters aboard the *Saratoga*.

"You know, I never thought I'd miss our quarters on the carrier," Brandon said. They each had a beer, the only non-ration item the ground mission brought with them. Several cases of beer were watched like a hawk by a sergeant with strict orders from Major Thompson to log every bottle.

It took all Brandon's years living in Vail, constantly negotiating with someone for something, to get three bottles.

Vail, safely tucked behind its walls in a safe mountain valley, didn't deal with or welcome outsiders. At least officially. Smugglers came and went all the time, and those in the know knew where to find them and negotiate for goods that were hard or impossible to get.

Lucy looked around the cramped space. "Yeah. Not exactly the Ritz."

Paco shook his head. "We spend most of our time in our suits. Who cares where we sleep? I'd sleep in my suit if I could."

Brandon waved a hand in front of his face. "Your crèche stinks already."

Paco frowned.

"Think we'll make it back home?" Lucy asked.

Both men leaned away, groaning. Brandon said, "You can't ask that."

"I just did."

"Of course, we'll make it back," Paco assured her.

"Taggart isn't. Making it back, that is."

Both men stopped, each looking down at the floor.

"Look, I'm just saying. We're a long way from home. No support. No carrier. No VarTech technicians to fix our suits. That's a lot of things stacked against us." She took a sip of her beer. "We're fresh out of the academy. This isn't a mission we should be on."

Brandon looked at her over the top of his own beer. Finally, he said, "Yeah."

"That's it? Yeah?"

He looked at her, then Paco. "We have a job to do. We do it. If more megafauna show up, we fight 'em. These things are invading our planet and doing a good job of taking it from us. There's no other option." He grinned. "And when we get back, we get medals, maybe promotions."

"Meanwhile, those creepy, bug-eyed things are out there watching us," Paco said. He took a sip of his beer. "Bet there's one watching us now."

"Creepy," Lucy said.

"Guess I'm not sleeping tonight," Brandon added.

"SO, WE'RE WHAT AGAIN?" Paco asked.

"A hunting party," Molly replied. Major Thompson assigned Alpha One to lead the hunting party. The order had annoyed Lucy and Brandon, but there was nothing to do but follow orders.

Over a direct channel, Lucy asked, "Are you still pouting?" It rankled Brandon, but he kept his mouth shut. That didn't mean his friend didn't know exactly how he felt.

"I'm not pouting."

"Uh huh."

The four suits were ranging out, a kilometer between each of them as they made their way south and east from the convoy. Before they separated, the flower tower had come into view.

"We're the hunters, right? Not the other way around?" Molly offered. Tacit Ronin made a knuckle cracking motion with each hand, and her head panned left and right, the sun glinting off her blue optic mesh.

"Have we ever seen anything like those big-eyed ones?" Lucy asked.

"The observers? No," Molly answered.

"That name creeps me out," Brandon said.

"Fitting, though," Paco said. "Those gigantic eyes. Just standing around watching while the dino-sloths—"

"Dino-sloths?" Molly interrupted.

Paco shrugged, even though Tacit Ronan was over a kilometer and a half away. "You know, looked like the ugly baby of a sloth and a stegosaurus."

Molly clucked. "Fair."

"You think the flower tower thing is what's causing the megafauna to be so different?" Paco asked.

"Entirely possible," Molly answered as Tacit Ronin pushed through a waist high thicket of sea-foam-colored plants with thorns as tall as a suit pilot. "Careful, these things are sharp," she warned.

"This feels like busy work," Brandon complained.

"You have other plans?" Lucy asked.

"I heard one of the VarTech folks talking this morning," Paco offered. "They were saying that the theory is the tower thing controls the monsters. The bug-eyed ones—"

"Observers," Brandon put in.

"Observers, *sí*. Those are the tower's eyes."

"That's not at all unsettling," Brandon said.

The four suits walked for three hours without seeing a single creature larger than a Category 1. Finally, Molly sent the halt command along with her visual feed. The tactical displays in the other three suits updated to show a pulsing red dot about one hundred meters ahead of Alpha One. Through the alien foliage, they could just make out a creature moving diagonally to their path, pushing aside meter-thick spine covered trunks. Its mottled gray and brown hide made it hard to distinguish any other features, except the enormous eyes.

"Think it's looking for us?" Lucy asked.

"Let's ask it," Molly said.

The four suits spread out, slowly making their way to surround the creature.

CHAPTER NINETEEN

OVER THE COMBINED TEAM CHANNEL, Molly in Alpha One said, "Okay, Bravo One and I will jump it. Bravo Two and Three, move on our signal."

"Technically, they haven't assigned Bravo One," Paco pointed out.

"Not the time, dude!" Brandon protested.

"Boys," Molly scolded. "Midnight Tango and I will jump it. Crusher Maverick and Valiant Azure, wait for the signal." Tacit Ronan turned her head toward Crusher Maverick. "Better?"

"*Sí*," Paco said.

Midnight Tango and Tacit Ronin made their way as quietly as two forty-foot-tall multiton metal monsters could, moving in behind and to each side of the wandering beast.

"Damn, that thing is ugly," Brandon said. He'd managed to get within two hundred meters of the observer creature. The lanky beast was pushing through megaflora with a purpose.

"Where's he going?" Lucy asked.

The bug-eyed monster had not deviated from its course since they found it. It was moving south.

"Not our mission," Molly replied. With a mental command, the matching chain blades deployed from their forearm storage. She didn't activate the blade, fearing the creature would hear it.

Midnight Tango drew one of his sidearms. Brandon sent his readiness over comms. Mentally, he flexed and the mechanism that readied his trimetal blade engaged.

"Go," Molly ordered.

The two lead suits charged. The megafauna spun toward Tacit Ronin as the paired chain swords spun to life. Ronin rushed in, arms spread wide, chain blades cutting through alien tree analogs with ease.

The observer creature turned toward the droning buzz of the two blades.

"They can hear," Brandon said, mostly to himself. He raised his right arm, the blade locking into position. He pulled back and sent the lethal weapon flying straight into the right observer's right shoulder. The trimetal blade embedded itself, sending the gangly creature sprawling forward with a deafening scream.

Molly ducked, swiping up. Her chain blade sliced up and through the off-balance monster's shoulder. The pitch of the observer's scream changed as its arm fell to the ground.

Brandon reeled the neon blood-soaked blade back in, letting it slide into place. The sensation in his arm still felt weird.

The observer got back to its feet, the wounded

shoulder spurting blood. It looked first at Tacit Ronin, then Midnight Tango, growling.

Before it could move, a bright purple beam of charged particles stabbed into the wound, instantly cauterizing it. While the creature was stunned, Crusher Maverick stepped up, massive armored fist slamming into the beast's face.

"KO!" Brandon shouted, raising both arms to cheer.

Valiant Azure walked up to the creature, nudging it with Azure's foot. "Now we need to get it back to camp."

MAJOR THOMPSON HAD his feet up on the conference table. It was the first time since the ground mission left the *Saratoga* that he felt, sorta, at ease. The four Wasps and two remaining suits had not seen a single alien creature between them. He was enjoying the book he was reading before leaving the air carrier.

Transport One was much the same as when they arrived, but the other three were nearly empty. Prefab structures filled the space between the four parked transports connected by tunnels of transparent plastic.

"Major? You in here somewhere?"

Thompson sighed, setting his e-reader down. "Conference room."

Dr. Erasmus took a seat halfway around the small table from Thompson. "You seem relaxed, Major." He nodded to the reading device.

"Until you're ready to leave, the *Saratoga* arrives, or

we're attacked, my job is done." He shrugged. "More or less."

The older man smiled. "True."

"You needed something? I assumed you'd be in one of the labs."

Erasmus nodded. "We've been working on isolating the proteins from those flowers. It looks promising."

Thompson smiled. "And?"

"Fine. I was bored."

"What?"

"My assistants are running tests. Their assistants are organizing the lab spaces." He clucked. "I've got nothing to do. At least until your suits return with one of those observer creatures."

Thompson chuckled as he shook his head. "Hope they don't let you down. Remember, not killing monsters isn't what they're trained for."

"I know. I know. It was a risk to send the suits out to find a monster and bring it back alive. We built the suits to fight and kill megafauna."

Both men sat in silence, watching one of the Alpha Team suits as it made its way past on patrol.

On a small rise a quarter kilometer from camp, Stalwart Rook was looking at the massive flower. The stalk was a matte gray with thornlike protrusions sticking out between armorlike scales. Sophie couldn't see any other features beyond the thorns all the way up to the top, where the glittering petals spread out in every direction.

"Wonder what's on the other side of the petals?" she mused.

"Stamen as tall as you," Victor answered as Void

Romeo made his way around the massive plant directly opposite Stalwart Rook.

"Huh?" The deep red and black suit turned toward Romeo, head cocked to the side.

The lithe suit looked over, making a shrugging gesture, its crimson optic mesh glinting in the sun. "What? I like botany," Victor said.

"The ladies love a plant guy," Sophie said.

"You know it, my dear."

Both suits continued their prescribed patrol route, walking a circle around the massive alien plant tower.

IT TOOK NEARLY three hours to fashion a suit-sized litter to transport the creature on. Lacking any other way to sedate it, they were forced to resort to Crusher Maverick punching it in the face whenever it woke up.

"I certainly hope these aren't the new models. So ugly," Paco said. Crusher Maverick was walking beside the litter while Midnight Tango dragged it. He looked down at the observer creature. "Oh, it's awake again." The creature turned its head toward Maverick. "Ew."

Tacit Ronin, bringing up the rear, looked down at the litter. "What?"

"It just turned and looked at me," Paco said.

"Maybe it thinks you're cute," Brandon offered.

The creature bared its teeth, what few were left after repeated punches from Crusher Maverick.

Maverick leaned in to knock the creature out again but stopped when a roar came from up ahead. All four suits stopped. Midnight Tango dropped the litter, causing the observer to howl and struggle against the bindings the team fashioned from alien vines they scavenged from the trees near where they attacked the observer.

"Form up," Molly ordered.

The four suits turned their backs on the litter, weapons deploying as their various sensor packages ramped up to full power.

"I don't see anything," Paco said.

"I've got him," Lucy replied. She pointed to the north, toward their destination. She mentally triggered Azure's sensors to zoom in, sharing her data feed. Azure's enhanced optics highlighted the parts of the creature visible between the massive tree analogs.

"It's just waiting for us," Brandon said.

The observer made a cackling-like call. The creature up ahead replied in kind.

"Uh...Are they talking to each other?" Lucy asked. She glanced down at the bug-eyed observer creature. It turned to the suit and made a different sound, like a laugh-growl-sneeze.

In her crèche, Lucy made a face. "Gross."

"Watch out!" Paco shouted as a Category 3 megafauna rose up from the alien forest twenty meters away. Another creature pushed its way out of the plant life opposite the new arrival. "Trap!" Paco shouted as he dropped into a crouch, arms up in a defensive posture bare seconds before a huge three-fingered beast slammed into them, raking claws down the armored forearms.

Lucy was able to bring her forearm beam cannons to

bear just in time to broil off several centimeters of skin, forcing the creature to veer off from its mad charge.

The observer thrashed and made more noise.

Brandon drew both of his sidearms. He was about to fire on the creature attacking Lucy when Molly shouted, "Third hostile inbound." He spun in time to see the massive pangolin-tiger creature bearing down on him at a full run. He took aim and opened fire.

The sound of his BFG-9000s was like thunder. Each shot vibrated the air. Rounds that should have ripped into the creature, destroying tissue and bone alike, bounced off the armored scales that covered the thing from head to foot.

"Oh, crap!" he shouted, diving out of the pangolin-tiger thing's path at the last moment. The tank of a monster skidded to a stop and in one swipe of a thick paw used a claw longer than the average man to cut through the vines holding the observer creature to the litter.

Tacit Ronin leaped onto the armored creature's back, clutching the armored scales for dear life. "Take those two out! I got this one!"

The pangolin-tiger reared back, roaring before bounding over its still prone fellow creature.

Brandon turned to face the creature currently locked in a grapple with Crusher Maverick. The creature's sides rippled and flexed. A pair of thickly muscled arms, covered in patchy bristle-like hair, unfolded from the creature's torso. Each new fist slammed into Maverick's core, the blows ringing like gongs.

"Oh boy," Brandon said.

"Little help," Paco said.

Brandon prepped his trimetal blade and charged around the massive creature.

The monster turned, and four deep set red eyes blinked, following Brandon as he moved to flank the beast. Below the eyes, almost invisible while closed, a mouth that spanned the width of the thing's head split open baring three rows of razor-sharp teeth. Before Brandon could get closer, it lunged, sinking its teeth into Maverick's shoulder. Paco howled, the sensors in his suit turning that input into pain.

"Paco, fall backwards. Now!" Brandon shouted, dropping into a low crouch and drawing his arm back. Paco's suit wriggled, freeing its shoulder from the creature's mouth and arching its back to pull him and the monster off balance. Shocked, the megafauna released the suit to avoid being pulled to the ground with it. The moment Paco was clear, Midnight Tango's blade pierced the creature's face, driving deep into its skull. All four arms quivered, then fell limply to its side. As the body fell to the ground, Brandon gave the thick cable spooling out of his forearm a tug, freeing the blade and sending it back into its housing in his arm. Alien gray matter and blood covered his arm. He knew Jennifer Morris was gonna be pissed when he eventually made it back to the *Saratoga*.

After helping Paco to his feet, he turned to Lucy to see Valiant Azure standing next to the empty litter. He cocked Tango's head.

Azure made the best approximation of a shrug she could. "It just left. I didn't notice the observer thing bugging out, but I guess once it was clear, my dance partner lost interest."

"Mine too," Molly said as Tacit Ronin pushed and cut her way out of the massive alien jungle.

"So, all of that was to free the bug-eyed monster?" Paco asked.

"So it would seem," Molly replied, adding, "Let's get back to camp."

"Dr. Erasmus isn't gonna be happy," Lucy said as the four suits fell into a loose formation.

BY THE TIME Brandon and the others returned to camp, it resembled a small town. The four transports were emptied out, the cargo holds empty of the prefab structures and equipment used to create the scientific village. The last of the equipment was scaffolding that was being erected around the giant alien flower tower.

Void Romeo spotted the group as they came over a rise. Victor keyed the comm system. "I've got the team on long range." He adjusted the zoom, pulling in tighter. Romeo's optics weren't as good as Valiant Azure's enhanced optical package, but they did okay.

"Did they bag one?" Thompson asked.

"Uh, I don't think so, sir. Just see the four mechs."

Thompson pursed his lips, looking around the command center for his comm. He tapped the icon to call Dr. Erasmus. He wasn't sure where the older man was, likely in the rabbit warren of laboratories between the four transports. The doctor had given the go ahead to begin erecting scaffolding around the tower the day prior, while waiting for the hunting party to return.

"Yes, Major," Erasmus said.

"They're back, Doctor. No joy on the mission, though."

The senior VarTech researcher frowned. "That's irksome, but the odds weren't high. Thank you, Major. We'll move forward with our explorations of the tower."

Thompson turned to a junior officer at a nearby station. "Have one of the Wasps go out to meet them and fly over watch. Don't want a random monster to stumble into them."

"Yes, sir," the young man replied.

They transferred the Wasps from the roofs of the transports to a small dedicated landing pad near the center of the camp.

Thompson watched the small craft rise into the sky, its four rotors tilting to send it shooting off toward the approaching hunting party.

While the suits made their way to base camp, Thompson exited the transport through an airlock that connected to the lab complex. After asking a few junior research types, he found Erasmus in a large, domed lab. Tables lined the outer edge. Equipment he couldn't even begin to name nor understand filled the middle space.

"How goes, Doc?"

Erasmus turned. "Well, my day freed up considerably without an observer to necropsy."

"You knew it was long odds," Thompson said.

The other man nodded. A junior VarTech woman came over offering a tablet. He took it, looked over whatever was on the screen, tapped a few things on the screen, and handed the device back. The young woman nodded and backed away.

"At least you can get to work on the tower," Thompson offered.

Erasmus nodded. "Indeed. I've been anxious to begin our examinations. With our full complement of suits back, I'm ready to dig in."

Back inside Tacit Ronin, an incoming signal indicator came to life near the top right of Molly's field of vision. Focusing her attention on the pulsing dot brought it into focus. "Miss us?" Sophie asked.

Ronin shook her head. "More than you know. I like a team where everyone knows their role. Two out of the three of them want to be Bravo One."

"What's Paco want?" Sophie knew exactly who Molly was talking about. Everyone who drove a suit knew.

"He just wants to drive a suit and smash monsters."

"Hoo raw," the other woman drawled.

"Looks like they got our little outpost all set up." Tacit Ronin could see the base camp and its defensive wall of locked down transports.

"Never been gladder to be in a suit. Avoided construction work." The big suit raised a beige with black trimmed arm to gesture at the camp.

ONCE THE AWAY TEAM WAS BACK AT camp, all six pilots were given some rest and relaxation time by the major. Wasps would keep an eye on things, and if the suits were needed, the pilots would know.

Since there wasn't any type of bay for the mighty war machines, each one took a knee beyond the wall formed by the transports. Each faced out, ready to go into action.

"Well, it's not the pilot's lounge, but it's better than nothing," Victor said as he collapsed into a folding chair in the cargo hold of Transport Four.

While Bravo Team and Alpha One were out trying to rustle up an observer creature, the remaining two members of Alpha had staked claim to the cargo hold of Transport Two, forcing out the ground troops that had tried to make it their hangout.

"So, they set a trap to spring one of their own?" Sophie asked. She grabbed a slice of pizza from the table in the middle of the group.

It wasn't really a slice of pizza. There was no pizza to be had this far south of the established border. Sophie collected a few different types of rations and mashed them all together into a generally pizza-shaped creation. Then, using a borrowed blow torch, she toasted it before slicing like pizza.

"Yeah, it was weird," Brandon said. He was standing next to the mini fridge that Sophie or Victor scavenged from who knew where. "Beers?" Everyone nodded, so he began filling his arms with ice cold bottles.

He really wanted to know how they'd filled the mini fridge, considering how much effort it had taken him to pry three bottles from Sergeant Tight-Grip.

Once drinks were distributed, Molly said, "It was weird. It was also well planned. They got us separated, freed the observer and then faded away. It was..." She shook her head. "Well coordinated."

"How is that even possible?" Sophie asked. She took a sip of her drink. "I don't even know what we do with that. I mean, our entire strategy around dealing with these things is that they're lone wolves. One wanders too close to the border and we deploy a few suits. If they're teaming up, coordinating attacks..."

Molly nodded her agreement. She took another sip of her beer, looking at but not reaching for her teammate's attempt at culinary creativity. Rations were bad enough. She couldn't imagine how toasting them would be an improvement, let alone mixing several together.

"They could get through the border by feigning an attack in one place," Brandon added.

"This is bad in all the possible ways," Lucy said.

Paco gestured toward a display that someone mounted on the wall opposite the large cargo door. It was showing a feed from a camera pointed at the massive flower tower thing. "And that's gotta be why, right?"

On the screen, the VarTech technicians and ground troopers helping them were completing the scaffolding. It only reached a handful of meters up the enormous plant. The transports all carried a few sections by default, but there was no way they had enough to even get a third of the way up the massive plant.

"How?" Molly asked. "It's a giant plant."

"A giant alien plant," Brandon said, his eyes glued to the screen.

CHAPTER TWENTY

THE NEXT MORNING, the camp was a hive of activity. The six suits stood around the flower tower thing, all on high alert, weapons deployed and powered up.

The four Wasps lifted off from their pad, slowly fanning out to ensure the immediate area was clear of megafauna.

Dr. Erasmus was with Major Thompson in Transport One's command center. None of the prefab lab spaces had anything that could be used for a command-and-control center, though all data being streamed from the suits and the four Wasps was being recorded exclusively on servers in Lab One.

Erasmus tapped his earpiece. "Wasp One, please proceed to Waypoint One."

"Copy that," the pilot responded. Ahead of the exploration of the flower tower, the senior VarTech researcher had mapped out the organism's structure, marking out waypoints for the exploration teams focus on.

The nimble attack craft made a slow spiral as it rose toward the first waypoint, about halfway up the alien stalk, a kilometer in the air.

"Incredible," Erasmus mumbled. He pointed at the large display showing the feed from the Wasp. "These scalelike objects. They're smaller here than at the base."

"That is interesting," Thompson said.

"You understand the significance?"

"Not even a little."

The other man made a series of disgusted sounding noises. "The scales must be a type of natural defense mechanism. The lower scales likely keep smaller creatures at bay. The taller the structure grows, the less risk. The scales reduce in side. I imagine they might vanish completely by the time we reach the flower structure at the top."

He tapped the earpiece. "Wasp Two, please proceed to Waypoint Two."

"Copy that."

The second waypoint was three-quarters to the top of the stalk. Everyone on the ground watched as the nimble airship left its circular patrol route, rising to an altitude of one and three quarters kilometers.

"Picking up strong EM readings," the pilot of Wasp Two said.

Brandon pulled up the Wasp's feed, putting it in a window in his field of vision. Regulations dictated how many floating windows a pilot should have in their visual field at any one time. Brandon figured that just standing around with no threats in the area, he could push the number, adding video feeds from the two Wasps and the other five suits forming the perimeter.

"EM readings are off the charts now," the pilot reported. "Ten meters from Waypoint Two."

The feed from Wasp Two was filling with static and visual artifacts.

Thompson turned to one of the junior officers. "Can you clean that up?"

The young man shook his head. "Sorry, sir. That's how we're getting it. Whatever it is, it's affecting the Wasp's cameras."

Dr. Erasmus looked at a secondary display. "Lots of exotic energy up there. Looks like it's spilling down from the flower."

"I'm going to pull back a few meters," the pilot of Wasp Two said. The feed from his craft cleared slightly. "At Waypoint Two altitude."

Erasmus nodded. "Your feed is considerably clearer, Wasp Two. Hold there. Wasp Three, you're up. Waypoint Three."

"Copy that," the pilot of Wasp Three said as she guided her craft out of the patrol route and began her ascent toward the top of the alien plant.

"Keep your distance until you're near the top, Wasp Three," Thompson said, adding, "Just in case."

"Copy."

Everyone with a pair of eyes in the command center, in a suit, or in one of the labs was glued to the feeds from the four Wasps.

Wasp Three was drawing closer to the alien flower's top. "Instruments are going haywire," the pilot said. For the first time, her calm voice was cracking. "Something is glowing or something. There's a lot of energy up here."

The nimble Wasp reached the same altitude as the enormous flower and slid closer to one of the massive petals. "The tops of the petals are reflective. Almost like metal or solar panels." As the pilot guided the craft closer, the four rotors pivoted, making minute adjustments to keep the aircraft level.

Brandon pulled up the live view from Midnight Tango's optical sensors, zooming in so he could see the light assault craft as it passed over the top of the giant alien flower.

Brandon watched the feed from Wasp Three, sending the mental command to increase the size of that window, while minimizing the other two. The feed from the Wasp was distorted, artifacts coming and going. Brandon could see the center of the flower; three-meter-tall stamen were waving in the breeze from the approaching craft's four rotors. They were a mix of pale yellow and pink.

Brandon could see arcs of what looked like blue electricity jumping from stamen to stigma and back. On the feed from the Wasp, a flash of blue filled the window a second before the pilot said, "What the hell?" The image went completely white for a few seconds before static overtook the audio and video feed.

Brandon flinched, Midnight Tango putting his matte black hands up over his head as debris—all that remained of Wasp Three—fell to the ground.

He glanced at his tactical display, making sure the

fully operational suits were still where they'd been. Not close enough to see him flinch.

All clear.

"Saw that," Molly Chen said on a private channel. Midnight Tango turned to spy Tacit Ronin almost directly opposite the giant plant from him. She raised one hand in mock salute.

Feeling his cheeks burn, he looked up at the flower. The blue arcs of electricity were visible from the ground now. Whatever had just destroyed the Wasp was still happening.

"All air units, maintain a safe perimeter. No-fly zone of fifty meters," Major Thompson ordered over the expedition channel. He added, "Suits, keep to at least twenty-five."

Aboard Transport One, the major turned to Dr. Erasmus. "Well, that went well."

The older man nodded absently, rubbing his chin as he rewound the footage from the destroyed Wasp. "It's building a charge of some kind."

"For what?"

The doctor stopped watching the replay and turned to the major. "Good question."

"GOOD MORNING, DOCTOR."

"Good morning, Major," Erasmus said as he took a seat at the conference table in Transport One's briefing room. With all of his underlings busy, the senior scientist had been loitering in Transport One more and more.

The major smiled to himself as he took a sip of his coffee, cherishing the bite. Coffee was getting harder to come by; things like cream and sugar were even more rare. A few years ago, he'd gone cold turkey as far as accouterments, taking his coffee black. "What've you got, Doc?"

"The analysis of the—" he ran a hand along his beard, smoothing it "—structure is ongoing. The bark is remarkably dense." He took a sip of his coffee. "Only our hardest drill bits have even made a scratch in it. If we can analyze it, it could make for the next generation of suit armor. It seems specifically evolved to protect the stalk from megafauna."

While that was interesting overall, the major didn't really care since that was all VarTech. They'd analyze and break down the plant's armor, duplicate it, sell it, rake in record profits, all that. He'd still be collecting his military paycheck.

"And the flower thing?" the major prompted. He was still sore that he'd lost a Wasp and its pilot. He hated have to write *that* letter and thankfully only had the one to write, so far. After Wasp Three was destroyed, he pulled the other two that were hovering near the stalk back and shut down any further explorations of the upper regions of the stalk.

The doctor stroked his beard again as he collected his thoughts to answer the major, with at least answer enough to satisfy the NACAF officer. "Obviously we can't send another Wasp up there." The major nodded his agreement. "We've sent a few remote drones. They've captured...energy readings, measured radiation..."

Major Thompson was getting tired of the old researcher's evasiveness. "And?"

"I don't know. The radiation it's emitting is across multiple spectra, including RF and EM, plus a half dozen we've only theorized the existence of."

"What about the idea that it's controlling them, the monsters?"

The other man shrugged. "It's certainly possible. We don't know what the purpose of any of the emissions are. They could be guiding the creatures." He shook his head. "For all we know, this thing is the catalyst for the recent evolutionary jumps."

"You think?"

"Anything is possible."

"That's not a great thought."

"Indeed."

The lighting in the room dimmed as the trim along the floor and ceiling turned red.

"Alert. Alert. This is not a drill."

Thompson was out of his seat before the first word left the speakers.

"Report," he demanded as he stepped into the next compartment, the command center. Out of the corner of his eye, he saw Erasmus moving toward the airlock that connected to the rabbit warren that was the lab complex.

The junior officer at the main sensor station turned in her seat. "Sir, the sensor net is picking up strange tremors."

"Strange? Tremors?"

She blushed. "Yes, sir. The computer is trying to pinpoint the source now."

Thompson was about to make a joke when the floor of the transport shook ever so slightly. He looked over at the coffee mug on the console next to her. The surface of the dark liquid inside was rippling. He tapped the commset in his ear. "Deploy suits."

BRANDON'S VISION took on a red tinge as the alert came in. His tactical display populated with three red circles.

"Deploy suits," Major Thompson announced on the squad channel. "Wasps lifting off now to provide air support. Bravo, you've got point until Alpha is on the scene."

On the suits-only channel, Molly Chen said, "We're suiting up now!"

Brandon turned to look toward Transport Three, spotting three small forms running toward the waiting suits kneeling a few hundred meters distant.

"What's the situation, Command?" he asked, panning his optics from side to side. He spied the remaining three Wasps rising into the air.

One of the Wasp pilots said, "We've got several Category 1s popping up on sensors. Like a nest or something." She sounded more stressed than Brandon would expect for Category 1 megafauna, the smallest of the categorized beasts. Then his tactical display updated. The three red circles he'd seen a second ago were now nearly two dozen smaller circles. He swore. Category 1 megafauna weren't much to worry about individually, but two dozen of them? That was another story.

Midnight Tango's weapon systems powered up. Glancing first to his left, then right, Brandon saw Crusher Maverick and Valiant Azure were equally ready for a fight; blades and cannons were deployed and locked in position.

"Bravo Team coming in from the right," Lucy announced. On the Bravo channel, she added. "Brandon, you split and fire a few rounds into the mass, break it up a bit. Paco, wade in and start smashing."

Brandon rolled his eyes at the play-by-play instructions but said nothing, priming each of his minivan-sized pistols.

So little was known about megafauna. Maybe this was a nest or a herd or some other grouping, or just a coincidence, but all two dozen creatures were the same: something that Brandon could describe only as scaly tigers the size of buffalo, with spines all along their backs and barbs on their tails.

"Watch your six, Tango!" Lucy shouted a moment before three of the diminutive monsters scaled his left leg.

"You could have just shot them!" he scolded as he tried to shake the creatures off.

"Well, hold still!"

Several beams of light split the distance between the two suits until three found their mark, burning holes in the sides of the scaly monsters trying to pull Midnight Tango to the ground.

"You're wel—" Six Category 1s leaped onto Azure's back, forcing Lucy to the ground. "Shit!" she shouted. She hadn't seen them on her tactical view.

"Alpha is coming in from sector four," Molly Chen announced on the mission channel.

Brandon glanced at the floating tactical view, spotting three green circles moving in quickly from the left toward the mass of red icons. He holstered both pistols and charged toward his downed comrade, a short blade deploying from his left arm behind his hand. He triggered the trimetal blade in his right, feeling the device engage.

Valiant Azure was thrashing under the weight of the attacking creatures. Lucy could hear the sound of their claws on Azure's armored torso inside her crèche. "Hurry up!" She got ahold of one of the creature's tails and hurled it away.

Brandon's trimetal blade stabbed into another creature. It released a gurgling scream. He pulled the tether back, sending the dead creature into the air in a wide arc. Another motion and he had the scaly tiger spinning like a flail at the end of his tether. He spotted an opportunity and adjusted his swing, sending the end of his line careening into two other creatures, sending them sprawling off of Valiant Azure.

Lucy shook off the remaining two creatures, grabbing one and tossing it while Brandon shot the other as it hit the ground.

STALWART ROOK DOVE into the middle of one of the groups of attacking creatures, her right hand in its war hammer mode. Each swipe sent creatures pinwheeling lifelessly through the air. One of the creatures leaped onto the thick built suit, clawing at the optic mesh covering the suit's sensors. Two powerful swipes sent creatures flying in both directions as the mighty suit cleaved a path through the relatively smaller alien creatures.

The suits were a flurry of activity—slashing, smashing, and blasting as nimble creatures jumped around and on them.

"How are there so damn many?" Victor shouted as he ripped a writhing creature in two. "They don't do this."

"They do now!" Molly called from her own five-on-one fight.

"Little help?" Alpha Two asked, turning this way and that. Two of the creatures were clinging to Rook's back, well out of reach of her thick arms.

Free of her own attackers, Lucy brought Valiant Azure in close. The forearm blades that were the suit's only close-in weapon sliced down and across Rook's attackers. Each released a gurgling cry, then fell, in pieces, to the ground.

Stalwart Rook turned. "Thanks," Sophie said, a second before reaching up to push Azure aside to slam a titanium alloy war hammer into an airborne tiger-thing. The creature erupted in a blossom of blue and orange gore that splashed across the ground.

"So squishy," Sophie quipped.

Brandon shouted a string of curses as he danced Midnight Tango into the midst of several of the creatures. Over his audio pickups, he could hear them snarling and hissing.

Brandon felt his balance shift as the weight of Midnight Tango shifted. Sensors embedded throughout the suit's body indicated that he'd picked up a hitchhiker that was currently clinging to the armored sail that protected the back of Tango's head. The creature was thrashing as it gnawed on the thick armor plating.

Reaching back, he felt Tango's hand grasp the creature, its spines piercing the armored fingers enough to register as pain. He had no idea how that was even possible. Suit armor was supposed to be nearly impervious to megafauna attack.

Wincing, he grabbed the thing and tossed it into the air. While the wriggling monster arced overhead, his right arm clicked and whirred as the trimetal blade engaged. He pulled his hand back, tracking the airborne creature's trajectory. He squinted, causing the multitude of cameras in Tango's head to zoom in on the creature. He pulled his arm back and made a pitching motion.

The reinforced blade shot out of its housing, the sensation of the high gauge tether unspooling behind it, like a twitch of his forearm muscles. The blade struck the monster, piercing it.

"Yes!" he shouted as he yanked his arm down, mentally triggering the winch in his arm to begin retracting the cable. The dead creature struck the ground with a thud. Before the winch fully retracted the blade, he spied another of the creatures creeping toward him. "Oh, yeah?" He flung his arm, and the deceased creature attached to it, to the side. The dead monster slammed into the living one with a wet crunch. Spines from both creatures pierced the other, locking them together. He was starting to like using these things as flails.

Elsewhere, Tacit Ronin was slashing both arms in wide arcs, chain blades whirring like a hive of angry bees. Several creatures, in multiple pieces, littered the ground near the dark gray suit. The ground and Ronin's legs were splattered with gore.

"It's a goddamned nest!" Paco shouted. Crusher Maverick was hip deep in an indentation in the ground. At least a dozen more creatures were clawing out of holes around the indentation, scrabbling to grab onto the suit's joints. Maverick thrashed this way and that, sending creatures alive and dead flying in all directions.

Valiant Azure jumped down into the shallow depression filled with angry monsters, her blades slashing this way and that.

"Okay, this is starting to be fun!" Lucy shouted as she ripped a creature from Maverick's back, driving one of her blades through it.

Two of the nimble Wasps buzzed overhead, strafing a group of creatures that were moving to surround the tower. "Command, Wasp Two. You seeing this?"

Brandon tossed a creature away, glancing at his tactical overlay.

"Copy that, Wasp Two," Major Thompson said.

Brandon watched as more Category 1 creatures

appeared on the tactical view. Instead of moving toward the suits spread around the tower, they were forming a perimeter around the structure.

"Uh...What's happening?" Paco asked as the creatures he was smashing with his thick fists backed away.

CHAPTER TWENTY-ONE

"ALL UNITS HOLD POSITION," Thompson ordered. He turned to Dr. Erasmus, eyebrows raised.

The other man shrugged. "We don't know what drives them. We saw coordinated action in San Antonio. This seems to be more of the same. Presumably, the tower is guiding them."

"Then we destroy the tower."

"Sir, Doctor! The tower," a young officer called out from one of the sensor stations. "I'm picking up increased output across all EM bands. Exotic radiation detectors are jumping all over the place."

"Where's it getting power from?" Thompson demanded.

Erasmus shook his head. "My theory is that there's a taproot that taps into geothermal power deep underground. It's the only thing that makes sense."

Thompson rubbed his jaw. "Guessing that's not something we can cut?"

Erasmus shook his head.

"Shit." After taking a deep breath, the major said, "We gotta take that thing down."

"The tower?" the other man asked, incredulous. "The bark is as thick as suit armor." He gestured to one of the monitors. "And now covered in armored creatures seemingly dead set on protecting it."

Thompson landed on the console before him. He didn't have the resources for a prolonged fight against megafauna. Not if they just kept coming. He glanced at the status display showing each of his six suits. All of them had damage; several were low on expendable ammunition.

A glance at the tactical display showed that all the remaining Category 1 megafauna had moved to surround the tower. His suits were standing off a few hundred meters. Neither side made a move toward the other. He tapped his earpiece. "All suits hold position. Report anything weird."

"Weird like a couple dozen Category 1s forming a wall around a glowing alien asparagus?" Brandon asked.

"Can it, Tango," Molly Chen said from Tacit Ronin.

Erasmus grabbed his comm and began tapping and swiping with gusto. "It must be moving into whatever the next stage is. It called these smaller creatures to keep us busy. Now it's increasing its signal output." He frowned, swiping more screens. "It's not just broadcasting wide now." He held his comm out for Thompson to see. On the screen, a sensor diagram of the alien flower tower was pulsing with energy. Unlike previous versions of the image, the top of the stalk was not just sending signals out in all directions. A strong energy stream was shooting from the flower into the sky—not straight up but at an angle, clearly aiming at something. Somewhere.

Thompson turned to the display they had been looking at. "Wasps, move into over watch position, two hundred meters out."

The three Wasp pilots acknowledged, their craft rising above the fight below to hover near the top of the flower.

"Lot of interference even this far out, Command," one of the Wasp pilots said. The channel was flooded with crackling static.

Thompson pulled up the feeds from the three aircraft. Each of the massive petals was glittering with energy. Lightning jumped from stamen to petal and back.

Dr. Erasmus was still busily working his tablet. He gasped. "We need to stop it."

Thompson turned. "I said that already."

"You don't understand. It's calling home."

The small command center fell silent. Thompson's mouth was hanging open. Finally, he regained his composure. "I'm sorry. What?"

Erasmus offered the tablet again. "Look."

Thompson took the table, saying, "Explain like I'm five."

Erasmus sighed. "The signal, it's aimed at the location in space we believe the original asteroid came from."

"All suits. Priority one. We need to destroy the tower!"

"ALL SUITS. Priority one. We need to destroy the tower!"

Brandon looked to his left at Valiant Azure, then right to Void Romeo. "Come again, Command."

"That thing is calling home. We need to stop it." After a pause, the major added, "Omega order."

Brandon swallowed. Switching to the Bravo Team channel, he said, "Omega order? What the fuck?"

"I kinda hoped my career would be longer," Lucy said. "Long enough to be named Bravo One, at least."

Molly Chen cut through their conversation. "Okay, everyone. Pair up. This won't be clean or easy. Cut through the little ones and get to the trunk. If you've got blades or ordnance, use it! Tango, you're with Rook. Maverick, you're with me. Azure and Romeo, you're team three. Go!"

Tacit Ronin broke into a run, both chain swords at full speed, high-pitched roars coming from each. Paco fell in behind her, slamming his enormous metal hands together.

"At least I'll die a suit pilot!" Brandon shouted as he broke into a run, deploying the blade in his left arm and mentally preparing his trimetal blade in his right.

Sophie said, "I plan to die a retired pilot!" She engaged her war hammer, her suit's right hand transforming into a heavy hammer. With her right arm engaged, she activated the slug thrower in her left forearm.

The Category 1 creatures reacted instantly. The outermost ring of creatures surged out to meet their attackers.

Brandon slashed as a pair of the spiny tiger buffalo monsters leaped at it. Both creatures fell to the ground, each in two parts. Three more were on him in a flash, clawing at Tango's legs.

One of the creatures on Tango's leg exploded, flying away from Brandon as Stalwart Rook fired another round at another creature. It flew off Midnight Tango, exploding.

Tango nodded to Rook as they continued toward the tower.

Lucy and Victor charged toward the tower, shoulder to shoulder. Both suits were blasting anything that moved. Romeo fought with his forearm-mounted plasma cannons and Azure with her shoulder-mounted particle cannons. Lucy also had her less powerful forearm beam cannons deployed. They wouldn't do much other than distract the creatures, but that was enough for the pair of suits' larger weapons to vaporize and flash fry the small megafauna.

While they waded into the mass of frenzied creatures, Void Romeo's shoulder-mounted slug thrower took aim on the tower, the zip-crack of the gun sending magnetically accelerated slugs at the tower.

The round struck the armored scales covering the tower. The scale that was struck glowed. Then the scales surrounding it rippled with energy.

"Well, damn," Victor said. He fired two more rounds at the same scale, causing it to glow brighter. The scales nearby crackled with energy, each glowing faintly. "Command, these scales absorb kinetic energy."

In Transport One, Thompson turned to Dr. Erasmus. The older man looked up from his tablet, frowning. "The energy is being channeled up to the flower."

"Of course it is," the older man snapped.

The major turned back to his display.

"Sir!" someone shouted from the rear of the command center. "Multiple contacts!"

"I should have been a dentist," Thompson said with a sigh. He turned to the junior officer. "How many?"

The young man swallowed. "A...a dozen, sir." The man's eyes were like saucers. "I think two of them are... They're Category 4s, sir."

"Fours?" Thompson turned to Erasmus.

"I think so, sir. The silhouettes are fuzzy but big. Bigger than the others."

"Distance?"

"Two kilometers and closing."

Erasmus groaned. "The tower. It's calling them."

Thompson glared at the older man.

THE TWO CATEGORY 4 monsters rose up behind the herd of Category 3s they were driving toward the camp. The mass of megafauna trampled brightly colored alien jungle without slowing down.

"Well, those're ugly," Sophie said as Stalwart Rook rose awkwardly from a pile of dead Category 1s, her left leg sparking from several cracks in her armor.

"And big," Lucy said.

"Like cowboys on a cattle drive. Horribly building-sized cowboys and cows," Paco added.

The taller of the two Category 4 creatures looked almost more plant than animal, vines writhing around its torso and limbs seemingly of their own accord. Its mottled black hide looked like wood. A thick tail that ended in a thorny burl swished through the jungle, destroying alien trees as it swiped. The creature looked around, spotted the distant suits, and roared an ear-splitting sound like what Paco imagined a dying animal would make.

The smaller monster looked like a gorilla with a turtle shell. It opened its fanged mouth, releasing a guttural growl as its long arms raised into the air, fists pumping. In places, its shaggy pale violet hair was matted. With what, Brandon didn't want to know.

The ten creatures before them lumbered on, seemingly oblivious to what was ahead of them. All of them were the big alien cow variety, six stocky limbs all ending in elephant-like feet. They typically moved through the deeper megaflora eating the tree analogs. Their hippo-like tusks made quick work of the alien tree trunks, even the armored kind.

Brandon glanced to his right seeing Void Romeo and Valiant Azure still fighting smaller creatures as the latter poured peta-joules of energy into the alien stalk that was their target.

Crusher Maverick and Tacit Ronin were back-to-back, the former firing what few energy weapons were available at the tower. They seemed to be having the same affect as Void Romeo's slug thrower. None. All the while, both groups were fending off Category 1 creatures as best they could.

Brandon's HUD flashed, highlighting Tacit Ronin in a bright red halo. The armor of Alpha Team's lead suit was cracked in multiple places, especially its chest plate. "Alpha One, hang back—your armor is compromised," he said over the squad channel.

"No chance, rookie." The damaged suit brought her arms up in front of her chest, then flicked them out to the side, chain blades snapping into place just in time to send two halves of a leaping Category 1 flying past her. The dark gray suit was splattered head to toe in orange and green bodily fluids.

Watching the lumbering monster cows close the distance with no concern for what was in front of them, Paco shook his head and muttered, "*Dios mio.*" Crusher Maverick's right shoulder sparked where one of the smaller creatures had managed to get under his pauldron to rip at the joint.

"We have to destroy the tower," Sophie said. Stalwart Rook slammed her war hammer into her open palm. "They're just going to keep coming."

Two Wasps buzzed overhead, raining plasma rounds on the stampeding creatures. The bolts of energy did little to slow the monstrous herbivores.

The two Category 4s dropped into a crouch, then charged their attackers. The turtle gorilla closed the gap the fastest, its long forelimbs allowing it to reach the camp in only a few long strides. The meager ground forces scattered around the rabbit warren of labs and connecting tunnels didn't stand a chance. The myriad pulse rifle fire rising up from the camp didn't faze the turtle gorilla—it didn't even seem to notice. Transport Three was batted aside, taking with it one of the prefab lab complexes that was connected to it.

Brandon wanted to look away, watching people he knew go flying through the air in every direction—and worse—disappearing under the creature's feet. Midnight Tango's computers started pinpointing potential weak spots on the creature as it closed the gap, eleven other creatures not far behind it.

"We gotta keep the fight outside the camp," Victor said as Void Romeo's shoulder-mounted cannon roared, sending an armor piercing round the size of a man's head into the chest of the turtle thing, staggering it back out of camp. "Tough bastard!" He fired another round, driving the creature further back.

"We'll try to divert them," one of the Wasp pilots said.

VarTech researchers and what remained of the NACAF ground forces were scrambling to disconnect the lab structures from the transports.

Brandon watched as Stalwart Rook's powerful slug throwers fired round after round into the black bark-like hide of the second creature, having little effect. Each round scorched the wood-like hide but didn't seem to faze the creature. It kept lumbering right at them just behind its friend.

"Well, damn," Brandon hissed. These things might be a problem. Panels on each of Tango's upper thigh slid open; frames slid out and locked into place, putting his

BFG-9000s within reach. They fired rounds with more punch than Rook's. Once the massive pistols were clear, the empty frames slid back into place, the armor panels closing up over them. "Guess we do this the hard way."

The plant thing let loose a rumbling cry as it dodged to the side to avoid Rook's next salvo.

"Alpha One, Valiant Azure. Focus on the tower!" Brandon ordered as he moved Midnight Tango into position to intercept the monstrous tree thing. He had both arms straight out, BFG-9000s at the ready. He was down to his last six rounds in each pistol. The downside of slug throwers, he guessed.

"Not in charge, rookie!" Molly called back, but added after a sigh, "Cover us." Tacit Ronin turned and made for the megaflora structure, Lucy in Valiant Azure on her six. The dark blue suit turned to look at Tango as he reached the tree creature.

Brandon was less than ten meters from the plant thing when the vine wrapped creature lunged for him, closing the distance in a flash. As Midnight Tango slid past the creature, Brandon fired both pistols. Two, then four, titanium-tipped, armor-piercing rounds tore into the mottled bark, sending splinters in all directions.

Before he could complete the turn that would carry him clear of the injured beast, vines lashed out, wrapping around an arm and leg. The vines tightened, causing several alarm pop ups to flash in his vision. The tightening vines triggered sensations in his arm and leg. Not quite pain, yet, but pressure. It was increasing. He was starting to dislike how reactive the pilots' suits were.

"I got you, *hermano*!" Two massive three-fingered

hands grasped the vines, tugging them until they snapped. Paco grabbed another bunch of vines, doing the same.

"Thanks," Brandon said, yanking the vines from his leg. He turned to see the gorilla turtle toss Void Romeo toward the megaflora tower like the multiton suit weighed nothing.

Brandon spied the cracks spider webbing the thing's front shell. He charged. "Let's end that ugly turtle!"

"Right behind you!" Paco said.

BEFORE MAVERICK and Tango could reach the gorilla turtle, Void Romeo was on his feet and charging back toward the long armed and armor covered creature. "That hurt, you ugly whatever-you-are!"

He leaped back onto the creature's shell and slammed a fist through the still glowing hot keratin covered bone.

While Paco, Brandon, and Victor traded blows with the turtle creature, Molly was doing a good job of keeping Tacit Ronin out of the plant thing's grasp, but her suit's damage wasn't just cosmetic. Beneath the ruined torso armor, the dark gray suit's power plant was straining along with several secondary systems.

Tacit Ronin spun out of the way of a claw only to stumble as her right leg gave out. The plant creature wasted no time falling onto the damaged suit.

Spotting Molly's predicament, Brandon broke from the gorilla turtle and ran toward the thrashing plant thing. "Oh, no you don't!" He reared back, his trimetal blade deployed and at the ready. The blade shot out of his forearm, the high strength cable trailing behind it.

The blade embedded itself in the thick bark-like hide of the creature, causing it to roar or scream, Brandon couldn't tell which. He also didn't care. In his left hand, he grasped the cable coming from his right arm and pulled with all the strength the suit's artificial muscle strands and their hyper torque drives could muster. The creature was pulled back, flailing to reach the jagged hook that was embedded between its shoulder blades.

Warnings went off around Brandon's peripheral vision as the creature spun, pulling on the cable. The winch in his arm strained. A warning flashed that the tensile strength of the cable was being taxed.

"Come on, you giant angry shrub," he growled, pulling the creature further away from Tacit Ronin, the cable digging into his hand palm. Every motor in Tango's body strained as he fought the creature.

"Thanks," Molly breathed as she regained her footing, barely. Ronin's right leg looked like it couldn't support the suit's full weight. That didn't stop Molly from hobbling up behind the vine covered creature and plunging her remaining functional chain blade into the monster's back. "Hold him!" she grunted, pushing her arm upward.

The creature jerked, and pale pink sap or blood or something gushed out of the increasingly long wound. Brandon released his grip on the cable and grabbed the thing. Vines lashed out at both suits. Brandon batted at them as best he could with one arm trying to hold the creature.

The plant monster spasmed, then stopped fighting. Brandon trained his optics on its face just as a chain blade burst through it, showering Tango in the pale pink sap-like offal that was mixed with the neon orange blood that pumped through all megafauna. The vines twitched, then fell to the ground a moment before the carcass did.

Midnight Tango tossed the last vines off and turned to Tacit Ronin, standing on her one good leg. Nodding, the suit turned to Crusher Maverick and Void Romeo still going back and forth with their armored opponent.

FIVE METERS from the alien tower, Valiant Azure had both particle beams pulsing into one section of the tower's scalelike bark. The individual scale being hit was bright white, and those nearest were orange and yellow from the heat. Both barrels were themselves glowing.

"Can't keep this up much longer," Lucy said.

Tacit Ronin was standing off to the side, both chain swords buzzing like a hive of enraged wasps. "Now!" Molly ordered.

The twin beams of charged particles snapped off, a haze of burned ozone lingering. Molly leaned back, then plunged her arms toward the still glowing section of the tower. Both blades struck the scalelike bark, shattering the white-hot chitin. As they chopped, more scales followed, falling in pieces to the ground. The chain blades bit, chewing deep into the material that made up the megaflora tower.

The entire structure shuddered. A deep purple sap-like substance oozed from the still white-hot wound, hissing and bubbling.

"Yes!" Molly hissed. She pulled her chain swords free of the tower, trailing pulp and alien sap. "Gross." She flung her arms as hard as she could to dislodge the goop covering both forearms. She glanced out toward the myriad battles being fought near the tower. "Oh."

"What?" Lucy asked.

Tacit Ronin pointed north toward the gulf. About a kilometer away, barely visible in a stand of alien trees, was an observer creature.

"Still creepy," Lucy said.

Ronin nodded. "Command, we've got an observer. Sending coordinates."

Crusher Maverick and Midnight Tango were on either side of the gorilla turtle. Fluids leaked from several cracks in the beast's shell.

"He's not looking so hot," Brandon said.

The megafauna turned its head slowly from side to side, looking at each metal monster nearby. It roared a challenge at Crusher Maverick.

Maverick nodded, slamming one thickly armored fist into thickly armored palm. "Let's finish it."

The two suits charged the monstrous creature; two armor-piercing rounds slammed into it, further cracking then shattering the damaged shell. The creature roared again, dropping into a crouch and lunging at Tango before he could fire another round. As gore pumped out of the ruined front shell, the long arms thrashed against Midnight Tango's chest. Brandon rattled inside the pilot's crèche. "Oh! Stop that!"

He deployed his left forearm blade. The creature spotted the blade and slammed its hand down, pinning the black armored suit's arm. It leaned down, ready to bite the face of its attacker.

"No, you don't!" Two three-fingered hands grasped the monster's head on either side. "That's my friend!" Paco twisted with all the strength his external pistol powered arms could muster.

A loud crack sounded. The creature went limp, slumping on top of Midnight Tango. Brandon tried to get his arms under the creature; his left arm was sparking. The creature's claws had done more damage than Brandon initially thought. "Little help?"

The dead monster rocked a few times, further covering Tango in blood and the random entrails that slipped out of the damaged shell, before tilting off to the side.

Getting to his feet, Brandon looked around. His friends were still fighting the large plant thing and dozens more of the smaller Category 1s. "Heads up!" he warned.

It was too late. One of the herbivore Category 3s plowed into Stalwart Rook, driving the heavy mech backward, her feet carving grooves in the hard ground.

The remaining seven creatures were all rushing toward the tower, surrounded by the surviving Category 1s. The plant thing was at the head of the pack.

"Guess that got their attention," Lucy said. She checked a floating status display in her heads-up display.

Both particle cannons were still too hot to use. "My canons are still offline." She looked around, spying Brandon and Paco a few hundred meters away, next to the dead turtle creature.

Brandon looked at his own diagnostics. Tango's left knee was flashing red; FLUID LEVELS CRITICAL flashed next to it. The left arm was orange.

CHAPTER TWENTY-TWO

WHILE CRUSHER MAVERICK and Midnight Tango slugged it out with the gorilla turtle, Void Romeo and Stalwart Rook rushed toward the ten new arrivals that were charging toward what remained of camp.

"Yeehaw!" Victor shouted as he unloaded his right forearm plasma cannon into one creature while his left fired at another. The plasma rounds didn't slow the creatures much but seemed to irritate their skin enough to divert them. Even the nonviolent variety of megafauna had hides like suit armor.

Stalwart Rook did what she was designed to do best. She waded into the new mass of Category 1 creatures, swinging her war hammer in wide arcs. Some blows staggered their recipients, while others did more damage, causing the suit to quickly become covered in neon orange bodily fluids. Several of the creatures lay at the mighty suit's feet, skulls caved in.

A pair of Wasps buzzed overhead raining energy bolts on the monster cows, keeping them too busy to charge the camp. Both crafts banked wide after their attack, heading north toward the gulf.

"Show off!" Victor said as he leaped onto the back of one of the cow monsters as it wandered toward him. The thing was startled by the sudden weight on its back. The beast's wide flanks heaved as it started bucking back and forth trying to unseat the metal monster on its back. It released a bellowing moan-like bleat. He felt a little twinge of guilt; these things were cows. Giant monster cows that stepped on houses and didn't notice, but cows all the same.

Releasing the thing's hide with one hand, he deployed a half-meter long serrated blade. "Sorry, my giant friend." He drove the blade into the beast's neck. It released another bleating cry, stumbling into a fall. Void Romeo rode the corpse to the ground, hitting the gore slicked dirt at a run toward the next nearest creature. "These things aren't as tough as I'd have exp—" The creature he was running towards reared on two pairs of legs while the front pair flailed about, one thick leg catching the running suit in the head and sending it sprawling to the ground.

Most of Victor's vision was obscured by static. "Ouch." He looked at the diagnostic details in the lower right of his vision. Void Romeo's head was sporting a large dent that damaged several sensors and cameras. The crimson optic mesh was torn and tattered.

The creature thundered past the downed mech, catching up with its friends.

"No lying down on the job," Sophie said, offering Stalwart Rook's non war hammer hand. Through the static in his vision, Victor reached up to accept the hand.

Rook's beige head tilted to one side. "You don't look good."

Victor reached up. The sensors in Void Romeo's fingers felt along the glossy black and red mech's head. "Explains my headache," he quipped.

Both suits turned to watch the remaining monster cows rumble toward the tower.

"All units, be advised. New contacts, one click out. Reading three Category 4s. Coming in from the west," Major Thompson said over the expedition channel. "Wasp Four, get eyes on."

"Copy that," the pilots replied as one.

"Command, target retreated into the jungle. No contact," one of the two Wasps that went after the observer reported.

Rook looked at Romeo. "This party keeps getting more crowded."

The glossy black suit nodded, sparks erupting from the damage to his head.

MAJOR THOMPSON WAS PACING the cramped command center in Transport One. "We can't keep this up." He glanced at the tactical display. The two Category 4s were finally fading dots, but every icon for a suit was flashing orange: damage. The Category 3 herbivores were dead or milling aimlessly half a click from the tower, unsure what to do.

Three more monsters would wipe out the entire expedition. Four, if you counted that ugly big-eyed freak lurking a klick out, watching everything.

"What if the Wasps kamikaze the tower? At the same point that Valiant Azure and Tacit Ronin caused damage?" Dr. Erasmus asked. He hadn't left the transport since the attack began, having his junior researchers handle the evacuation of the camp and return to the remaining transports.

"Their reactors are pretty powerful. Time the impact just right...maybe..." Thompson said, nodding slowly as he ran the numbers in his head.

"Worst case, three pilots die for nothing?"

Thompson spun to look at the other man. "Would you send three of your people to their deaths?"

Erasmus shook his head. He wanted to say, yes, but knew he couldn't.

"Sirs, they could eject. The pilots," one of the junior officers offered.

Thompson shook his head. "Their flight suits aren't radiation hardened. It was risky enough every time they went from the transport to their craft."

"The suits could catch them, rush them back to the nearest transport?" the young woman offered.

Thompson was thinking it over. The suits were still dealing with random Category 1s attacking them. They'd be fully engaged with the new arrivals in a matter of minutes.

"Command, Wasp Four."

"Go ahead," Major Thompson said.

Everyone in the command center stopped what they

were doing. The feed from the Wasp popped up on one of the larger displays. "So, uh, these things are ugly," the pilot reported.

The suit pilots tuned into the feed from the fighter.

"Oh shit," Molly said.

Three megafauna were lumbering toward them. All were Category 4.

"Guess these three were just late," Sophie said. She was leaning on the alien flower tower.

The three new megafauna were a mixed bag; one looked like a furry lobster, one looked like a fringed lizard with spines along its limbs, the other was...a salamander with a ridge of bone and horns behind its head. All three were moving with purpose.

Panting, Brandon said, "Are there any megafauna left in South America?" He looked down at the Category 1 creature he'd just skewered. It looked like a mole with scales and stubby spider legs that each ended in little claws. He shook his head. His skin suit was soaked through with sweat.

The tactical overlay floating in the corner of his vision updated with three red icons: T1, T2, and T3. All three icons were on the move. An icon appeared a kilometer or so off: T4. He turned to zoom in on the new icon —the observer creature the Wasps were sent to drive off or kill. How it evaded the fighters, he didn't know. Crafty, ugly bugger.

LUCY KILLED HER PARTICLE BEAMS. Tacit
Ronin made a series of single arm slashes using all the
mech's strength. Each slash into the white-hot scales sent
plant matter and whatever the sap-like substance was
flying.

Molly got three good slashes and a fourth not-as-good
slash in before whatever the tower was made of cooled
enough to be impervious to Ronin's blades.

"This is going to take forever," Molly said. She
glanced at the tactical display that she kept in the lower
left of her field of vision. The three new arrivals were
closing in fast. She toggled a comm channel. "Command.
We're not going to chop this thing down any time too
soon, this way."

"Do you think a Wasp power core would do the
trick?" the major asked.

Molly turned to Lucy, who shook Valiant Azure's
massive head. "No, sir."

Lucy looked around. The barren ground around the
tower was littered with the bodies of dozens of
megafauna. Neon colored gore was everywhere, pooling
in shallow areas. She doubted anyone in the NACAF
had ever seen so many monsters in one place, living or
dead.

She glanced at her tactical display. T4? The observer.
She'd forgotten it was there. "Command, what if we take
out the observer?"

"Come again? The Wasps are trying to drive it off,"
Thompson replied.

"Yes, sir, but the plant can't see what's happening.

That thing is telling it. If we kill it, the plant won't know how to direct the new monsters."

In Transport One, Major Thompson looked at Dr. Erasmus, eyebrow raised.

The older man made a face, then nodded. "She has a good point. It's possible—likely, even—that in all the instances of coordinated action, one of those was lurking nearby."

"Lurking? They're thirty feet tall."

Erasmus cocked his head, shrugging.

Thompson tapped the comm system. "Valiant Azure, think you can take it?"

Lucy grinned. "Yes, sir."

She turned to Tacit Ronin. "Be right back."

The dark gray suit inclined her head. "Good luck."

Valiant Azure strode off toward the small jungle covered rise the observer creature was hiding behind.

The three new megafauna reached the open ground. The five suits and three Wasps stood between the creatures and the alien tower.

"I haven't even caught my breath from the last group," Sophie said. Stalwart Rook was favoring her left leg.

The three creatures charged.

Major Thompson and everyone else in Transport One held their breath.

The five NACAF suits rushed to meet them. "Team up! Two on one where we can," Lucy ordered. She added, "Azure, get your ass back here as soon as you can."

"Copy," Lucy answered. She was already half a kilometer away moving at a wide angle to where the observer creature was lurking. She glanced at her tactical overlay as her friends clashed with the three enormous monsters. She spied the three Wasps buzzing the melee. A glance at her suit status display, floating in another window in her vision, didn't deliver good news. Valiant Azure was in better shape than most of the other suits, but that wasn't a very high bar.

"UH. COMMAND?" The pilot of Wasp One was calling in.

"Go ahead, Wasp One," Thompson said.

"Sir, I just picked up four new contacts."

"Of course. Category?" Thompson looked at the tactical display. Wasp One was nearly at the same altitude as the top of the flower. The new arrivals were red dots moving toward them three kilometers out.

"Get eyes on," the major ordered.

"Copy."

He turned to look at the camera feed. Tacit Ronin was down, her left arm and part of her upper torso a tangle of shredded metal and artificial muscle strands. Crusher Maverick was kneeling not far from Ronin, his right arm dangling uselessly, the already damaged pauldron gone.

The furry lobster creature was wounded, one claw gone and several chunks of chitinous exoskeleton caved in.

A Wasp dove, peppering the creature with blaster fire. It banked away and exploded. The fringed lizard creature's tongue stabbed right through it in the blink of an eye.

His teams weren't going to last. He ran a hand through his hair, looking up at the vehicle's ceiling.

"Uh, Command. You seeing this?"

Thompson pulled up the feed from the small aircraft. "What the hell?" The four unknowns were four suits. They were striding toward the tower and camp with purpose. "Those ours?" He leaned forward, zooming in.

"I don't think so, sir," the pilot replied.

Unlike NACAF suits that tended to be built with specific mission profiles in mind and therefore varied in physical appearance, the four new arrivals were identical: mottled matte green and brown with what looked like an energy weapon on the right shoulder and something else on the left. Both pointed up in a standby position. Each arm sported forearm deployable blades, barely visible in their stored position. The optic mesh on each suit formed a wide and shallow V of glossy black.

"High gauge chain gun on the left, particle beam on the right," the Wasp pilot announced.

"Who the hell are they?" Thompson wondered out loud.

"No IFF, sir," one of the junior officers reported. All NACAF units from suits and Wasps, even the transports, all the way up to air carriers and other airships, broadcast an Identify Friend or Foe signal.

"The Syndicate," Dr. Erasmus said, adding, "It must be."

Thompson looked at him, a blank expression on his face. He snapped his fingers, remembering the mystery organization the townspeople of Libertad said protected them. He had initially dismissed the idea outright, then when enough reports came in, he adjusted his thinking, assuming whatever suits this Syndicate had would be stitched together homemade affairs.

The four suits striding toward them were anything but homemade.

"Well, shit." He composed himself before tapping an icon on the control panel in front of him. "Unidentified suits. Please identify yourselves." No reply. He repeated his demand. Nothing.

LUCY SHRANK the tactical display in her heads up, wanting to focus on the creature she was now less than two hundred meters from. As far as she could tell, it hadn't noticed her. From the glimpses she caught, it was still intently watching the rest of the suits fight the Category 4 monsters.

As she made her way closer, she wondered if the plant-tower-thing was somehow sentient. Was it directly controlling the monsters? Or simply signaling needs that they responded to? Had it caused the observer creature to evolve and appear? Until this mission, there were no reports of creatures that looked like it. Of course, there also weren't reports of megafauna acting in any coordinated way, and they'd seen examples of that several times since leaving what was left of Texas.

The alien plant life was thick enough that Lucy had to stop every few meters to slice her way through orange and purple trunks studded with thorns that could pierce armor plating.

"Okay, you ugly creeper," she whispered. Both particle beams were primed and ready.

The observer was ten meters away. She glanced at the tactical display; the icons for Tacit Ronin and Crusher Maverick were orange. Thankfully, the small icon next to each suit for pilot vitals were both still green.

Pushing aside one last thick trunk, she cleared a path to the bug-eyed monster that was somehow guiding or helping to guide the attack on her friends. It turned.

"Shit," she swore, firing both particle beams. The ozone frying purple beams snapped into existence, connecting with the creature's chest. The flesh boiled away with a sizzle. The creature fell backwards and to one side, screaming.

The twin beams disengaged, and Lucy strode forward, forearm blades locked in position. "Time to die, Peeping Tom." The creature was thrashing on the ground, split alien tree trunks all around it. As she got closer, it lashed out, raking long claws along her left leg. Alarms screamed inside the pilot's crèche.

Valiant Azure swayed to the side away from the creature while bringing her right arm down, cleanly removing the thing's hand from its arm.

Hearing the noise the thing made, Lucy grinned. "Didn't like that, did you?" She checked her suit's status; the left leg was flashing orange—several hydraulic leaks and a few severed artificial muscle strands, but still functional.

The observer was back on its feet. It wobbled

unsteadily a moment before leaping right at Valiant Azure. Lucy braced herself, bringing both blades up in a defensive position. A second before they would have clashed, her opponent made a sharp turn, pushing through the alien trees.

It was running away.

Lucy swore. These things weren't fighters. She slashed through the trunks, giving chase. She switched her particle beams to single barrel and fired. The beam stabbed through a thick alien tree trunk but missed the observer. The second shot clipped its shoulder, sending it crashing against a tree, splintering several thorny branches.

Before it could raise its remaining hand to attack, she plunged both of her blades into the warped and burned chest. The creature's massive eyes grew even wider as it gurgled. Its face was barely two meters from Azure's.

Lucy saw the light fade from the enormous eyes as if she was looking it in the eye herself.

She stepped back, and the creature slumped to the ground. She looked down, then up at the sky, taking a deep breath of the not-great-smelling air in the pilot's crèche. She turned back to the battle.

"ALL UNITS. The new arrivals are suits," Major Thompson announced as he pushed the updated tactical data across the battle space.

"Suits?" Victor asked between deep breaths. He had managed to cut off the fringed lizard creature's tongue after it nearly punctured his chest armor. The creature wailed, but still lunged in to attack. He was holding it off, barely.

"Angela's friends, the what-was-it?" Paco said. He was using Maverick's meager long-range weapons to take potshots at the attacking megafauna.

"Syndicate," Brandon answered. "Sir, do we know what they want?"

"Negative, Midnight Tango. They haven't replied to hails."

Brandon ducked under the salamander creature's barbed tail. He made a grab for it, but the creature's skin was slick to the touch. He couldn't feel the sensation but knew it was gross.

"Tango, watch out!" It was Lucy.

Brandon opened his mouth to complain about her need to give orders, but stopped as he spotted the wounded lobster charging him. He ducked under a swipe from its remaining claw.

While Lucy watched Brandon duck the attack, she didn't take her eyes off her own surroundings. She saw the fringed lizard creature moving toward her to leap at her. Azure sidestepped the attack, catching the beast by the throat.

Before she could end the creature's life, it lashed out with a hand that ended in three jagged two-meter-long claws with barbs along their edge. The attack caught her in the head, crushing several cameras and sensors. Stunned, she released her grip.

The thing took a small step back, the fringe around its head fluttering as it prepared to strike, ready to cave

Valiant Azure's head in, but stopped short when one of Void Romeo's blades pierced its side, between the thing's scales.

Through the static, Lucy watched the creature retreat. "Thanks."

"Don't mention it!" Victor didn't wait, giving pursuit.

Catching his breath, Brandon pulled up the feed from Wasp One. The lobster fell back as soon as he ducked its attack, and he fired a round from his pistol into its face. The shot didn't end the creature but did blow its mandibles to pieces.

Midnight Tango shook his head. "Angela wasn't wrong. She said they didn't look like ours. They look less 'robot-y.'"

"But no less armed," Paco said.

"Cut the chatter," Molly ordered. She and Paco were doing their best to keep the surviving cow-creatures from forming a stampede with their long-range weapons.

Brandon blushed. Alpha One was right, now wasn't the time for gossiping. He'd assumed Angela was lying about the Syndicate suits, or at least misjudging. Even though more than one person, including the major and Dr. Erasmus, had heard about the Syndicate that night, no evidence was seen or offered.

Looking at the four suits coming to a stop a half kilometer away, he saw that Angela was right. The machines looked less martial. Softer, despite their weapons. Their armor rounded where NACAF suits were more angular. He had no idea how they got those suits, but they weren't homemade, another thing he had assumed when he first heard about unlicensed suits being used down here.

Without saying a word to the NACAF forces, the four new suits broke into a run toward the nearest of the Category 4s.

Valiant Azure turned to the tower. "My cannons are cooled down enough for another try."

Tacit Ronin nodded as she struggled to her feet. "Let's do this. Maybe if we move the beams a bit, create a wider hotspot. Maybe I can cut through more of it?"

Lucy nodded. "Worth a shot."

Brandon watched the four new suits descend on the lobster creature. They started with energy weapons as they closed the gap, then deployed blades and fell on the creature en masse. It screamed through gruesome mandibles as blade after blade pierced its exoskeleton. One of the suits cut the remaining claw off, sending neon orange goo spraying from the wound like a fountain.

The creature spasmed and did its best to scream through its ruined mouth a few more times, a pool of orange forming around it and its assailants. Finally, it fell silent and all four suits stepped away.

"Damn," he whispered to himself. They were efficient, to say the least.

WATCHING the four suits make quick work of the giant furry lobster, Major Thompson whistled. "They know what they're doing."

Dr. Erasmus nodded. "They likely don't have much access to spare parts and repairs. Our pilots often fight one on one because their suits get repaired when they return to base."

The major turned to the senior VarTech man. "Yeah, guess VarTech doesn't have an Exclusion Zone service center set up." At the look he got from Erasmus, he smiled. "Unless you think these suits aren't VarTech? VarTech, the sole manufacturer and distributor of combat suits, worldwide." The other man said nothing, so Thompson nodded and turned back to the display he'd been looking at.

Stalwart Rook stumbled, her left leg giving out. The fringed lizard creature rushed in, sensing its opportunity. Before any of the still standing NACAF suits could intercede, a missile streaked in, blowing the massive creature into several large, gooey pieces that pinwheeled in all directions.

"Holy shit!" Brandon shouted.

"They have missiles?" Lucy asked, looking around with what few sensors were still functioning. She couldn't fathom how Victor was still fighting as well as he was, his own suit's head being equally damaged.

"All NACAF forces. Incoming fire. Repeat, incoming fire," a voice called out over the ground expedition channel.

"Little late for that," Sophie quipped.

Every suit turned to look for the source of the missile, following the fading exhaust trail.

"It's the *Saratoga!*" Paco exclaimed. Crusher Maverick pumped his fist in the air.

CHAPTER TWENTY-THREE

SITTING IN HIS COMMAND CHAIR, Captain Bartell leaned forward. "Fire again." He watched as a missile streaked toward the remaining Category 4 creature. It looked like an axolotl to him, but with barbed claws and bony plates all over. And of course, it was nearly sixty feet tall.

The creature dodged to the side at the last second, the missile exploding behind it, sending dirt and flames high into the sky.

"Guns. Take that thing out," the captain ordered. He turned to his first officer. "Looks like we got here just in time, Linc."

Lincoln Willis nodded. "Yes, sir." He pointed to the four suits standing off to one side of the NACAF suits. "Looks like our kids made friends."

The captain nodded. "Yeah. Who the hell are they?"

Willis shook his head. "No idea. They don't look like they're ours. Not that there'd be other fire teams this far south, anyway."

Bartell turned to his XO. "None are NACAF suits?" Both men knew what that would mean and where those suits would had to have come from.

"That can be later today's problem," Bartell said, turning back to the forward window.

The axolotl creature didn't last long against the *Saratoga*'s rail gun fire. The creature blew apart in a shower of orange gore that rained down on everything within a hundred meters.

Watching the herbivore megafauna disperse, Bartell said, "Open a channel to Transport One."

"*Saratoga*, are you a sight for sore eyes," Major Thompson said as soon as the connection was established.

Bartell and Willis exchanged smiles, the former saying, "So, you missed us?"

"You could say that, sir," the major answered. His voice sounded like he was smiling ear to ear. "Thought were doing our own Little Big Horn down here."

"Well, sorry it took so long. Those winged nightmares did a lot more damage than we thought." The captain glanced at one of the monitors near his seat. "We're dropping Charlie and Delta Teams now."

"Copy that, sir."

BRANDON WATCHED the *Saratoga* settle to a stop half a kilometer from the tower. He watched as hatches along its underside opened, disgorging five shiny suits all in perfect working order.

"Hey, guys. Miss us?" Stacy Decker asked as Viridian Slammer struck the ground. Valor Ascendant dropped next to Slammer, and the two suits made a beeline for their colleagues. She extended a metal fist that Midnight Tango banged his own against.

"You could have at least saved some monsters for us," Brady Davidson, Charlie Three, said.

Molly got Tacit Ronin to her feet. "Sorry. Maybe next time." The battered suit hitched a thumb over her shoulder. "We did make some friends, though."

The white and gold suit leaned to the side. "Who?"

Molly turned. "What the hell?" Tacit Ronin panned her head around. "Where'd they go?"

The Syndicate suits were nowhere to be seen.

Brandon checked his sensors and tactical view. Nothing. "They can turn invisible?"

Lucy shook her head. "Idiot."

She extended a hand toward Paco. "Let's get up to the ship."

Crusher Maverick nodded.

Aboard the hovering *Saratoga*, captain Bartell was rubbing his chin. "Say that again. It's calling home? The Syndicate, whatever that is, has suits?"

The overhead speaker crackled. The radiation from the tower was wreaking havoc on the air carrier's systems even at a half kilometer distance.

"Correct, Captain. The tower is some sort of transmission apparatus," Dr. Erasmus said. He continued, "I believe it is building to a charge to send a pulse or signal back to where asteroid LV-426 came from."

Major Thompson cut in. "The suits bailed us out. Never spoke a word to us."

"And now they're gone?" Commander Willis asked. How four suits could slip away, he had no idea. Between the transport's sensors and *Saratoga,* that shouldn't have been possible.

"Right now, all that matters is the tower," Dr. Erasmus insisted.

"For what? Why's it calling home?" Commander Willis asked.

"Do we want to find out?" Major Thompson asked, then added, "Sir?"

Bartell smiled. "Good point, Major." He turned to the officer at tactical and nodded. "Major, get your people clear."

"Copy that, sir."

Thompson turned to the command center staff. "Send the word to all forces. We're rolling out."

"YOU HAVE THE FIRING SOLUTION?" Commander Willis asked.

The lieutenant at tactical looked up. "Yes, sir. Forward guns locked."

Willis turned to Captain Bartell and nodded.

"Fire."

The two guns on the lower forward section of the *Saratoga* twitched as the gunners made minute adjustments. The barrels of the two massive guns glowed briefly, then with a deafening crack, sent a pair of high-density, armor-piercing rounds down range at the speed of sound.

The round struck the base of the alien tower, sending pieces of armorlike scales flying in all directions. The enormous structure swayed. The wounds from the two railgun rounds oozed.

"Tough bastard," Captain Bartell commented. "Fire again."

The tactical officer nodded. The forward guns zip-cracked, sending two more rounds into the flower's base at the same location as the first two rounds. The wound erupted in sap again. More scales flew.

"Command, the top of this thing is getting really bright," a Wasp pilot reported.

Captain Bartell looked at a screen that was showing the inside of Transport One's command center, Major Thompson and Dr. Erasmus both in frame. "Doctor?"

"We don't know anything about it, but that plant out there seems to be at least minimally sentient. It surely knows it's being attacked."

"So, it's rushing to finish whatever it's doing?" Commander Willis surmised.

The doctor nodded.

The captain removed his cap. "Fire. Don't stop until that thing falls."

"Aye, sir," the tactical officer said.

The guns zip-cracked, then zip-cracked again. The explosions blew more and more of the alien structure's base to pieces, causing it to sway.

"Contact! One megafauna, Category 3," someone at the sensor station announced.

From Transport One, Dr. Erasmus said, "Calling for help."

The guns continued to fire. Each loud zip-crack echoed through the ship as magnetically charged rounds shredded more and more of the alien structure.

The tower began to sway more visibly, a pile of deformed, depleted uranium shells littering the ground around it.

"Tough son of a bitch," Willis said.

The massive alien tower shuddered with each impact. The armored scales shattered, and the interior material erupted in a pulpy splatter. There was an intense flash of light from the top of the tower as it began its fall.

"Timber," someone whispered.

Bartell and Willis held their breath.

Thompson and Erasmus did the same.

Down on the ground, the suit pilots watched as the giant stalk first slowly, then with more speed, crashed to the ground. The sound was deafening, and the ground shook.

As the dust cloud from the fallen alien stalk cleared, Brandon turned to watch a recovery cable pull Void Romeo up into the guts of the *Saratoga*.

"You're up next, Tango," the controller aboard the *Saratoga* called. The thick deployment cable lowered from the carrier, ready for its next passenger.

CAPTAIN BARTELL TURNED in his chair. "Where'd that contact go? The one that popped up before the tree thing fell."

"Lost it, sir." The captain frowned. "The moment the tower thing fell, it seemed to lose interest. Stopped, then turned and left."

Commander Willis cocked his head. "Well, that's weird."

From the screen connecting Transport One to the ship, Major Thompson said, "Oh, we've seen weirder."

Behind Captain Bartell, Commander Willis chuckled. He was looking forward to hearing about the ground expedition's adventures since leaving the damaged *Saratoga* a week earlier.

Dr. Erasmus nodded, then said, "Captain, I'd like to get my people back out to the Impact Zone to take samples now that the top of the flower is accessible."

After a few moments, the captain nodded. The threat board was clear, and between the *Saratoga* and her complement of functional suits, he was sure he could hold the area. For now, at least. "Go ahead, Doctor."

Down in the hangar, Midnight Tango settled into his cradle along the wall, next to Crusher Maverick. As soon as Brandon locked the grime-covered suit in place, he issued the shutdown command. The suspension material all around him loosened. He sagged in the crèche as the various hatches behind him clicked and whirred, slowly opening to free him from his suit.

The hangar was even more hectic than normal. All of the expedition suits were aboard while Charlie and Delta

Teams were patrolling down on the surface, keeping the VarTech science teams safe.

VarTech technician Jennifer Morris was waiting for him on the deck as he slid down the ladder. "Thanks for bringing it back in," she looked the once black suit, "in mostly one piece." She turned to look at the other suits, both docked and making their way to their docks. "You all had an adventure."

Brandon nodded. "To say the least." Brandon watched Valiant Azure and Tacit Ronin help Stalwart Rook into her docking cradle. It was odd to see two massive and damaged metal mechs helping a third through the hangar. Heavy thudding footsteps clanged through the cavernous space.

Paco met Brandon and Jennifer at Midnight Tango's foot. The team technician nodded. "Glad you all made it back." She gestured to each of the team's suits. "Obviously, you're not going anywhere, anytime soon."

Valiant Azure stomped by, stepping back into her cradle. The faint hum of her power plant faded as Lucy issued the shut down command.

"Down time sounds good," Brandon said. Paco bobbed his head in agreement.

Lucy rode the lift down, joining them. "I need a long nap."

AGAINST CAPTAIN BARTELL'S WISHES, Dr. Erasmus kept the *Saratoga* on station at Impact Zone Five for another week while his people dissected the various megafauna corpses littering the area and took samples of the alien tower from all along its length.

The flower turned out to be a treasure trove of rare and unidentified elements, biological circuitry, and what could only be described as a powerful transmitter, made of mostly plant matter and the unidentified elements the tower created.

Hangar Two had several of the tower's petals laid out on the deck. They had to leave the transports behind to make room for the various samples being returned to NACAF Command and VarTech.

The trip back to Libertad was uneventful. Not a single megafauna showed itself, which was both a relief and cause for worry among the ship's senior staff. Of the mysterious Syndicate suits, there was no sign.

Miguel welcomed the ship and its crew with open arms. "I am glad to see you again, Major, and you, Doctor. I was asked, should you pass this way, to thank you once again for saving Graciela's caravan."

Thompson nodded. "She's already gone?"

Miguel nodded. "She doesn't stick around one place very long, that one." Turning, he led the group to the same establishment he had taken the NACAF group to the last time they were there. Over dinner, Major Thompson shared the tale of their trip from Libertad to the Impact Zone, the battles along the way...the battle that, he was certain, was going to be their last.

"So, you met some of the Syndicate's fighters? We told you they were a force for good."

Major Thompson inclined his head. "We only wish they'd stuck around to accept our thanks."

"They're not here in town at the moment, are they?" Captain Bartell asked.

Miguel shook his head. "No. Two of their people arrived shortly after Graciela, but upon hearing about you and your destination, they departed. I presume to collect reinforcements."

The crew of the *Saratoga* enjoyed a few days of R&R in Libertad before continuing on to Denver.

AS THE *SARATOGA* NEARED TEXAS, Captain Bartell called Bravo Team to his ready room.

As the lift doors slid open, the three of them took in the view. The captain's ready room was to the left, but dead ahead of them was the main command bridge and the expanse of transparent aluminum that gave the captain a sweeping view of the ship and the sky beyond.

"So beautiful," Paco whispered.

Lucy nodded. "It really is."

Brandon cleared his throat. "Think we're in trouble?"

Paco looked at him. "For what? We've been on R&R most of the last two weeks. None of our suits are mission capable." He stopped. "You don't think someone found the—"

"No!" Brandon assured him.

Lucy looked at her two friends. "I don't even want to know. But whatever you're talking about, keep it away from my room." She nodded toward the hatch to the captain's ready room. "Let's go."

The captain was sitting behind his desk when the trio walked in.

The three young officers stood at attention before him. Brandon said, "Bravo Team, reporting as ordered."

Captain Bartell stood. "I've read Major Thompson's reports as well as those of Alpha Team." He came around the desk to stand in front of the three pilots. "The three of you performed your duties admirably in the best traditions of the North American Coalition Armed Forces."

He looked each of them in the eye. "All without a clear team leader." He grinned, seeing two of the three straighten a little more. He turned slightly to pick something up off his desk.

"Pilot first class, Brandon Sinclair," he nodded to the young man, "you showed strong tactical thinking and initiative in challenging situations. You'll be Bravo Two." Brandon's smile faltered momentarily. He turned to Paco. "Pilot first class, Paco Molina. You're a steadying influence on the field and your hand-to-hand skills may very well be top of the list among the *Saratoga*'s suits. You'll be Bravo Three." The young Hispanic man beamed.

Bartell turned to the third and final member of Bravo Team. "Pilot first class, Lucy Jones." Bartell smiled at the young woman's expression. "Your performance on the battlefield showed true leadership. You'll serve as Bravo One." He offered her a fire team leader pin in a small case. The pin: a stylized fist clutching a lightning bolt.

Lucy's grin was ear to ear. "Thank you, sir."

The captain turned to Brandon and Paco. "This is in no way a reflection upon either of your performances."

"Of course, sir," Brandon said. "If I'm being honest with myself, Lucy deserves it. She was great out there." He turned to Lucy. "Happy to follow your lead, Luce."

Paco nodded. "Sí, amiga. Lead the way."

ONCE THE *SARATOGA* reached Denver and docked at the NACAF Base tower, the entire crew was given shore leave while the repair crews crawled all over the hull and the suits inside the suit bay. Between the ship's engineering department and the NACAF Denver engineers, they estimated that the *Saratoga* would be out of the fight for three weeks—two, if a miracle or two took place. Captain Bartell wasn't pleased but didn't push.

The line to disembark was progressing at a snail's pace. Brandon nudged Molly Chen. "So, you think we'll ever hear anything more about all that stuff they collected at the Impact Zone?"

All four fire teams were together in the queue to take the lifts down to Denver. Grace was pushing Alec Lefebvre's wheelchair. He was banged up but, according to the *Saratoga*'s doctors, out of the woods. Brandon thought the wheelchair was a bit much but said nothing.

Molly shook her head. "Unlikely. I heard that the moment we docked, VarTech shuttles were hovering outside Hangar Two, waiting for the door to open so they could retrieve the collected samples. It's all long gone now."

Alec nodded, craning his head to look behind him

and Grace. "We'll get new armor or other tech in a few months or so. That'll be it."

"What about all that talk about a poison from those flowers?" Paco asked.

While the crew made its way off the ship, Captain Bartell stood in the forward hangar face to face with Dr. Erasmus. "What do you mean, classified?"

The bald-headed scientist shrugged. "I'm sorry, Captain. Everything we collected has been classified. Highest level."

"Even that flower? The one you think might make for a poison?"

Erasmus nodded slowly. Bartell swore.

"And those suits?" The captain had his hands on his hips. "We both know what the existence of those suits means."

Erasmus sighed. "I don't know what to tell you, Captain." He looked around the cavernous space. Lowering his voice, he said, "All I can tell you is that VarTech has contractors that provide us with samples of megaflora and fauna from time to time. I know nothing about it beyond that, however." He leaned in. "I'd guess this Syndicate, whomever they are, are those contractors."

Bartell was furious. He had avoided this argument with the VarTech man during their trip north, but having VarTech lock down part of his ship was too much. He looked around the forward hangar. He was the only non VarTech person there.

"I'm sorry, Captain. I really am. You know how it is." At the open end of the hangar, a cargo shuttle was settling onto the deck. Several of the ship's VarTech contingent were guiding carts containing the various samples from the giant alien flower-tower thing toward the shuttle.

After a moment, the captain released a breath. "I know." He turned on his heel and left the hangar. Tapping his commset, he said, "Make an appointment for me with Admiral Leera."

TWO BLOCKS from NACAF Denver tower, Major Thompson and Commander Tanner were at a cafe watching *Saratoga* crewers flood out into the city. Normally, ship crewers hitting the streets were happy, laughing, and clapping each other on the back as they made their way to bars, cafes, restaurants, and more. Most of the *Saratoga* crewers that day were sedate, at best, downright beleaguered, at worst.

Turning from the depressing sight, the senior ground force commander took a sip of his overpriced something-or-other with oat milk and said, "So, the captain put you in for a promotion."

Thompson set his cup down. "What? Really?" The other man nodded. "Wow."

Tanner smiled. "That wasn't nothing you did down there. Five days overland in no-man's-land? Finding that town, the tower? Some impressive shit, man. You brought most of your people home."

Thompson smiled. "But in the end, mission failure." He took a sip of his black coffee. "The tower sent its signal."

Tanner shrugged. "You didn't even know that was a thing when you left the ship." He tapped his mug absently on the tabletop.

"True. Any word on that other signal?"

"All I've heard is that it wasn't sent into space. The scuttlebutt I heard was that it was low level, likely traveled around the globe, bouncing off of some level of clouds or whatever."

"To the other Impact Zones? Flowers there?"

"We don't know yet. I hear Command is in talks with the other alliances to mount missions to each of the Impact Zones."

The two men continued to sip their drinks, watching NACAF personnel filter out into downtown Denver, both thinking to themselves that things were about to get a lot more interesting for the people of Earth.

EPILOGUE

"GOOD EVENING. I'M KENT ROLLINS," the handsome blonde-haired news man said.

His cohost added, "I'm Leslie Green." She smiled and continued, "Tonight, we have news out of VarTech headquarters. Researchers have discovered a protein compound that is showing promise as an effective poison for megafauna."

Kent smiled. "Perhaps humanity's long nightmare is nearly over?"

Leslie nodded her agreement. "If we're lucky, and none too soon."

"That's right, Leslie. NAC Command has released an after-action report from an expedition that recently went south of the border all the way to Impact Zone Five and discovered an alien plant that, it's reported, was an organic transmitter."

Leslie's expression fell. "I guess this toxin was discovered at just the right time."

"Indeed. The NACAF and VarTech haven't

confirmed if the plant structure sent a signal or not, but we'll keep you posted."

The lights in the studio faded. The two newscasters exhaled as one. Kent turned to Leslie. "Think it called for reinforcements?"

The journalist leaned her head back, looking at the ceiling. "Even if it didn't, there are four other Impact Zones..."

THANK YOU!

If you enjoyed Invasive Species, I'd love it if you left a
review. Seriously, reviews are a big deal.
Reviews help readers find authors.

Unfortunately, just tapping the stars on your reader,
doesn't cut it. Those don't go anywhere. You gotta write a
review.
It doesn't have to be wordy, even "I liked it" works!
Every review has a big impact. Thanks!

OFFER

As they say, there's no harm in asking, so here we go.

If you can help connect me with someone who can get Space Rogues on a screen (Big or Little) I'll cut you in for 10% (Up to $10,000) of whatever advance is paid.

Send me an email and we can discuss.
rights@johnwilker.com

STAY CONNECTED

**Want to stay up to date on the happenings in the Galactic Commonwealth?
Like free short stories and more?**

Sign up for my newsletter at
johnwilker.com/newsletter
Visit me online at
johnwilker.com

If you like supporting things you love by sporting merch or buying direct, well you're in luck! I've launched a Shop, take a look. **Use, discount code "Ghost" and you'll save %15!**

ABOUT ME

I've loved writing since I was a kid. I entered writing contests in 2nd and 3rd grade. I read books and wrote book reports for my parents (It helped that I got a new G.I. Joe for each book report). From that point on I've told stories wherever I could.

I hope to keep telling the story of Wil and his friends for as long as people enjoy reading them.

Tell your friends, tell your family, tell the person next to you on the plane that just looked at you funny for laughing out loud. You see where I'm going with this. :)

The Space Rogues Series. Wil Calder and a bunch of alien misfits somehow keep finding themselves in the thick of it. No one ever checks qualifications when it comes to saving the galaxy!

The Grand Human Empire Series. Jax, Naomi and the droids are just trying to get by. New droid parts ain't cheap after all.

ACKNOWLEDGMENTS

I couldn't do this without an amazing group of people who sign up to beta and/or ARC read for me. The Beta readers in particular have to suffer through an early draft to help shape the story.

Below are some of these awesome people (If I missed your name, email me and you'll be in the next one :D)

- Beta Readers
  - Felix Muller
  - Scott Jann
  - Richard Lindsay
  - Marcus Zarra
  - Roger Gilmartin
- ARC TEAM
  - Gregory Jump (extra special thanks!)
  - Dave
  - Felix Muller
  - Marcus Zarra
  - Meenaz Lodi
  - Jim Stiles

Thank you so much, all of you!